The Final Sacrifice

Book 1
Visions Series

By
Teresa A. Leighton

Copyright © 2003 Teresa A. Leighton. All rights reserved.
No part of this book may be reproduced in any form or by any electronic or mechanical means including information and retrieval systems, websites or Internet without permission from the publisher in writing.

This is a work of fiction. Names, charachters, places, and incidents are either the product of the author's imagination or are used fictitiously, and any resemblance to actual persons, living or dead, business establishments, events or locals is entirely coincidental.

Library of Congress Control Number:2003100838

Teresa A. Leighton 1962 -

ISBN 0-9723376-3-6

ORIGINAL COVER ARTWORK: Tamara Northcutt

Printed in the United States of America

Address all inquiries to
**Teresa A. Leighton
via E-mail
TALeighton@hotmail.com**

Write to **Print**
P.O. Box 1862
Merrimack, NH 03054

DEDICATION

To my sister Elizabeth Miller, who lives in Crater Lake National Park and wasn't much of a book reader, but spent countless hours on the phone and online going through each chapter with me,
I dedicate this book to you.

Thank you James, Liz's husband, for taking care of the house and keeping the children busy.
I appreciate your patience.

To mom and dad for being my parents and being there for me. I love you. Thank you Jeffrey, my loving husband, for giving me the time to write. To Amber and Erica, my daughters, for believing in me.

Endora, my best friend, thank you for letting me escape to your house when things got too hectic at mine. Sarah, Amanda, Josh and Marisa, thank you for reading it in its early stages.

Tamara Northcutt, artist and a resident of Crater Lake National Park, thank you for doing a fantastic job on my book cover and hopefully having many more to come.
Thank you Michelle W. for calling me when you did.

CHAPTER ONE

Dreams are defined as "A series of thoughts or images passing through the mind in sleep."

I once had a dream. No. . .a nightmare. About my parents. They were in their car driving down a busy highway on their way to see me for the Fourth of July holiday. My mother had the map unfolded in front of her so she could tell my father what exit they needed to take next. My father took his eyes off the road for just a second. One-sixtieth of a minute. One second too long.

It happened two times more after that and even though I mentioned it to them, they still left. It was only a dream after all. . .and dreams aren't real. It took me over a year to build the walls around the guilt I felt after they died. A year to go back to pretending. . .that dreams aren't real.

That's what I told myself as I turned from the woman who slept so peacefully on my couch and walked slowly towards my bedroom door. My hand hovered over the doorknob and I turned once more to look at her before. I walked into a bedroom I didn't recognize.

A crystal chandelier hung from the center of the ceiling and bathed the room in a soft, warm glow of light. The drawers of an oak dresser were open. Clothes hung from them, some thrown carelessly around the dresser. Perfume and make-up from the top of a glass vanity were swept off the top and lay scattered about on the hardwood floor.

A large, canopied bed took up most of the room. Its headboard centered against the far back wall. Thick velvet curtains, the color of blue cornflower, draped its frame to hide anything that might be happening on it. A night stand near the bed lay knocked over on its side. What sat on top of it, now lie sprawled out on the floor around it.

"Hello?" I asked. My voiced sounded shaky. "Is anyone here?" I had to try didn't I?

I felt the first stirrings of panic wash through me as I walked slowly towards the bed and around the side. Some the curtains had been pulled from the rod near the night stand. My pulse quickened as I ran trembling fingers along the folds of the curtain and pulled it back to reveal what could be hiding behind it.

She lay there. So still. . . .so lifeless. Her right arm down by her side and the other lay up near her face. It was almost like she had found a comfortable position to sleep in. The bed covers and sheet where a knotted mess. She wore a blue T-shirt that went up to her waist exposing the upper thigh of her bare leg. My eyes went slowly to her neck where a silk stocking had been tied tightly around it. Blood ran slowly from the corner of her parted lips. It made a trail on her cheek and dripped onto the pillow. Her long, red hair and dark eyebrows stood out against her pale face. Deep-blue eyes stared blankly up at the canopy and I could still see the fear in them as if her spirit still lingered, hoping to be re-united with her body.

    My eyes widened and my hands flew to my mouth as a sick taste came to the top of my throat. I screamed into my hands and turned away. My scream caught in my throat and I nearly jumped out of my skin as I stood before the very person who took her life.

CHAPTER TWO

    I woke to the sounds of my own screams, the face in my nightmare still visible in my mind's eye. My hands shook as I wiped the tears from the corners of my eyes and my heart beat hard against my chest. I took deep breaths to calm myself, sat up and looked quickly around the living room. My eyes stopped at the closed bedroom door. I got up, grabbed my blanket and walked slowly towards it. I turned around. . .the couch was empty. It was all just a dream.

    I let out a breath I didn't know I was holding and went into the bedroom. The same bedroom that had always been there. A nervous laugh escaped my lips as I went into the bathroom. I turned the light on and my heart flew to my throat when I saw the person that looked back at me.

    There were black and green bruises on my neck, decorating it like the plague. A red rash topped the bruises and the skin was torn and caked with dry blood. I had a

Chapter Two

cut on the left corner of my mouth and the blood that dried left a stained trail down my chin.

My eyes widened as I brought a trembling finger up to touch the cuts on my neck. I stopped short when my sleeve slid up to reveal bruises that blossomed around my wrist. My ring finger was swollen and torn at the knuckle. I backed away from the mirror and stopped when I hit the wall. "No, this can't be happening again," I whispered to the person staring back at me. "It wasn't real. It couldn't have been real."

The memory of the dream flashed through my mind and the woman's face appeared slowly before me in the mirror. Her deep-blue eyes stared out at me, but they were eyes that held no sign of life — and I remembered her face — from past dreams.

A sudden wave of nausea washed over me, leaving a sour taste in my mouth. I made a mad dash for the toilet and lost what little I ate the night before.

When I was through, I turned the faucet on and rinsed my mouth out. As I stood there with my face over the sink, the memory of my parents' accident came back to haunt my thoughts. Could I have saved them if I had done it differently? I would never know. Was it possible to save this woman? Maybe. I only hoped I wasn't too late. I couldn't live with myself if it was too late.

I ran to the kitchen and snatched the cordless from its cradle. Panic prickled along my skin, sending a cold chill through me. My breathing came in short gasps as I dialed the police.

I leaned on the counter listening to the other end ring. "God, please don't let me be too late."

"911," the man's voice said.

"Yes, I'm calling to report a possible murder," I said hastily.

"Okay, slow down ma'am. Tell me your name and where you are."

"My name's Julie Summers and I'm home but. . ."

"Give me your address."

"It's 30043 Club House Road. I saw him, you need to. . ."

"Are you in a safe place right now?"

"Yes, I'm safe. I told you I'm home. It's not around here," I said quickly. I was tired of being cut off. They needed to find this man.

"Okay Miss Summers, just calm down and stay on the line."

"I am calm. You're not listening to me," I said through clenched teeth.

"Please, Miss Summers. . ."

I jerked around and dropped the phone when I heard a knock at my door.

"Is someone there?" I asked. My voice had a nervous lilt to it.

"Virginia Beach Police ma'am," the man said from behind the closed door.

That was fast. Were they waiting in my driveway or something? I left the phone on the floor and went to the door. My hands shook uncontrollably and it took me three tries to get the chain to unlatch.

There were two officers standing on opposite sides of my door when I opened it. They were both well over six-foot, the uniforms they wore looked as though they had poured their bodies into them. Muscular thighs pulling at the material in their legs that led up to narrow waists. They wore dark-blue, waist-length jackets that added to their broad shoulders. It was as if they both did the same workout program at the gym. One had dark-brown hair and chocolate-brown eyes. The other, sandy-blonde hair and light-blue eyes. Like night and day.

Chapter Two

They stood there looking like they were ready to draw their guns at any second. Well, I did say something about a murder didn't I?

The dark-haired officer glanced in the door then looked down at me. "I'm officer Reilly, this is officer Hayes. Did you call the police?" he asked.

"Yes, I did. Please, you have to hurry. You have to find him before it's too late," I said as I paced to the couch and turned around.

"Slow down Miss. . ." Reilly paused.

"Summers," I said.

Hayes walked over to the kitchen with his hand on the butt of his gun. He peered in as if someone would jump out from behind the counter.

"Miss Summers, we can't help if we don't. . ." His brows furrowed as he looked down at my neck and brought his hand down as if to touch it. "Are you all right?"

I backed up and glanced over at Hayes who was now headed for my bedroom. His hand still on the butt of his gun. "Of coarse I'm all right. It's that woman who won't be, if you don't do something soon. I told them that she was going to be murdered."

"What woman?"

I looked up at him as if he should've understood me all along. "The one I saw on the canopy bed. He strangled her with some kind of silk stocking. I can give you a description."

Hayes came back in from the bedroom. "There's nothing here."

I turned to look at him and felt a frown forming on my face. "I never said it was here. I don't know where it is. I only know what he looks like."

Hayes picked the phone up from the floor. "We got it," he said then hung up and put the phone on the counter. He looked at Reilly and his brow rose.

"When exactly did you see this, Miss Summers?" Reilly asked.

"Last night— this morning. I don't know when. I saw it in my. . ." I looked at him, at Hayes, then back at him. "I saw it in my dream."

Hayes choked back a laugh and walked by me to the door. "I'll be out in the car." He glanced back at me, his lips curled up and he left.

"Listen, Miss Summers. Police time is valuable. Calls like this can take us away from more important ones that require immediate attention."

"Calls like what? I didn't call just for the hell of it. I'm telling you this woman is going to die or could already be dead."

He looked down at me and something moved behind his eyes. Was it pity? "Would you like us to take you to a hospital?"

I took a deep breath through my nose and let it slowly out my mouth. They didn't believe me. "No, I don't need a hospital. I need you to believe what I'm saying."

Hayes came to the doorway and peeked in. "We got a call."

"Okay," Reilly said and turned back to me. "Are you sure about the hospital?"

"Positive."

"Don't make anymore calls like this one. It could get you into trouble." He took one more look around. "Have a good day, Miss Summers," he said and left.

I slammed the door behind them and stared at it for a few heartbeats. What was I going to do now? The only people that could help didn't believe me. They probably thought I was some kind of nut case, which is exactly what I figured.

I needed to talk to someone. Someone who would believe me at least. I looked at the clock on the TV. It was nine o'clock. She would be at work by now. I picked up the phone and decided to call Elaine.

Elaine was the only friend I had in Virginia Beach since I moved here six years ago with Scott, my ex-fiancé. I was a mere twenty years old. He was tall, handsome and a smooth talker. There's a relationship I'd like to put down on paper and burn to ashes. He talked me into moving here from my hometown in Brainerd, Minnesota. He said we'd do better without the parents — meaning mine — interfering. In other words, it was him or my parents. I was in love with him, so I said goodbye to my parents.

We rented a small, one-bedroom, one-bath house off Rosemont Road. It wasn't much, but we where happy— so I thought. Three months later I came home from shopping and found a "Dear Jane" letter on his pillow in our bedroom. The TV, stereo and his clothes went with him. . .he left the hangers. He said he needed some time alone to figure things out. I found out later the little blonde he worked with left with him. So much for alone time. I stayed here because I couldn't afford to move and I wasn't going to ask my parents for help.

I met Elaine about eight months later at Sam's Diner, where I work. She came in asking for directions to Anderson's Technology. She had an interview there the following day and wanted to know where it was ahead of time. I sat with her to give her directions and we have been friends ever since. She got the job. Three years later she changed her name to Anderson. I hope to be as happy as her someday.

"Anderson's Technology, this is Elaine speaking," she said through the phone.

"Elaine? Can you come by on your lunch hour?" I asked.

"What's wrong, hun?"

"Something's happened and I need to talk to you."

She must have heard the panic in my voice. "You want to tell me about it?"

"No, not over the phone."

"Are you all right? You're not hurt are you?"

I lied, sort of. "No, it's nothing like that."

"Okay, how's eleven sound?"

"That'd be great. Thanks"

"No problem, hun. See you then."

"Okay, bye."

I hung up and felt a little better knowing I could talk to someone who would believe me. She was my best friend and we've always tried to be honest with each other.

CHAPTER THREE

I decided to take a quick shower to freshen up and maybe soak some of the dried blood off my neck. I pulled my favorite blue sweatshirt out of the bottom drawer of my dresser. It had a picture of Tigger on it, my favorite character from Whinnie The Poo. I grabbed a pair of gray sweatpants off a hanger in the closet and I was all set. Comfort was first on my list and I wasn't due in any beauty pageants anytime soon.

A half-hour later I headed to the kitchen to brew a fresh pot of coffee, although most would call it a kitchenette. I call it a closet. It's a nine-by-ten room. The cabinets are white, the counter a light gray and the linoleum floor was white with gray diamonds on it. A refrigerator, stove, and sink with two cabinets over it took up one wall. Four small cabinets over a counter that served as my kitchen table divided the kitchen and living room. There was just enough room to move around. You get more than two people in it and you're stepping on each other's toes.

I sat at the counter sipping my first cup of coffee for the day and wondered how I was going to explain all of this to Elaine. I never mentioned the dreams about my parents to her or to anyone else for that matter. The only people who knew, are no longer alive. I was afraid to tell anyone after that. Afraid people would think I was so consumed with grief that I was loosing my mind. That was the last thing I needed or wanted.

The doorbell chimed just as I was getting up to get some more coffee and the cup nearly fell out of my hands. I didn't bother looking at the clock. I just assumed it was Elaine, so I opened the door. I'll give you three guesses as to who it wasn't.

My brows rose. "Did you forget something, Officer Reilly?"

"Actually, I need to see you about our visit earlier."

"I don't understand."

"If you don't mind, I'd like you to talk to Detective Stuart, who's in charge of the investigation."

I didn't like the sound of that. "In charge of what investigation?"

"Please, Miss Summers, he just needs to ask you a few questions."

"Well, I suppose it's okay."

Reilly left me standing in the doorway, and a few seconds later, a tall, slender, black man came to the door. He wore a gray suit, light-blue, button up shirt and a blue and gray, pin-striped tie. He wore the suit well and looked to be about forty or so. He had light-brown eyes and a neatly trimmed mustache. His hair was cut short and graying on the sides.

He held his hand out to me. "Hello, Miss Summers."

I shook his hand, motioned for him to come in and peeked around the door. Reilly and Hayes were sitting

Chapter Three

in a cruiser in my driveway. It was parked next to my piece of shit, 89 Ford S/10 pick-up. There was a dark-blue car parked behind my truck, but I couldn't make out what kind. I was assuming it belonged to the detective.

"Are they coming back in?" I asked.

He pulled his pant legs up and sat on one of the stools at the counter. "No."

Not very talkative is he?

I closed the door and sat on the arm of the chair in the living room. "What can I do for you, Detective Stuart?"

He sat there for a few heartbeats and eyed me from head to toe, stopping at my hand and neck for a short period of time; as if memorizing me. I felt as though I was being measured for the right size prison attire.

When he was finished, he grabbed a pen and notepad from his inside pocket and flipped it open. He scribbled a few things in it and looked over at me. "What can you tell me about this woman you saw murdered?"

"I can't tell you anything about her, I don't know her. I only know what she looks like."

"That'll be fine."

"Well, she's about my height I guess. I couldn't tell because she was lying down. Long, red hair and blue eyes. She wore a blue T-shirt." I bit at my bottom lip as I visualized her from my dream to make sure I didn't forget anything. "I guess that's about it."

His brows rose. "And you got all that from a dream?"

"Yes, from a dream."

"Can you describe the bed you mentioned to Officer Reilly earlier?"

I took in a breath and let out a sigh. I was wishing they would get to the point. "I can describe the whole room." His brow rose at that. I had his undivided attention so I continued, "There was an oak dresser, drawers open and clothes thrown around it. A glass vanity that had been swept clean. Everything was on the floor. The night stand by the bed was knocked over. It was a canopy bed with blue bedding and curtains."

He scribbled the last of what I said in his notepad and looked over at me again. "Anything else?"

"No," I said.

"And you don't know this woman personally?"

"No."

"Where were you at around three AM this morning."

"Asleep on the couch."

"Was anyone here with you?"

"No, I live alone."

I thought I saw his lips twitch. "That's not what I asked you."

My eyes narrowed. "The answer's still no. I live alone and I'm not involved in any relationships."

There was that twitch of lips again. Almost as if there was a secret and I was the only one who didn't know. I didn't like it.

"Where did your injuries come from?" he asked.

"I woke up like this."

"So, you're telling me you got those from a dream also?" He used his pen to point at my neck.

"Yes, I am. Listen, Detective Stuart, I've been through this 'I think you're crazy' routine with Officers Reilly and Hayes. Am I under arrest for something?"

"No, Miss Summers, you're not under arrest for anything. I'd like you to give our sketch artist a description of the man you saw."

I could feel my eyes going wide. "Are you serious?"

Chapter Three

He closed the notepad, slipped it back into his inside pocket and got up. "Yes, I am."

I walked over to him. "Why the sudden interest in the 'crazy woman's' dream of a murder?"

"We can talk about this after you give the description." He started to leave.

I walked in front of him. I wanted to know and he wasn't leaving until I did. "She's dead, isn't she?"

He looked down at me with eyes that were blank of any meaning.

My stomach tightened. "I was too late wasn't I?" Silence and that damnable blank stare. "Tell me!" I yelled.

"Yes, she's dead. Her sister found her around eight forty-five this morning. Now, please give us the description so we can go on with our business." He walked around me and left.

CHAPTER FOUR

The sketch artist was a small, slender woman of about thirty. She had black hair tied so tightly up into a bun that it stretched the skin back on her face, which made her brows lift and her eyes slant back slightly. Small, wire-framed glasses covered her hazel eyes and the dark-blue pants suit she wore was tailored perfectly to fit her tiny frame. She was short and to the point when it came to asking me the questions she needed to sketch the man's face. She and the detective could use a few lessons at the local charm school.

"I think that will do it for now, Miss Summers," she said and got up. "I'll let Detective Stuart know I'm through here." She put the sketch in a folder and left. No bye or handshake. I guess courtesy isn't in the manual.

Elaine came rushing in, almost bumping into the sketch artist as she was going through the door. She had on a black mini skirt, red button-up silk shirt and a blazer to match the skirt. She wore black flats instead of heels.

Chapter Four

Elaine was five-seven; a good six inches taller than I was and all leg. Her dark, chestnut hair was shoulder length and tied up in a hair clip. Her usual hair style. I don't think I've seen it down more than a dozen times since I've known her.

"Julie! What's going on?" she asked through quick breaths. She stopped short when she saw me. Her brown eyes went wide and her mouth dropped open. I kind of expected that. "What the hell happened to you? I thought you said you weren't hurt!"

I held my hand up to stop her as she threw her purse on the chair and started to come towards me. It worked. "Don't ask until everyone leaves."

She started for me again with her fingers pointing to my neck. "But. . ." She stopped when Detective Stuart came to the door.

"I think that'll be all for now, Miss Summers," he said.

"What do you mean for now?"

"We'll be in touch if we need anything else. You're not planning to go anywhere anytime soon are you?"

Now I felt as though I was a suspect and was just told, in so many words, not to leave town. "No, I'm not going anywhere, but I'll be sure to let you know when I'm going to pack up and skip town."

There was another slight movement of lips again. "We'll be in touch," he said and left.

I walked over to the window by the entertainment center, moved the blinds to peek out and waited for everyone to drive away. When they were gone, I turned and looked at Elaine. A deep frown formed on her face and her hands were folded across her chest.

I walked by her and went into the kitchen. "Let me make a fresh pot of coffee and I'll explain everything to you okay?"

She sat down at the counter. "All right, but you'd better explain everything."

I started with the dreams of my parents and how they were accurate right up to the unfolded map they found lying on the floor of the car. Virginia Beach was circled in red pen. Then I told her about the dream I just had, the ones before it, and I ended at the point when she walked in the door. She knew the rest from there.

Two cups of coffee and an hour later, Elaine sat staring down into her empty cup. I sat silently and waited for her to digest everything I had told her.

She looked up at me finally. Her eyes held a sadness I've never seen before. "God, Julie. Why didn't you tell me?"

"Would you have believed me?"

She seemed to think about that. "Maybe. Probably. Oh hell, I don't know. It's just too fantastic to think about."

"That's exactly why I didn't."

"I hate that you couldn't tell me. What you must've gone through when. . ." She let the thought tail off.

"It's over now. I dealt with it and went on. Don't beat yourself up about it."

"Is that why you refuse to take the money they left?"

I just looked down at my hands.

She grabbed me and hugged me hard. "Oh, Julie. I'm so sorry."

I held onto her tightly, not wanting to let go of the comfort it gave me and let the tears flow freely. People believed me. . .now that it was too late. It's always too late. She pulled away from me and wiped my face with her hand.

"Do you think it'll happen again?"

Chapter Four

"I don't know. I hope not. I didn't wake up with stuff like this the last time."

"Do you want me to stay with you tonight? I could tell Frank you need me."

"No, I'll be fine. And please don't tell him about this."

"I won't, if you don't want me to." She got up and grabbed her purse. "I have to get back to work, but I won't leave if you don't want me to."

"No, go ahead."

I walked her to the door, gave her a quick hug and stood staring at the closed door.

It was over. I finally was able to get out in the open what happened over a year ago and I felt as though my shoulders weighed a lot less than before. It didn't change the fact that my parents and the woman I saw were dead. Nothing would bring them back. Nothing.

I bandaged my neck and finger and spent the rest of the day inside. No one else came to the house after Elaine left, which was good because I didn't want any more company. I spent the rest of the day walking around the house doing the things I had planned to do. It was just another normal day in my life. Ri-ight.

When I finished everything there was to do for the day, I made some tomato soup and cuddled up next to my bon-shaped pillow on the couch. With nothing else to occupy my mind, I thought about the dreams again. Could it happen again? I didn't know the answer to that question. There had to be a way to find out what was happening to me. Some way to stop or control it. Hell, I didn't even have a word for it. I put my soup on the coffee table, reached under the couch, and grabbed the phone book.

I flipped through the pages, stopping when I saw the book store section. I figured it was a good place to start. I ran my fingers down the columns and stopped when I saw *Mystical Tools*.

"Mystical Tools? What the hell is that?" As if someone was going to answer me.

Under it was a line that read *see add display, page 185*. I turned back a page, found the boxed advertisement for the store and read a summary of what the store offered. It was a "New Age" store. Just a different way to say occult I think. I ripped the page out of the phone book and set it on the coffee table. I had no doubt that a store like that would have a book about things like this. I curled up on the couch and went to sleep with a little more hope than when I started this day with.

CHAPTER FIVE

  I managed to sleep through the night without a problem and woke to the sound of the phone screaming in the kitchen. Elaine decided to call me before work to tell me she would stopping by on her lunch break to check in on me. I told her I was going for a walk and I should be back before she got here. I didn't tell here where I was going. I felt a little awkward going as it was.

  The store was only about a mile or so and I was looking forward to some fresh air. I threw on my black jeans, a pair of comfortable sneakers, and a high-collared, black and red sweater to hide the bandages on my neck. I tied my hair back in a braid because I didn't feel like spending an hour putting it up. Finally, I grabbed my wallet off my dresser and shoved it into my back pocket. I don't carry a purse, it's too bulky and I like to have my hands free. I carry money, a credit card, and license. What more did I need?

I didn't wear a coat because although it was early October, Virginia Beach's fall weather is pretty mild. The morning air was cool, but not bone chilling. I enjoyed the cool breeze and watched the leaves fall from trees and seemed to float on invisible strings to the ground, coating it with a colored blanket of rust, orange, yellow and red.

The store was on the corner of South Lynnhaven Road and Lynnhaven Boulevard. It was situated in the middle of a sports bar and a Seven Eleven. Tucked neatly away, almost as if it was trying to hide its secrets from the world. The outside of the building was white with a sign above the door done in plain, black letters that read, *Mystical Tools*. I could just imagine the possible "tools" they would be selling in a store like this. Maybe a magic wand to wave my troubles away.

There were two rooms to the store; the front room had wall to wall books, crystal balls, candles of every size, shape and color and a variety of other items. There was a shelf containing cone incense that overwhelmed the senses with rose, thyme, peppermint, clove, and every other fragrance you could think of. The second room was to the back and was hidden by a black, velvet curtain. I have to admit I was curious, but not *that* curious.

A woman sat on a stool behind a glass counter that held raw gemstones, scented oils and amulets. She was reading a book and looked to be about my age. She wore a large, loose fitting black sweater. She had short, jet-black hair that framed a round face. Her hair and sweater enhanced her pale skin as did her black eyebrows and thick lashes. She seemed to be engrossed in what she was reading. That was fine with me. I just wanted to look and leave.

There was only one other person in the store and she seemed to know exactly what she wanted as she pulled things off the shelves and stacked them carefully in a

Chapter Five

wicker carrying basket. She had on a long, black cloak that tied at the neck. Shoulder-length, dark brown hair fell loose over the hood of the cloak. I could see the hem of what was probably a long, blue skirt peeking out from under it. Talk about trying to look mysterious. She had my vote. She looked over at me and I turned quickly away. I hated when people did that. It embarrassed me.

I turned my attention to the books on the shelves nearest the door, making sure I could "high-tail" it and run if need be. I started at the top, scanning the titles. Every book I saw had to deal with witchcraft and the occult. Definitely not the kind of books I would settle in for the night to read. I felt a sudden tightness in my stomach that I couldn't quite put my finger on, so I turned to leave. "Trust your instincts," my father always said.

"My name's Christine, can I help you with something?" Came a voice from behind me.

I jumped and turned. Nervous? Me?

I found myself looking into the deepest, sapphire-blue eyes I had ever seen. She had on a long, sapphire-blue skirt to match the color of her eyes. She was actually not much taller than I was. Imagine that? Someone I didn't have to look up to.

I shook my head. "No, actually I was about to leave. I don't think you have what I'm looking for," I said and turned again to leave.

"I'm sure we have what you need to help you with your problem."

Instincts. Yup.

I stared at her and my eyes narrowed. "I never said I had a problem."

She smiled. I didn't like it. I turned to leave for the third time. I was sensing a pattern here.

"You are just now coming into your powers."

That stopped me. She had a way with words don't you think?

"Is this the sales pitch you use when sales are down and you're desperate?" My voice was as mild as honey.

She walked by me to the bookshelf I was standing near earlier, glanced sideways at me, and smiled. She grabbed a book without really looking at it and walked back over to me.

She held it out. "I believe this is the one you want to read."

I wanted to wipe that polite smile right off her face. Instead, I smiled back at her with all the sincerity of a snake about to strike, and took the book from her hand. I looked down at it. The title read, "Psychic Dreaming." I felt a cold chill run up my spine.

"How?" I whispered.

"How did I know?" she asked.

I nodded.

"I felt your essence the moment you stepped up to the door. Your aura is a very powerful one, it does not lie about your abilities."

"I don't believe. . ."

"Why do you pretend not to see what is right in front of your own eyes?"

She reached out, but stopped short of touching my arm. Instead, she brought her hands down and folded them in front of her. It was as if she wanted to touch me, but was afraid to.

I shoved the book into her hands. "Listen, thanks for your help, but I think you've been inhaling the incense in this place a little to long."

I turned to leave and bumped into the woman I saw in the store earlier. If she hadn't grabbed my arm, I would have fallen backwards.

Chapter Five

When I met her hazel eyes, they washed over me like a water fall over a cliff on an exotic island. For just an instant, I felt as though I was being covered by a warm, thick blanket. The warmth penetrated every pore in my skin and I thought I could lie down in that warmth forever and never want for anything else. Then, as quickly as it washed over me — the warmth — the feeling of security — was gone. It was gone like a kiss blown in the wind. I blinked and I was smiling as if coming back from a pleasant dream of promises yet to come.

"Sorry." I heard myself say from somewhere at a distance.

"That's quite all right," the soft, seductive voice came echoing back.

I squeezed my eyes shut and shook my head. It helped. When I saw clearly again, she was standing there, watching me.

"Did I say I was sorry?" I asked.

She smiled and it never quite reached her eyes. "Yes you did. That's quite all right."

"Are you all right?" Christine asked from behind me.

I kept my eyes on the woman standing in front of me and nodded. "Yeah, I'm fine." I hadn't noticed until now that she was still holding my arm. I shook free and headed for the door. "Thanks again for your help," I said over my shoulder as I opened the door to leave. I wanted out of this place as fast as my legs would take me.

"I'm here if you. . ."

I closed the door before I heard the rest.

CHAPTER SIX

I arrived home to find a black Durango in my driveway. It looked as though it was just driven off the damn lot. Great. Just great. I wasn't in the mood for company. I walked up the driveway and saw a rather tall, well-dressed man standing on my porch. He looked as though he was getting ready to leave. Someone's got perfect timing. I turned to leave, hoping to disappear before he saw me.

"Excuse me?" the man asked in a deep, rich voice.

Not fast enough. Maybe that's why I never tried out for track in high school or chose a life of crime.

I turned around and tried to look like I hadn't a clue he was standing there. "Who, me?"

He stepped off the porch and walked towards me. "Are you Julie Summers?"

I came up to just below his shoulders when he stood near me. The gray suit he wore was tailored to fit his trim waistline and broad shoulders. My eyes traveled up his neatly trimmed beard and mustache to see steel-blue eyes framed by dark eyebrows and lashes. His black hair was just past his shoulders and had the effect of being cut close to the head, but was actually tied neatly back in a pony tail.

"Who are you?" I asked.

"I'm Detective Kyle Sanders of the Virginia Beach Police Department."

Another cop. Great. I resisted the urge to run to see if he'd chase me.

I debated with myself whether I wanted to lie or tell the truth. I settled for being honest, although I was sure I wasn't going to like the results it gave me. "Yeah, I'm Julie."

He smiled, a smile of even, white teeth that could have blinded a person if the light hit them at the right angle.

"Is there something about that you find funny, Detective Sanders?"

His smile widened. "He was right. You are quite the package."

Did he just call me a package? I didn't care if he was a detective. He could be Santa friggin Clause for all I cared. I didn't have to stand here and listen to this shit.

"If you've got a reason for being here, detective, state it. If not, you're wasting my time and I've done enough of that already."

His eyes faltered and his smile slipped. Point for me.

"I need to talk to you," he said.

"About what."

"Can we do this inside?"

"Listen, Detective Sanders, unless you have some kind of warrant, I don't have to talk to you, let alone invite you into my home," I said as I walked past him. I turned around before I walked up the steps to my porch. "And unless you tell me what it is we're going to "do" inside, you can either stand out here or leave. It makes no difference to me." I walked up the steps and shoved the key into my door.

"Miss Summers, please."

I held the doorknob and my brow rose as I turned to look at him.

"I need to talk to you about the picture our sketch artist did for you yesterday," he said.

"I've been through this twice already, Detective Sanders. Read the report."

I started to go in and he grabbed my arm. "Please, it's important," he said.

I looked down at his hand on my arm, then up at him. He let go. I don't know whether it was the please or that I wanted to get rid of him as soon as possible because I pushed the door open and motioned for him to go in. This was the most company I've had since I moved here. I'm on a roll.

He stood just inside the doorway, scanning the room like it was one of his crime scenes and he was looking for clues. I brushed by him and went into the kitchen to make myself some coffee. If he wanted to sit, he'd sit. I already had a slight disliking for the man and wasn't going to offer anything more than I had to.

I didn't join him until my coffee was done brewing and I had a cup in my hands. He had found his way to the chair by the couch. Good boy. I wanted to ask him to roll over and play dead, but thought better of it. Instead, I sat on the couch, took a long sip of my coffee and made him wait. He just sat there watching me intensely as if I was one of his suspects in for interrogation and he would try staring me into a confession.

"Okay, Detective Sanders," I said, "what is it again you need to talk to me about?"

Chapter Six

He smiled and shook his head. "The sketch our police artist did for you yesterday."

I didn't say anything.

"This sketch was made from a likeness of a man you. . ." He stopped as he fumbled around in his inside coat pocket and pulled out a small notebook. He flipped it open to a page that was paper clipped, "The likeness of a man you saw in a dream?"

"Why are you asking me questions you already know the answers to?"

"I'm just making sure we have the facts straight, Miss Summers."

"The facts are already on paper, detective. If you have another form to fill out, copy the information from the original. I'm not answering the same questions over again." I was back to calling him detective. Not good.

He blinked and just stared at me. Guess he didn't expect that, but he'll learn. Well, there's always hope.

"Why don't I just get to the point then," he said.

"I was wondering when you were going to."

Something moved behind his eyes. "Things such as this are rare and most people who claim it are phonies or just plain nuts.

Did he just say what I think he did? So much for hope eh? I'm glad I didn't ask him to play dead earlier.

"Get out, detective." My voice sounded calm as I slowly stood up.

His eyes widened and his brows rose. "What?"

He had the nerve to look surprised.

"I don't think I want to talk to you anymore. Now get out!" I said the last part through gritted teeth.

He rose from the chair. "Listen, Miss Summers."

"No, you listen!"

Then, just at that moment, the door opened and we both turned at once to glare at whoever was there.

"Hey, Julie. Who's. . ." Elaine stopped halfway through the door, her hand still on the doorknob. Her eyes flicked from me, to him, then back to me. Her mouth hung open and her unfinished words hung in the thick silence.

She came in and leaned against the door so it closed with a soft click, as if she thought any loud noise would set off a ticking bomb. She picks up on things fast don't you think? The detective, on the other hand, could use a few lessons.

I turned my attention back to him. "Elaine, this is Detective Sanders. He was just leaving." At least I was being polite about it.

"Hello. . .I think," she said.

He stared back at me and his eyes narrowed. "Nice to meet you, Elaine. Actually, I'm not leaving just yet," His lips turned up into a half-smile as if daring me to say otherwise. . .who am I to pass up a dare?

"You say that as if you had a choice," I said and marched over to the door. Elaine moved aside rather hastily as I swung it open and caught the knob before the door hit the wall. "You don't."

"What's going on here?" she asked.

We both stood there, still glaring at each other. Guess he wanted to have a contest of wills. He sure wasn't going to be bringing home any blue ribbons today.

"Nothing that I can't handle." I opened the door more.

He didn't move. Instead he reached into his inside pocket and took a six-by-nine manila envelope out. "Maybe you'd like to take a look at these."

I felt my brows crease and my eyes narrowed. I looked at Elaine and she gave a shrug with her eyes so I closed the door. Curiosity and all.

Chapter Six

Elaine let her breath out loudly and flopped her purse on the counter. She sat at one of the stools with her hands folded in her lap. I hopped up onto the one next to her, not a graceful way to do things, but I wasn't out to impress anyone.

"What is it?" I asked.

He went into the kitchen to the other side of the counter. Elaine and I turned in our seats to face him. He opened the envelope, pulled out some pictures and tossed them onto the counter top. They slid on its surface and lay spread out; the top picture stopping in front of me.

All I could do was stare. I felt my heart jump into my throat and an icy chill ran over my skin. "Oh my God."

I knew she was dead. They told me she was. But it still didn't seem real. . .until now. It never seems real until you see.

The top one was a morgue picture. I knew just by looking at it. Her face was blocked out with a large black square, but I knew it was her. It was her neck that got my attention. The bruises and cuts were a mirror image of my own. Right down to the size and length of each one. I ran my finger across the smoothness of the picture, tracing the wound across her neck. Without realizing it, my hand went up to my own neck and felt the bandages I had put around the cuts.

"Is that the woman you saw?" Elaine whispered.

I just nodded slowly. I was afraid to speak as I pushed the first picture aside, revealing the second one. It was another morgue picture but of her left arm and hand. Again, the same exact wounds. The third was of the bedroom. The very one I saw in my dream. She was lying there, the same woman, the same way I remembered. The sheets — her T-shirt — the silk stocking.

I pushed the pictures aside. I'd seen enough. I closed my eyes, still seeing her face in my mind. And I wished I could have saved her, but I waited too long. If I had said something when the second dream came to me, she could still be alive. It was the same as if I had killed her myself.

"They picked him up early this morning," Kyle said.

I just stared blankly up at him.

"The one Julie saw?" Elaine asked.

"Yes, the one she saw in her dream. Miss Summers' wounds are an exact duplicate of the victims'."

"My God, Julie," Elaine said.

The victim. It sounded so final. I got up from the stool, walked over to the couch and leaned my hands on the top of it. I took a deep breath, let it out slowly and turned around. "What's your point in all of this, Detective Sanders." My voice was flat. It sounded alien even to me.

He scooped the pictures up and put them back into his pocket. "I'm sorry I had to do it this way, but I wanted you to see the importance of it."

He was talking in riddles and I could feel a rush of anger building. "The importance of what?"

"Well, Miss Summers, about four years ago many states included psychics as expert witnesses in criminal trials. It was only a little over a year ago that Virginia had included them, but only those psychics that undergo and pass certain. . .tests are accepted."

He must have seen the confusion on my face. "True and natural psychic abilities are far and few so we'd like you to undergo the testing."

My eyes went wide and I wondered if he knew what he was asking. I didn't want to be in some scientific lab so they could do experiments on me. Twice now it's happened and twice someone has died. I didn't care if I ever had another dream again. If they didn't need me anymore for this one case, I was through with it all.

Chapter Six

"Are you serious, Detective Sanders?" Elaine asked. There was an excited lilt to her voice. I guess she thought it was a good thing. I certainly didn't.

"Yes," he said and looked over at me.

"Did they pick that guy up based only on my information?"

"What?" he asked.

"You heard me."

His eyes narrowed suspiciously. "No. We had the evidence we needed. Your description helped find him."

"So, you don't need me to convict this guy right?"

Elaine looked at him, then at me. "Julie, what are you doing?"

I ignored her. "Answer me."

He looked at me and I watched something move behind his steel-blue eyes. He knew what I was doing. "No, we don't need you to convict him." His voice was somehow strained.

"I'm sorry, detective. Thanks, but no thanks."

Elaine came over to me and grabbed my arm. "What's wrong with you, Julie? They're asking for your help."

I shrugged her hand away. "Elaine, please." I walked over to the door and opened it again. "You have my answer, detective. Now you can leave."

"I believe you're being a little too hasty here," He said.

"I don't give a damn what you believe, detective."

He stiffened and his eyes grew dark. "You have a gift, Miss Summers, which should be used to overcome the obstacles that we run into."

"A gift?" I choked back a laugh and walked over to him. "You call this?" I pointed at my neck. "A gift?" I was more angry with myself than anyone in the room. "I didn't ask for this and I sure as hell don't want it!"

I walked back over to the door. "You can. . ."

I stopped in mid-sentence as it hit my body. It was like I had stepped outside into a cold winter's morning. My skin grew cold and my body tingled as inch-by-inch, it slowly grew numb. Everything around me faded to black and I groped around to try to find something real to grab hold of. The aroma of incense filled my senses, making my breath catch in my throat. I was being laid down on something hard that was covered with a material that felt like velvet against my naked skin.

"Where am I?" I asked hearing my voice echo back to me.

"Don't worry, it will be all over soon." An older woman's voice echoed. Her voice was soft; somehow comforting.

I smiled, took in a deep breath and sighed heavily. "Okay." I believed her. I would believe anything she said.

"That's a good girl. It's best if you just lay still."

The voice was getting clearer. It was like a drug was wearing off and my brain was coming back from a deep dark place only your mind could take you.

I felt something cold and wet being placed on my forehead. My eyes fluttered open and I was no longer lying down. The room was empty and the walls were covered with black velvet curtains. I stood near the side of an altar covered in cloth made of the same material as the curtains. A woman lay naked on top of it. Her long, dark-auburn hair spilled over the sides of the altar. Delicately arched dark eyebrows and thick lashes framed closed eyes.

She was a tiny thing and looked pale against the darkness of the cloth. There was black and red silk cord wrapped around each of her ankles and was threaded through holes in the altar and tied off underneath. Her hands lay stretched above her head, tied just below the wrist in the same fashion as her ankles. Wrapped tightly

Chapter Six

around her palms was more of the same silk. It was tied off on the legs of the altar making her hands stretch back at a painful angle so her wrists were fully exposed. Her pale-green eyes fluttered open and immediately went wide with fear. A fear that only thoughts of impending death could bring.

My stomach tightened and my pulse went into my throat. I swallowed it back down and tried to move, but couldn't.

"It's just another dream," I told her.

She never looked my way. She seemed to be looking by me — no — through me to something else. I turned my head in the direction she was transfixed on. There was nothing there. Why would there be?

The woman whimpered and squeezed her eyes shut as some invisible force painted a symbol in black soot on her forehead. Tears spilled out of her eyes when she opened them. I watched as her eyes grow wide again and her breathing came in rapid gasps. She took a deep breath and screamed, trying frantically to move her hands. I didn't know why she was screaming until I saw it.

Slowly and deliberately, something that could not be seen was cutting along one of her wrists from one end to the other. My eyes widened and my pulse raced as I watched it start out as a thin line of pink. It then turned a deep shade of red as the blood came rushing to the surface to spill out of the cut and down her wrist. She screamed again as the other wrist began the same process. . .this time I screamed with her.

CHAPTER SEVEN

"Julie!" Elaine's voice came echoing from outside the deep recesses of my mind.

"We need to get her to a hospital." A deep voice echoed.

"We have to get her out of this first."

Her voice seemed a little closer this time and the coldness slowly subsided. There was a dull throbbing in my wrists as the feeling in my body came back and I started to feel like a human inferno.

"Julie!" Elaine yelled. Her voice sounding shaky.

Then Elaine's face was there, inches from mine, her eyes filled with unshed tears It was as if she had appeared from out of nowhere.

I found myself lying on the couch covered in blankets with Elaine kneeling beside me.

"Christ, Elaine. You don't have to shout," I said. My voice came out a little ragged.

She hugged me. "You scared me half to death."

Chapter Seven

I tried hugging her back but my arms felt weighted down.

"Can we take her to a hospital now?" Kyle asked.

I looked at Elaine. My brows knit together. "Hospital? I only fainted. I don't need a damn hospital. And get this shit off me, I'm sweating my ass off."

Elaine moved aside and I found myself staring up into the softly frowning face of Detective Sanders. Sweat stood out on his forehead and he was holding my wrists wrapped in a dish towel that had been fastened tightly with his belt. The towel was wet with something dark. It was blood. . .my blood.

I tried to sit up. "What the hell is going on here!"

He pushed me back down and held me easily. "Oh, no you don't. Elaine, take my keys out of my left coat pocket and go start my car. We're taking her to the hospital." His deep voice held no room for argument.

I watched as Elaine got up, fished through his pocket and left to do his bidding.

"Excuse me? Don't I get a say in this matter?"

A half smile formed on his lips. "Actually, no."

I tried again to get away from his grip. "And how exactly am I going to explain this to the doctor? They're going to think I did this to myself," I said through gritted teeth.

He pushed me back down. "I'll take care of everything. You're just going to behave yourself," he said as he raised my hands up, put his knee on my stomach and used his weight to hold me down.

I stopped struggling and just stared up at him. There was a look in his steel-blue eyes and his mouth curved up as he switched both my wrists into his left hand, leaving his right hand free. He shoved his hand into his right pocket and fished out a cell phone. He flipped it open, pressed a couple of buttons and put it to his ear. It was as though he knew some dark secret and I was the only one left out in the cold. It reminded me of my meeting with Detective Stuart. I didn't like it — Not one bit.

"Hey, it's me," he said into the phone. "It's an authentic piece, Sir." He paused. "I saw it myself, but I'm afraid I have to take a trip to the hospital first." More silence. Yes, Sir."

"The car's ready," Elaine said. Her breath coming fast as she came running through the door.

"Hold on, Sir," he said into the phone and looked over at Elaine. "Go open the passenger side door for me, I'll be right out." He glanced down at me with those beautiful eyes and when Elaine left, his attention went back to the phone conversation. "Okay, I'm back." More silence. "Consider it done." He stared down at me then, his eyes were intense and there was a darkening behind them. "No, Sir, I won't." And with that, he hung up. At least this "Sir" got more respect than I was getting at the moment.

He slid the phone into his pocket and before I knew it, he scooped me up in his arms in one fluid movement.

"What the hell do you think you're doing!" I yelled.

I tried to twist myself out of his grip. Not easy when your wrists are tied together in a towel. I couldn't get any leverage and all I succeeded in doing was letting him get a firmer grip on me so he was holding me closer to his body.

"You've lost a lot of blood. I can't chance letting you walk, so stay still or I'll drop you."

He held me tighter so that my face was buried in his neck and I was cradled in his arms like a helpless baby. I could feel his heart beat vibrating against my body and the sweetness of his cologne sent my senses reeling. The nearness of his body made my breathing come in short gasps against his neck. I felt his body tense and I suddenly wanted to rip his throat out. How dare he do this to me.

"Put me down you sick son-of-a-bitch!" I yelled into his neck as he carried me down the steps of the porch.

"Something wrong?" Elaine asked.

"No, nothing I can't handle," he said. His deep voice vibrated through his chest. His breathing was slow and even, as if my struggling wasn't phasing him in the least.

"I'll go grab her keys and lock the door," she said.

I found myself being lowered gently into the passenger side of the car. It took me by surprise because I half expected to be thrown in. I glared up at him as he closed the car door on my face. I lifted my leg and kicked his dashboard as hard as I could. The pain was sharp and immediate.

"Fuck!" I cursed under my breath.

He slid into the driver's seat and closed the door. After starting the car, he glanced sideways at me and there was a pleased look on his face. "Did anyone ever tell you, you have quite the extended vocabulary?"

"Only when I'm angry or around someone I don't particularly care for."

Something crossed his face. Was it anger? I certainly hoped so.

"What is that suppose to mean?"

I shrugged. "You're the detective, you figure it out."

He opened his mouth to say something and closed it when Elaine jumped in the back seat.

"All set. Let's go," she said.

He stared at me for a few heartbeats, his eyes as dark as the clouds in a summer storm. He slammed the car into gear and pulled out of the driveway. A little bit too fast for my taste. Oops, I'm sorry. Did I hit a nerve?

Elaine hadn't noticed. Maybe she just thought he was in a hurry to get me to the hospital. I sat back against the seat, closed my eyes and felt the corners of my lips curving up.

CHAPTER EIGHT

The ride to the hospital was a quiet one. Elaine never said a word. I couldn't really blame her. Anyone with half a brain could feel the tension in the car. It was as though any noise outside of the car's wheels humming on the pavement would start a chain reaction causing mass destruction.

I was happy with that. I needed time to think anyway. I had to figure out how to get out of this mess I was in. If I went in there like this, they would think it was an attempted suicide. No one would believe otherwise. I don't know what the detective had in mind, but I know it had nothing to do with what I wanted. He was quiet. . .a little too quiet. He has his own hidden agenda and I refused to be a part of it. I suppose jumping out of a moving car isn't an option.

My heart quickened as we drove into the emergency entrance of the hospital. I was out of time and out of options. Not that I had many options to choose from. He pulled into the farthest parking spot he could find. Two rows from the very rear of the parking lot. Not a good sign — I saw at least three open spots near the entrance.

Kyle turned the engine off and turned sideways in the seat, glancing my way before looking back at Elaine. "Could you go get a wheelchair, Elaine? She shouldn't be walking."

Without a word, she got out of the car and went to do as he asked. Who did he think he was? Captain friggin America?

He turned his attention back to me after Elaine got out. The look on his face serious and his eyes as dark as polished jewels. My heart skipped a beat. Shit.

"You're going to listen to me and do exactly as I say," he said finally.

I felt my stomach tighten. Nope. Not a good sign at all, but I wasn't going down without a fight.

"What makes you think you can tell me what I can and cannot do detective." My voice sounded calm. I could do this. Really I could.

His lips slowly curved up. "I've asked you nicely to help us and it's plain that you will not voluntarily do what we want you to do."

"That's because I have a choice, detective."

He shook his head. "Actually, I'm afraid you don't anymore. You did when I first asked you, yes. That's because you were only a possible candidate. Your options ran out the moment I saw what happened to you today. You have a true and natural gift, little jewel. From now on you will be using that gift to aid me in anyway I see fit. When we are done getting you patched up, you are going to tell me what you saw today."

I sat there listening quietly to what he said. Taking it all in. I could feel the fear creeping up on me. It was like

Chapter Eight

a snake was hiding in the tall grass, waiting for me to come within striking distance. . .and Kyle was the snake. I swallowed my pulse back down my throat and decided to give it one last try.

"There's a word for what you're doing, detective. Elaine's here. She's not going to let you do this," I said. My eyes narrowed, daring him to continue with this little game he was playing. Good for me.

"Yes, I suppose there's a word for it. But do not doubt that I can and will use whatever means necessary to get what I want. And as for Elaine, believe me, you don't want to drag her into this." His voice was soft; somehow threatening.

I frowned. I felt as though someone had ripped my life out from under me and I never saw it coming. I was that wild animal in the jungle, caught in a net and thrown in a cage; to live its life on the wrong side of a locked door. Never having the freedom to do what it was meant to do.

He must have seen the light of freedom dimming in my eyes because he smiled, pulled the keys out of the ignition and stuffed them in his pocket.

I watched him as he started to get out of the car. This was my chance. My one and only chance to get out. I pulled the door handle with my fingers, gave it a quick shove with my shoulder, and stumbled my way out of the car. I kept my footing by leaning on the car door and took off running when I gained my balance. Where was I running? I had no idea, but anywhere was better than here.

Two rows of parked cars and I would be out of the parking lot. I ran to the first row and slipped between two cars. One more row and I'd be near the main road. The main road and lots of people. My heart pounded against my chest as the thought of not making it ran through my head. Please, let me make it.

I could feel him at my back as I reached the second row of cars. He was either real quick or I was too slow because of the condition I was in. My wrists were tied together and I was weak. I didn't turn around to look. You see too many people in movies do it. They almost always get caught. It either slows you down or you run into something in front of you. So, I didn't look back. If I was going to get caught, it wasn't going to be because of stupidity.

As I started to slip through the last row of cars, I felt a sudden chill flow through my body. A wave of lightheadedness washed over me in a surge of starry darkness. I stumbled and leaned on a car for support to wait for the feeling to subside — but I couldn't wait because I could feel him right behind me. No time to wait. . .I had to run.

I pushed myself away from the car, intent on getting away. . .away from the impending doom of never having my life back. I struggled awkwardly on shaky legs and was grabbed by my braid of hair. He yanked me backwards against his warm, solid chest. It felt good against my cold skin. My legs started to go numb and it felt like I was standing on two stumps. Tiny pinpricks nipped at the skin as if they were waking from a deep sleep. I started to fall but was held up at the waist and then lifted up into a pair of strong arms.

"Why do you fight this? I can't believe you would rather die." His deep voice came from far away.

I opened my eyes. Through the fast growing haze and darkness, I looked up into steel-blue eyes framed by a frown of wrinkling dark brows. I resisted the urge to close my eyes as he carried me back the very way I fought so hard to run from. Too weak to move, let alone struggle.

He sighed heavily. "Well, you've made it easier for me anyway."

I managed enough strength to glare at him for just a heartbeat and closed my eyes to let the darkness encompass my mind.

"You are very special, my little jewel."

His voice faded away as I fell into the dark hole of nothingness. It was a wonderful feeling of emptiness. It was better than the reality I would be forced into.

CHAPTER NINE

I woke slowly. My eyes fluttered at first as they tried to adjust to the dimness of the room I was in. The smell of antiseptic stung my nose and I could taste it in the back of my throat. My brain felt like it was floating outside my skull on invisible wires. I turned my head and saw that the bed I was in was surrounded by a wall of white curtains. I was in the hospital. I remembered now — he brought me here.

I struggled to lift my head, but it was as though someone opened it and filled it full of lead. Every part of my body felt foreign. They had given me something. How the hell was I going to get out of here if I was pumped full of drugs? I'd have to wait for it to wear off a little. Bide my time. How much time did I have? I had no clue. I had no idea what was going to happen to me after today. No clue where he was going to take me or what he was going to do. I refused to be a lab rat. I didn't care how noble they thought their cause was.

Chapter Nine

I heard the lock on my door click and the door open as someone walked quietly into the room. The only sound was the soft hush of the door closing. My pulse jumped. Great, just friggin great. They keep the door locked.

It was him. I knew it. . .I sensed it. Every nerve in my body felt him. I closed my eyes, hoping to fool him into thinking I hadn't come to yet. I concentrated on keeping my breathing slow and even. No easy task when your nerves are about as tight as the string on a bow. If it meant getting out of here in one piece, I could do it.

I heard the curtain nearest my head being drawn back, sending a soft breeze across my face. I fought not to flinch at the sound. I had to concentrate. Don't move. Then Something tugged at my hair. .He was touching it. He was actually caressing the ends of my braid. It took every ounce of self-control I had to keep myself from reaching over and breaking that hand. I felt my body start to stiffen and quickly stopped myself, hoping it wasn't noticed. Please don't notice.

The door opened again and another rush of air blew at my face as another person walked quietly in the room. Great. More company to poke and prod at me. I didn't know if I could stand another person touching me. His hand moved quickly away. I almost let out a sigh from the breath I didn't know I was holding, instead I let it out slowly and evenly. My mind screamed for them to leave. I was losing my self-control. I was never big on self-control and this was a true test.

I heard him walk away from the bed and close the curtains. Relief flooded my senses and I slowly — cautiously opened my eyes. They were standing on the other side of the curtains, their silhouettes casting gray shadows along the curtains. One tall and broad, the other a little shorter and thin. I didn't have to guess which one was which. I could watch and listen and not be noticed. Things were looking up.

"So, what's the deal, Shawn? Can we do it when she comes to?" Kyle voice was a deep whisper.

I think it's quite hard for a deep voice to actually whisper without it sounding hoarse, but he did it quite well. It sounded like the soft rumbling of a thunderstorm off in the distance; dangerous, but calming. I wonder how much he had to practice to get it like that. Under different circumstances, I would have asked.

"I don't think it's a good idea," Shawn replied.

"Why the hell not?" His voice rose just above a whisper and then he lowered it again. "We may not have a lot of time here."

"If she goes through the same thing she did today, she may not live through it. Not this soon after."

"How soon?"

"Her wounds heal fast. It's remarkable how fast. The wounds she received the other day are almost non-existent now and modern medicine had nothing to do with it." He paused. "She needs at least twenty-four hours from the time of each incident."

"That woman was reported missing as of nine o'clock last night. For all we know she may already be dead," he said. His voice sounded tired and weary. He sighed heavily. "We have to know if this woman is the person she has seen in this recent encounter. I want her under no later than ten o'clock tomorrow morning."

"Christ, Kyle. You're playing with fire here. This girl is very gifted and I'm certain her powers haven't even scratched the surface. You're taking the chance of loosing a prize piece of psychic ability. You know as well as I do that they are far and few in between, let alone as special as this one. She is the only one we have right now."

"Just do it! And keep her under sedation until the appropriate time. I guarantee you she will run if she has the chance."

"Fine. It's on your head if something happens to her."

"Did you take care of Elaine."

"I told her Julie needed rest and she could come see her on Thursday."

"That's good. We'll have her out of here by then." Shawn opened the door to leave. "I'll see you tomorrow."

"Don't forget the sedation, Shawn." Kyle said flatly.

Shawn sighed heavily. "Don't worry, I'll take care of it."

The door closed and I quickly closed my eyes, the anger I felt threatening to boil to the surface and explode. If he didn't leave soon, I would end up inflicting as much harm to him as I could manage and then I'd be stuck here. I needed time between his leaving the room, that's if he ever did leave and Shawn coming back to shoot me up with sedatives again.

I heard him come back through the curtains and could feel his presence close to my head; could smell the scent of him. He ran his finger gently along my temple. Did I flinch? I hoped not. His finger traced a line down my cheek, along my jaw and to my lips. I resisted the urge to bite that finger and tear it of his hand. Down girl. Maybe later.

His finger caressed my top lip, tracing its shape, then he did the same to the bottom. His finger lingered there for what seemed an eternity.

"See you tomorrow, my little jewel," he whispered as he ran his finger once more along my bottom lip.

He stood there for another couple of heartbeats and was gone. The only sound was the door sighing as it closed and the soft click of the lock slamming home. I was beginning to feel like that wild animal. . .desperate for freedom.

I waited for what seemed an eternity before trying once more to get up. My head still felt heavy, but my arms and legs were mine again. I sat up and waited for the rush of fog to clear my brain. My wrists were neatly bandaged; it looked like I was ready to go play a game of tennis. I was also hooked up to an IV, makes it easier to give you the drugs you need. In my case, the drugs they needed to keep me from being coherent. I tore the tape off the top of my hand and winced as I slid the needle out slowly while applying pressure to it with my other hand.

There was one of those adjustable eating tables on wheels by the bed. The ones that you can never quite get to adjust to the right height. I reached over, grabbed some tissue out of a box on top of it and taped it over the bleeding hole. I slipped off the bed and when my legs stopped trembling, I padded my way to a metal cabinet by the bathroom. The door opened with a low moan. My breath caught in my throat and I froze. The only sound I could hear was my pulse thumping in my ears. So, I stood there. . .waiting to see if someone would come and shackle me to the bed.

No one came. I guess the room was pretty sound proof when the door was shut. That would be a good thing — for me. I swallowed my heart back into my chest and peeked inside the cabinet; afraid to open the door any further. There lay my jeans, sweater, bra, and socks. All folded neatly on the bottom shelf with my sneakers next to them. I let out a deep breath and could feel a smile of triumph forming on my lips. I guess they weren't as smart as they thought they were. I sure never said they were.

The cabinet door was open enough to reach in and grab my things off the shelf. I searched frantically through

Chapter Nine

my jeans' pockets for my wallet. My heart sunk to the pit of my stomach and I felt the cold rush of fear crawling up my spine. It wasn't there. That dirty son-of-a-bitch. I guess after tonight, my life wasn't to be mine any longer, but not if I could help it. I was going to get out of here. I threw my clothes on, and with trembling fingers, I fastened my jeans. The effect of whatever they gave me was almost gone and I knew I stood a fifty-fifty chance now of getting out in one piece.

I went over to the door and tried to open it. No luck. Did I expect it to be unlocked? No, but it was worth a try. The lock could have gotten stuck. Ri-ight.

My feet padded softly around the room as I looked for something to defend myself with when Shawn came back to do Kyle's bidding.

The only furniture was the bed, the adjustable table, the metal cabinet, and a heavy chair that sat in the corner on the opposite side of the bed. My pulse quickened and my stomach tightened. I felt the beginnings of the hot sting of tears in my eyes. I went back over to the bed. Nothing, unless I wanted to have a pillow fight with him. Maybe, if I was lucky, he'd be allergic to feathers and he'd sneeze to death.

I decided to try the bathroom. Toothpaste, plastic cup, mouthwash and a small bar of soap on the sink. At least I'd have fresh breath when I screamed for mercy. I pulled the shower curtain aside and there it was. One of those shower chairs for people who can't quite get around on their own. I grabbed it, went into the main room and waited by the door. Listening for the approaching footsteps. . .Shawn's footsteps.

CHAPTER TEN

I stood by the door with my ear against it; waiting . . .listening. The only thing I could hear was the quick beating of my own heart against my chest. I held my breath to slow it down to try to get my anxiety in check. If I didn't hear him approach the door, I wouldn't make it. When I calmed myself enough, I put my ear back to the door and heard it. Someone was coming and that someone was very close already.

I rushed around to the other side of the bed and hid behind the curtains. I picked the shower chair up and held it over my shoulder. Like a batter would a bat before swinging and believe me — I planned to come out swinging. Swinging objects at another person was new to me. I didn't want to kill him and I hoped that I didn't. I could never do that to another human being. I just wanted him out long enough to get away. This was going to work. I hoped.

Chapter Ten

I heard the lock click and the door swung open, sending in a breeze of warm air from the hallway. The curtains around the bed swayed gracefully like trees in the wind.

His footsteps tapped softly on the bare floor as he walked towards the bed and swung the curtain aside to find the bed empty.

"What the. . .," he said and stood there for a breath before he ran over to the metal cabinet and flung it open. "Shit!" He rushed to the bathroom, coming out moments later. "Shi-it, shi. . ."

He stopped when he saw me standing in the shadow of the curtains. He stood there. . .frozen. As if waiting to see if I'd move. When I didn't, he walked slowly; deliberately towards me. Like a hunter bearing down on a frightened animal he had just wounded. He reached carefully in the large pocket of his medical coat, pulled a syringe out and held it down to one side. It was as if he thought any sudden movement would frighten his prey off.

He reached me in just a few heartbeats and stopped. His eyes grew wide when he saw what I held in my hands. "Julie," he whispered.

My lips curved up. "Hi," I said and swung the chair around hitting the side of his head and shoulder with a resounding thud. He fell sideways onto the end of the bed and into the curtains; its force ripping some of them off their rods. He slipped off the bed and onto the floor in a slumped heap, taking some of the curtains with him.

I stood there frozen and my breathing came in heavy gasps as I let the chair slide out of my hands and drop to the floor. I had never done anything like this before. The sound and feel of the metal hitting flesh and bone made my stomach want to heave.

I took a breath, knelt down and put my hand near his nose. I let out a deep sigh when I felt his soft breath on my hand. I checked his head and my hand came back dry. He was just out cold. He wouldn't bleed to death anyway. I silently prayed that I would never be put in a situation to do this again.

I felt around in his coat pockets, pulled out a cell phone and laid it on the floor beside me. My hands trembled as I felt around his waist and found the keys hooked to a belt loop. They went next to the cell phone. I quickly rummaged through his pant's pockets and found his wallet. It had a license, credit cards and money. I closed it, snatched up my other treasures and got up. The keys went on my belt loop; the wallet and cell went in my back pockets. The cell was one of those compact, slim jobs. I was grateful for that because I felt I needed it and didn't want to carry it in my hands. I needed my hands free.

When I had everything there was to find, I started to leave. Shawn moaned and it stopped me in my tracks. I looked over at him, then to the syringe that lay on the floor near the wall. I felt a sneer forming on my lips. I picked it up. Could I do it? Why not? He was going to do it to me.

His arm felt like dead weight as I lifted it off the floor and pushed his sleeve up. I had never given anyone a needle before, but there's a first time for everything eh? It's not like I don't know which vein it goes in. I found the vein, slid the needle in and sent its contents spilling into Shawn's arm.

Satisfied now, I got up to make my escape, but not before seeing a chart hanging off the end of the bed. I plucked it off the hook, shoved it under my arm and padded over to the door. There would be time to look at it later. When I was far away from here.

I opened the door just a crack, to see if anyone was around. The hallway was dark and quiet. I glanced to my left. Two doors down from my room on the opposite

Chapter Ten

side, was an emergency exit. The hallway to my right went down about six more doors and turned off the left. If I was going to get out, I'd have to do it quick or I'd be caught.

The keys jingled softly as I took them off my belt so I gripped them tightly in my hand to make the noise stop and slipped through the door. There were about ten keys on the ring and I hoped I didn't have to fish through them all to lock the door. I looked at the lock. It was brass colored so I went for the brass keys. It was worth a try. The worst thing that could happen, is that I would end up going through all of them. There were four brass keys. I carefully took the first one, holding the others together so they didn't jingle, and tried it. Didn't fit. I did the same with the rest. It was the last key I tried. Figure's huh?

I slipped through the emergency exit door and practically stumbled my way down the stairs. Four flights of stairs later, I was in the hall of the emergency room. All I had to do was walk out the automatic doors. Just a few more feet and I would be free.

The fresh air hit me like the first rain in spring. It felt invigorating. I stood there for a moment. . .breathing deeply. Fresh air and freedom. You can't top that.

Where was I going from here? He knew where I lived, what my truck looked like and he knew my friend Elaine. What options did I have? I couldn't go to the police. That was definitely out. I could hop in my truck and just drive. Out of this state and out of their reach. Out of his reach.

That was the plan. A good plan. I used Shawn's cell to call a cab and paid for it with his money. Kind of ironic isn't it?

I got to my door and realized that I didn't have my keys. I never kept a spare hidden because I was always afraid of someone finding it. . .or me forgetting where I put it. So, I went around back and through an unlocked window. I don't lock my windows, but I lock my door. Makes perfect sense to me.

I climbed through the window without much trouble. Being small has its rewards. The clock over the TV read 11:33 PM. I wouldn't be able to drive very far before pulling over. The events of the day and the sedatives I had been given would take their toll sooner or later. Right now I was running on pure adrenaline.

My gym bag was in my closet. I grabbed it and rushed through the house, throwing things in it, making sure the hospital clipboard went in with everything else. I went to the kitchen, pulled one of the drawers open and grabbed any paperwork I may need later on. The second drawer contained a second set of keys to my house and truck. With keys in hand, I was ready to "hi-tail" it. I grabbed my gym bag, flung it over my shoulders and headed out. I was sure he wouldn't come looking for me until either Shawn woke up and someone heard him in the room or ten o'clock tomorrow morning rolled around. I was hoping for the latter.

I was just about to unlock the truck when the phone in my pocket vibrated against my body. I dropped my keys and nearly jumped out of my skin. I stood there as it vibrated again and again. If it was Kyle calling Shawn, I would be found out. I reached in and pulled it out, my hands shook as I opened it up to see if there was an incoming number. My stomach tightened and my breath caught in my throat. It was the hospital. I couldn't think of any reason the hospital would call this number unless they knew I was gone. I did the only thing I could think of. I pressed the talk button. I had to know.

CHAPTER ELEVEN

I held the phone up to my ear, not saying a word. My breathing the only thing the person on the other end could hear.

"Julie, my little jewel. What have you done? I came back because I missed you and you weren't here," Kyle said. His voice was low and deep. Its dangerous edge made my pulse quicken and the hair on the back of my neck stand up. It was as if his words held the promise of the things I would suffer without actually saying it.

I took a deep, shaky breath. "I'm afraid I won't be making our ten o'clock meeting tomorrow morning, detective," I said. My voice was laced heavily with sarcasm. Sarcasm works for me.

"So, you were awake?" It wasn't a question.

"Very much so."

"I have to admit, I was surprised to find that you had recovered so quickly from our — treatments."

"I'm sure Shawn thought so too. By the way, how's he doing?"

"He's sleeping it off. I'm afraid he won't be with us for a few hours."

"That's too bad," I said with all the sincerity of a black widow.

"We'll have to make sure your treatments are more...potent next time." There was that edge to his voice again. My heart skipped a beat. Shi-it.

I swallowed my pulse back down my throat. "I'm afraid there won't be a next time."

"Where do you plan to go, my little jewel? There's nowhere for you to hide. You're life is not yours any longer. I've seen to that."

I could feel the anger twisting deep in the pit of my stomach. Anger was much better than fear. It was an emotion I was familiar with. "What the hell is that suppose to mean?"

"You haven't looked at your chart yet?"

Shit. The chart. I hadn't thought to look at it until I was well on my way out of state.

"I'll take your silence as a no," he continued. "I will sum it up for you then. What that chart pretty much says is that you are a danger to yourself and society. I have taken the liberty to add a few extras to your past history of psychotic behavior. It also states that Shawn has been your acting psychiatrist for the past ten years. By attacking Shawn, I'm afraid all you've done this evening is show how very dangerous you really are."

"You can't do that," I whispered.

"It's already done. You belong to me now, my little jewel. Accept that fact and things will go a lot smoother for all of us."

"Stay away from me you — sick—fuck!" I yelled.

Chapter Eleven

I heard him laugh, deep and rich. I hung up, threw the phone across the yard, leaned against the truck and let the tears flow freely. My life vanished before my eyes and I was alone. I didn't know where to go or whom I could trust to talk to that he didn't know about. I had no family and he knew the only friend I had. I couldn't chance putting Elaine in any danger. Who knew how far these people would go. Maybe I should have said yes. If I did, where would that have gotten me? In a lab like a rat. Only to be let out when they needed it for an experiment or two. In my case, it would be when they needed me to help them find someone dangerous. It was a worthwhile thing to do. The problem was, that this "thing" I have is dangerous to me. This last episode was worse than the first. They could find someone else.

I pulled myself together, picked up the phone and decided that a motel would be best for the night. I couldn't stay here or take my truck. I didn't want to be sitting here in the open, so I walked the back roads to the Boulevard and called a cab from a pay phone.

The hotel room was small. It was all I could afford. It had a bed, three-drawer dresser, a night stand, a chair near the window and a TV on a small stand by the dresser. The whole room was done in a putrid green color that looked like someone through buckets of pea soup all over it. The walls were green, the bed spread had large green leaves with gold outlines and the carpet was a dark, forest-green. I'd never buy another thing that had green in it after today.

When I was settled in, I took a hot shower and washed my hair. I felt a hundred percent better. I sat on the edge of the bed and combed my hair out. No small task with it down to my waist. I thought about the woman I saw on that altar. Her pale-green eyes so engulfed with fear and her naked body stretched out like an animal ready for slaughter.

I sighed heavily, picked the cell up, and stared down at it. It was possible to help her and not have to submit to his demands. I didn't need to be with him to help, although I didn't know what else I could do for her. I didn't know where it was. It could be a hundred miles from here for all I knew.

I flipped the phone open and found the address book. Kyle's was the only number on the list. I pressed talk and listened as the phone on the other end rang.

"Hello, my little jewel. It's nice of you to call me back so soon." His voice caressed my skin like the soft breeze of a cool spring evening. It sent chills down my spine and reached to deeper parts of me. Damn.

"If you want to continue this conversation, I suggest you stop calling me that. I'm not anyone's little jewel, let alone yours."

"Fine, Julie. To what do I owe the honor of this call."

Did I detect a bit of hostility in his voice? It was certainly better than the alternative. I could deal with this.

I decided to get right to the point and end this conversation as soon as possible. "The woman I saw was about five-five, hundred-fifteen pounds, green eyes, long dark-auburn hair."

Silence. This was not going to end it soon. All I heard was his soft breathing on the other end.

"Where?" he asked finally.

I shrugged and realized he couldn't see it. "I haven't a clue. It was inside."

"I need to find you, Julie."

I frowned into the phone. He sure liked to piss me off. "Don't start that shit with me again, detective"

Chapter Eleven

Silence again, although I could hear a faint clicking sound over the phone. I was either being taped or traced. I've seen enough movies to know.

"With our help, you'll be able to see things you wouldn't normally see yourself. At least until you could control it on your own."

"With what? Drugs that'll fry my brain in the process? I don't think so. Accept that I was willing to call you at all and give you what I know. The only other thing I can tell you is that she was on an altar of some sort. It was as if..." I stopped myself. The black velvet table cloth and curtains. The symbol. Witchcraft? I needed to pay another visit to Mystical Tools.

"It was as if what, Julie?"

"Nothing."

"You can't go off doing something on your own. It's too dangerous."

"No more dangerous than what you have planned for me."

That silence with the clicking sound again.

"I will find you, my little jewel. You can only hide for so long," he said finally. His deep, rich voice was laced with threats of things more harmful than any dream I could possibly have.

"I don't see you breaking my door down, detective. Try and trace *this* you bastard!" I pushed the end button on the phone and threw it on the bed.

He was right. I couldn't hide for long and there wasn't much cash in Shawn's wallet. My parents had left me money, but I had to go through a lawyer to get to it. I never bothered after they died because it wasn't their money I wanted. I never got a checking account because I hated the thought of carrying a checkbook around with me. The savings account I got was just so I could cash my checks from work. I think there's a whole five dollars in it.

I always paid for things in cash and got money orders for my bills. All the money I had and my one credit card was in my wallet. I think when this is all over I'll change my mind about checkbooks and bank accounts.

I opened my gym bag and found the clipboard that I took from the hospital. I glanced at the top page. Vitals, medications and prognosis. They had pumped me up with some drug called propofol. Whatever it was, it didn't work as well as they thought it would. I guess there were certain advantages to my having these abilities. I healed fast. A nice thing to know — and my body recovered from the effects of drugs a lot sooner. A fact they didn't know about until it was too late. Things were looking up.

The prognosis was just as Kyle said it would be. My arms stiffened and I gripped the clipboard so tightly that my knuckles blotched. I glared up at the ceiling and took a deep, cleansing breath.

"I'm not fucking crazy!" I flung the clipboard across the room. It hit the wall and fell to the floor. The papers it held came out and fell like leaves in the wind.

I stared at it for a few heartbeats, my heart racing like I had just done the mile in ten seconds flat. "You'll pay for this, Kyle Sanders. I don't know how, but you will." I said to the clipboard. My voice was just a whisper. "Tomorrow's another day."

I thought about my plans for tomorrow and I only hoped that this next visit to Mystical Tools would help in some way. I braided my damp hair and went to bed — I left the light on.

CHAPTER TWELVE

There was a cold front pushing through and forty degrees was below what we normally would have at this time of the year. I wore jeans, a black sweater and my black winter jacket. Once again, I was glad it was colder so I could hide my many war wounds. I took my hair out and it fell down my back in tight waves because of the braid it was in all night. I kept it down to keep the chill off my neck and fastened the sides back to keep it out of my face.

I took the bus this time. Shawn's money was running out fast and I only had enough for one more night in the motel. I looked out the large window of the bus and watched as people went on with their daily routines. Either oblivious or ignorant to anything corrupt that could be happening. I hoped that one day my life could go back to blissful naiveté. So far this week I've gone from one problem to the next. I had to find a way to stop this shit from happening to me, find this woman before anything happens to her and take my life back from Kyle. And it was only Tuesday. Just your normal everyday problems. Ri-ight.

I hesitated at the door with my hand hovering just above the doorknob. The door opened and Christine stood there. She wore a loose fitting, red dress to her ankles that tied at her small waist.

"Come in. Please," she said.

I looked into her sapphire eyes. There was a blankness there that told me absolutely nothing. I brushed by her and walked into the heated warmth of the store. My first breath caught in my throat as the smell of incense bit at my nose and I had to swallow hard to get the bitter taste out of my mouth. This would definitely take some getting used to.

She closed the door and followed me into the store. "I knew you would come back."

"What was it that you were saying when I left here yesterday."

"I said I would be here if you needed any help."

"I'd like to ask you something."

"Sure."

I turned towards the back room and the black curtain that covered its entrance. "What's back there?"

"More. . .advanced tools and supplies. Mostly for those of experience." She walked by me towards the curtain and opened it from the side. "Would you like to see?" she asked.

My first answer would be a definite. . .no. "Yes, I would." I walked over to the curtain and hesitated as I remembered the blackness of the curtains in my latest adventure — the blackness of the cloth against her white skin.

"It's okay. There's nothing back there that'll bite you."

Chapter Twelve

I peeked in through the opening. It was just another room. No black velvet curtains on the walls or altar with a naked woman lying on it bleeding to death from slit wrists. Just more items for sale. Did I expect to see what I thought I would see? Yes. But we won't go there.

I sighed. I think I was relieved, but that meant I still didn't know where the woman was. "Thank you for letting me have a look."

"What did you expect to see?"

"Nothing," I lied.

"Come," she said and motioned towards a chair near the glass cabinet, "sit down and we can talk."

I thought about that for a moment and walked over to sit down. I came here to get information after all and she seemed willing to give it to me. She hopped up onto the stool behind the cabinet and put her hands in her lap.

"My name's Julie by the way."

"What can I do for you, Julie?"

"I'm very limited on time and I need some questions answered."

She nodded. "Sure, if I can."

"Can you find someone that's missing?"

"Well, if I could, there wouldn't be any missing people. No. I'm sorry, I can't."

Strike one. "You're a witch aren't you?"

She smiled at that. "Yes, but I don't have that kind of capability and I don't know anyone who does."

She answered my second question. Strike two. I had a feeling she wouldn't be able to help me with that part of it.

"If you knew about my problem when I walked in here yesterday, then that means you can. . ."

"No. I can't. I am not a psychic. I told you I knew from your aura. You are a very powerful individual, although you haven't reached your full potential yet."

I frowned at that. "There has to be other people around that have the same thing," I said. I felt foolish. Witches. Auras. Psychic powers. What's next? Flying saucers? I didn't believe in this bull shit.

"I have been reading auras for a little over thirteen years and I have never seen one like it."

Not really the answer I wanted to hear. I was hoping she'd have the decency to lie to me. That's strike three. Do I get another strike just for luck?

I took in a deep breath and let it out slowly. I was getting answers, but I didn't like them. Now for the ten million dollar question. "Can you help me stop this from happening?"

"I've never heard of it. That doesn't mean it isn't possible. I only know of ways to enhance and induce psychic abilities of those that have it naturally."

That's sort of a maybe answer. Should I give her five mil for it?

"If I can't stop it, is there a way to control it? Every time it happens I end up like this." I pulled up my coat sleeves and showed her my wrists. They were just faded pink lines now. My other injuries were already gone. Pretty amazing.

Her eyes went wide and her jaw dropped. "This happened while you were having a vision?"

"Well, it was actually worse yesterday, right after it happened. It looked like I took a razor to them, but I guess I heal fast."

"You have healing abilities also. I guess you would have to in order to be subjected to these kinds of injuries each time."

Chapter Twelve

"Is there a way to control these visions?" I asked again. Vision. Geeze. I felt like I was in some kind of science fiction movie.

"I'm afraid you can't control what happens in them, but I think you can control what you do in them when they happen. I could help you and with a little practice and meditation, you could be better prepared."

Better prepared she says. How do you prepare for this shit? Are we ready? Sure, I've got my meditation music and armored suit.

"It's better than nothing I guess." I looked down at my wrists and felt my heart sink into my stomach. This would never end and would probably only get worse. I didn't like it. I was running out of time as far as that woman was concerned. I knew it. I could feel it. If Christine couldn't help me, I would call Kyle and tell him where I was.

Christine touched me gently on the shoulder. "Are you okay?"

I sat silently trying to figure out how what I saw could help in anyway. "I saw a symbol." I whispered.

"What?"

"I saw a symbol in yesterday's vision. The whole thing looked almost ceremonial."

Her eyes widened, her mouth opening slightly. "Could you draw this symbol for me?"

I nodded. "Sure," I said and got up. I grabbed a pen and piece of scrap paper from near the cash register and drew the symbol. When I was done, I held it out for her to see.

Christine froze and just stared at the piece of paper I held in my hand. As if she wished she could set it on fire and make it disappear with just a look. Her eyes widened and her face went deathly white. After a few breaths, she reached out a trembling hand and took it from me. "You saw this?" she asked. Her voice cracked.

A shiver ran up my spine. It looked as though the devil himself reached in and snatched her soul from her body.

"Yes, I did. What's wrong?" I asked.

"If this is what I think it is. . ." She stopped herself and looked into my eyes. "I need to do some research on this. Can I get back with you?"

"Listen, I'm pretty much pressed for time here. I have one other problem besides these visions that I have to contend with."

She must have seen the distress on my face. "Do you want to tell me about it? I'd like to help you as much as I can."

"I think this is something only I can resolve." I looked into her eyes. The sincerity was as plain as a baby's smile for its mother. I sighed heavily. What the hell. I could tell her part of it anyway. "I'm pretty much desperate right now. I don't know who I can trust. I can't go home, don't have any money left and after tomorrow, I have nowhere to stay. I can't tell you why, only that it all has to do with this so-called "gift" that everyone says is so damn special!" I started off calm enough, but by the time I finished my anger had gotten the best of me. My hands were in fists at my sides and my chest was heaving.

I turned and walked away from the counter. "This is so not fair." I turned back around to look at Christine. "I just can't figure out why it has to be me."

"Do you trust me?"

I thought about that for a moment. I nodded. "Yeah, I do. For some reason that I can't figure out, I do." It's that instinct thing.

"Okay. Tell me where you're staying. I'll get this research done quickly and come to you so you don't have

Chapter Twelve

to go out anymore today. It should only take a few hours." She looked down at her watch. "I'll close the shop early and see you around five okay?"

Five? That was seven friggin hours from now. "Okay. I guess that'll have to do."

At least she was willing to help me. She was probably the only one they didn't know that I could trust at this juncture.

I wrote the motel name and room number on a piece of paper and put it in her hand.

She gave my hand a squeeze. "I'll be there. I promise,"

I smiled. "I know."

For the first time since this started I felt as though I wasn't alone. I walked to the door and turned once more to look at her. "See you at five."

I put my hand on the knob to open the door when someone opened it and walked right into me.

I stared into pale-blue eyes. Eyes the color of a cloudless winter sky. Eyes I could jump into and swim around in. Their depths swallowed my mind and brought me to a place where cool breezes blew ocean waves against rocky cliffs. A place where I could stay forever. I could close my eyes and let the sounds lull me into a deep and peaceful sleep. And I let those sounds lull me. I wanted them to — needed them to. The peacefulness crept slowly up my body until something from somewhere pulled at me to come back. It was like I was being pulled out of the dark depths of the ocean floor.

"I said, are you okay?" Christine asked from somewhere far away.

"Huh?" I heard myself say. I squeezed my eyes shut for a second and opened them to see the woman was still standing in front of me.

Another woman in a black cloak. Geeze. Was there a fashion trend I wasn't aware of?

I turned around. "Yeah. I'm fine, I think. I must be tired is all."

"Can I get by please?" the woman asked as she slipped her hood off her head revealing long, ash-blonde hair.

I moved aside. "Oh, I'm sorry."

She glanced at me sideways and I could see her lips curving up. I felt my stomach tighten. Shi-it.

"I'll see you later, Christine." I said and left before she had a chance to say anything.

I walked outside and welcomed the cold breeze that blew at my skin. Things were getting weirder by the minute. Did I have the word "freak" written on my forehead?

I walked over to the mall, got a charger for the cell and then to Seven Eleven and bought a cold sandwich and cup of coffee. I ate while I waited for the bus. Looked like I was going to be eating on the run for a while.

By the time the bus came, two more people stood with me. One was a man who was a good foot-and-a-half taller than I was. He had long muscular legs that practically ripped the seams of his tight jeans. He was solid muscle and had dirty-blonde hair tied back where it fell to his narrow waist. He kept glancing my way, dark-gray eyes caressing my skin; his lips curving up into a half smile under a neatly trimmed mustache. I felt as though he was seeing and touching parts of me that only a lover should. I was relieved when the bus finally pulled to the curb and I sat to the rear, as far away from him as I could get. I didn't feel comfortable having him at my back.

When I got off the bus, I looked up at the window where he was sitting. He smiled at me and leaned back in his seat. I stared at the bus as it drove away. Yep, it's gotta be the sign on my forehead.

CHAPETER THIRTEEN

I shoved the key in the motel room door and walked in. I was still in the same position I was when I left. No answers and time was running out. The feeling of dread spread through my body like an electric current. I was going to have to call Kyle. I couldn't let that woman die because of my pigheadedness. After all, what was my freedom compared to someone's life?

I looked over at the cell phone on the night stand and a thought came to me. I picked up the phone book and got the non-emergency number for the Virginia Beach Police Department. I used the hotel phone in my room and dialed the number.

I waited while the phone on the other end rang.

"Virginia Beach Police Department, Officer Williams speaking," came the voice on the other end.

"Is there a Detective Kyle Sanders there?" I asked.

"Hold on please."

Chapter Thirteen

I twisted the phone cord around my fingers as I waited. I needed something to do with my hands or I'd end up chewing all my nails off.

"Can I get your name?" he asked.

"I just want to know if he's there. You don't need my name for that do you?"

"Where are you Miss Summ. . ."

I hung up. My heart skipped a beat. Shi-it. I stood there with my hand still on the phone. How would they know it was me? Maybe he wasn't a detective and the mention of his name gave me away. Who the hell was he?

I plugged the charger in the cell, flipped it open and dialed his number.

"Hello my little jewel," he said. His low voice kissed my skin and sent goose bumps down my arms. Damn it!

He just answered the phone and I could feel the anger building like a tidal wave heading for its target. "I asked you not to call me that!"

"We don't always get what we ask for."

Sarcasm. I think that was a first for him.

"Who the fuck are you really, Detective Kyle Sanders? Or is that even your real name?"

Silence and that damnable clicking sound. The silence confirmed my suspicions. I wanted to know who he really was and having a time limit pissed me off.

"It's my real name, yes."

"You're not a detective though. Who the hell do you work for? The C.I.A? F.B.I? What?"

I heard him choke back a laugh. "Now *that* was insulting."

Now I wasn't sure if I wanted to hear it. "Answer me!"

"I, my little jewel, am the one that takes care of certain problems that otherwise would not be able to be resolved. I have the consent to do what it takes and am non-existent when, and if, circumstances should turn out to be less than desirable."

I wished I never asked. Things were actually worse than what I thought. It was bad enough thinking he was a detective with pull. Now he was some friggin ghost with unlimited power and resources to do what he wanted. . .to whomever he wanted.

I swallowed hard. "I don't believe you," I lied. I was hoping maybe I still had a chance.

"Believe what you wish, but I'll tell you this. You have been assigned exclusively to me and I will not stop until I have you." He said it so softly that his deep voice practically purred through the phone.

"Go to hell!" I screamed as slammed my finger into the end button and let the phone slip out of my hand. I felt lost and defeated. I hated what was happening to me. Powerless to stop it and no one to help. Not even Christine could help me with Kyle. I threw myself on the bed and cried myself to sleep.

CHAPTER FOURTEEN

I woke to the soft rapping on my door. My eyes were held shut with dried, unshed tears. I peeked through the curtain, unlocked the door and let Christine in.

"You look terrible," she said.

"Thanks, it's much appreciated."

A soft frown formed on her face. "I'm sorry, I didn't mean it that way."

I went over to the bed and sat on the edge. "It's okay. Really. I just got some rather bad news earlier and decided I deserved a good cry."

She sat next to me and put her hand on my arm. "Anything I can help you with?"

I looked into her deep, sapphire eyes and wondered if I should take the chance. I didn't think getting her involved would be wise. Elaine was safe as far as I knew. She wouldn't even know I was gone for another two days, when Shawn told her she could see me. I couldn't take the chance calling her. The less anyone knew about this the better off they were.

If all else fails, change the subject. "Did you find anything out?"

She frowned then. The look in her eyes held a seriousness that made my stomach knot up.

"I'm afraid it's not good news. The symbol you showed me has to do with the God Olakla. There are many rituals paying homage to him, all of which require human sacrifice, which is why the book is rare. This particular symbol is a symbol of three. Three human sacrifices so his worshipers gain his favor and are granted powers of some kind." She paused. Maybe to see if I was grasping it all. "I can't find the details of the ritual itself because I don't have the book."

I sat speechless as my eyes widened. Witches. Great. Just great. Now I had not one, but three people to worry about. And the hits just keep on coming. "So, there is no way to find out when this thing is going to take place is there?"

She shook her head. "No, I'm sorry. Not without the book or more details from you."

"I've described to you everything I saw."

"I know and I'm sorry, but it's just not enough."

Not enough. I thought about that. I took a deep breath and sighed heavily. "I have to make a phone call. I want you to tell this person everything you've told me. Maybe he can figure something out."

"Who?"

"This person is my. . .other problem."

I grabbed the phone, threw the cord in my bag, and sat back down next to Christine. "His name is Kyle. At least that's what he tells me. Please, don't tell him your name." Her brows rose and she opened her mouth to say something. I held my hand up to stop her. "Telling him

Chapter Fourteen

your name would only make it harder on me. So, please, promise me." I stared at her hard. I wanted her to know how important it was she do what I say. "Promise me."

She nodded. "Okay, I won't."

I gave her a quick smile and dialed the number.

"I see you still haven't thrown the phone away," Kyle said.

I ignored that. "Why haven't you turned the service off?"

"Have you called to tell me where you are, my little jewel?" His turn.

I ignored the "little jewel" part. Good for me. "No, actually no. I have someone here that would like to give you some information."

That irritating silence and clicking. Guess he hasn't learned yet.

"Do you think it was wise to involve an outside person?"

No, I didn't think it was wise. "Yes, I do. Do you want the information or not? You don't have a lot of time to talk." Hinting might help.

"Okay, I'll listen."

I put my hand over the mouth piece of the phone and turned to Christine. "Make it as fast as possible. Just tell him everything you told me and then give me the phone back." I started to hand her the phone and stopped. "And remember, don't tell him your name." I stressed the last part. She needed to understand.

"Don't worry, I won't," she said.

I gave her the phone.

"Hello," she said into the phone. She glanced at me and said, "No, I'm sorry, I can't do that."

I smiled satisfied. I knew he would ask her. I sat and listened intently to the rest of the conversation. I listened to her explain everything she said to me earlier.

"It's poss. . ." I snatched the phone out of her hand before she could finish.

"I think that about covers it," I said flatly.

"I believe this information could help," he said.

"I'm glad I could be of service."

"You do realize I will only play this game with you for so long." His voice held an edge of anger.

"I don't know what you mean," I said in my best innocent voice.

"I *will* find you."

Yup. Anger. . .definitely anger. I was actually enjoying it.

"So you've indicated."

"You don't want to do it this way, Julie." His voice was low and menacing. It was like a razor's edge. The barest pressure on the blade and it left you bleeding.

"At least I'm getting the job done. Which is more than I can say for you." I had to rub it in. Couldn't resist.

"Time is on my side where you're concerned."

"I wouldn't. . ."

I dropped the phone. The coolness was like a rush of arctic air on a sea of icy water. The numbness overtook my body one piece at a time while blotches of blackness formed in front of my eyes. Reality slipped from my grasp as I felt my arms being stretched above my head and my ankles being wrapped in silk and tied down. The incense burned at the back of my throat leaving a bad taste in my mouth.

"I'm dreaming again," I heard myself say.

"Hush, little one. Your time grows near and soon you will be set free," the woman whispered to me. Her voice was as tranquil as a field of flowers swaying wistfully upon the breeze a warm spring morning.

I sighed and smiled. I would be set free. I wanted to be set free. "All right."

Chapter Fourteen

"Such a good girl. This will be quick I promise you."

I opened my eyes to see the woman that would set me free. Free from all that was happening to me. I wanted to see her face. To remember.

I opened my eyes to see a room with black velvet curtains on the walls. There were black and yellow candles scattered about the room. Their flames sent shadows across the walls, floor and ceiling. It was like I were in a deep, dark dungeon somewhere in a faraway land. I stood near the side of an altar covered in black velvet — and I remembered. The feelings of comfort fled and were replaced by something that tightened my stomach. It sent my heart into my throat.

I stared at the woman who lay naked on top of the altar. Her hair was long like the other woman's was, but dark-brown. Her golden-brown eyes were open and wide with the fear of her life being swept away. She was just as tiny, but her skin was tanned and healthy looking. She already had the symbol painted on her forehead. I guess I was a little late getting here.

At the head of the altar there was a five-foot high candelabra with four candles. The candles it held were yellow, white, red and purple. The white candle was the only one lit.

I looked down at the woman, wishing I could tell her everything would be okay. I knew by now that talking to her wouldn't work. "I'm sorry," I whispered.

The woman whimpered and her eyes followed that invisible force around until she was straining to see behind her head. And then, as if by magic, someone appeared near the head of the altar. The person's back was to me and was covered in a hooded, black robe. It had the same symbol on the robe as on the woman's forehead, along with other designs I didn't recognize. It looked as though they were hand-sewn into the cloth. She screamed high and loud. I couldn't see, but I knew what was happening. Without seeing. . .I knew. And I screamed with her. I wanted this to end.

CHAPTER FIFTEEN

"Julie!" Christine yelled from a faraway place. "Please, come back!"

I felt myself being shaken and Christine's shock-stricken face was there. Poof! Just like magic. The same as it was when Elaine brought me back.

I got up from the bed. "This is annoying the shit out of me," I said. My voice sounding hoarse.

Christine's eyes were wide and glistening with unshed tears. "I can't believe I saw what just happened." Her voice cracked. "Are you sure you should be getting up?"

"I'm fine. Really." I reached up to wipe the beads of sweat from my forehead and saw that my right wrist was wrapped in a hand towel. The towel grew dark with my blood. I looked at my left wrist. Nothing. "I stopped it."

Her brows wrinkled. "What are you talking about?"

I stared into her eyes. "I'm not sure, but I think I left before I was suppose to."

"You're learning how to control it."

"Yeah. It's about time something good started happening." I scooted to the edge of the bed and slid my legs over the side. I looked down at the floor and saw it lying there near the bed...still open. My pulse jumped and my skin grew cold. I reached down and cautiously picked the phone up off the floor as if it might burn me if I touched it. "How long have I been out Christine," I whispered.

"Fifteen, maybe twenty minutes, why?" she asked and watched as I brought the phone up for her to see. Her eyes widened. "It's not still on is it?"

I brought the phone up to my ear. I could hear his rushed breathing and something else. The sound of traffic whizzing by an open window in the background. That was the first time I heard anything like that. My eyes widened and my heart sank into my stomach. He was in his car.

I pressed the end button, shoved it into my back pocket and grabbed my coat off the chair near the window. The panic was plain on my face as I looked over at Christine. "Grab my bag. We need to get out of here."

I stopped and my stomach knotted at the sound of squealing rubber on pavement outside the room. I reached out and grabbed Christine's arm before she could grab my bag.

Her eyes went wide. "What?"

I just shook my head vigorously and backed up from the door towards the back wall, pulling her with me.

We stood silently and listened as heavy footsteps rushed by the door, then back again and then silence. I took in a breath and held onto Christine's arm. My body trembled with the panic that surged through my veins. I looked at her and felt a frown forming on my face. Her

Chapter Fifteen

eyes went wider as she bit down on her lip. She had no clue who was standing outside that door. But I knew.

I jumped and Christine screamed as the door was kicked open so hard that it slammed into the wall. He stood there in his dark-blue tailored suit and his black trench coat and stared at me for a few breaths. His steel-blue eyes were as dark as the deepest depths of the ocean and his brows came together in a deep scowl.

Christine ran after him as he started towards us. "Leave her alone!" she yelled.

I saw his hand pull back. "No, don't!" I screamed as I tried to stop her.

The sound of his fist hitting flesh vibrated in my ears as the force of it turned her whole body around before she hit the bed and landed on her face beside it. I rushed to her side, dropped to my knees and turned her over on her back. She was still breathing, but blood trickled slowly from the corner of her mouth. If she was lucky, the worst thing she would get out of it was a badly bruised cheek. I only hoped that nothing was fractured.

Hot tears stung at the back of my eyes as I wiped the blood away with trembling fingers. He could have hurt her badly. He did this to Christine without hesitation. Without a second thought passing across his eyes. I felt my stomach tighten and a flush crawl up my skin. . .and I wanted to kill him.

"I told you not to do it this way." His deep voice was dark with a dangerous edge cutting through it.

I didn't look up at him right away. I didn't want to give him the satisfaction of seeing me cry, so I forced the tears back and let my rage come to the surface.

I took a deep, shaky breath through my nose. "You cold-hearted bastard," I said through gritted teeth.

He grabbed my arm and pulled me up from the floor, my feet feeling air for a brief time before I came to stand face to face with him. His eyes were a dark pit of nothingness.

"If the need calls for it, yes," he said.

I swung my hand, but he caught my arm before it could connect with his face. He gripped it tightly so that his fingers dug into my skin, but I didn't flinch. I stood there and glared into his eyes. The rage refusing to let the pain register to my brain.

He held my arm up to look at my wrapped wrist. "I see you've been busy."

My eyes narrowed and I did the first thing that came to mind. I brought my knee up as hard as I could and planted it between his legs. It was something he didn't expect. He let go and went down to his knees. His hand flew to his groin and a loud growl escaped between his clenched teeth. A deep red flush crawled quickly up his face and blue veins pressed against his neck.

I stepped back, not wanting to give him time to recover. He brought his eyes up to meet mine and I saw the murderous look in them before my foot connected with his chin, sending him falling onto his back near the dresser. Whoever said that watching TV wasn't educational?

I heard Christine moan, but I had to make sure it was safe before I went to her. I took a step closer to him and kicked him in the leg. When he didn't move or groan, I rushed over to Christine and dropped to her side.

"Christine?" I asked. My voice held the edge of hysteria as I fought to keep my emotions in check.

She opened her eyes and looked blankly up at me, then recognition started to wash in. "Julie?" she whispered.

"Can you get up? We need to get out of here and I can't carry you."

Chapter Fifteen

She frowned up at me for a few heartbeats and as the realization set in, she nodded her head and groaned. "Yes, I think so."

I helped her to her feet. Her legs were unsteady and we almost fell on the bed. I held onto her waist and put her arm over my shoulder. I heard a deep moan from near the dresser and glanced quickly over at Kyle. He was moving.

"Please, Christine, we have to get out of here," I urged.

We still had to make our way pass Kyle who was lying between the dresser and the end of the bed. I held my breath as I scooted us sideways by his slowly waking form. I grabbed my bag, flung it over my shoulder and gave Kyle one last glance before walking out the door.

The Jetta was parked two spaces down. By the time we got to it, Christine was able to move on her own. I helped her to the passenger side and opened the door.

She reached into her coat pocket and pulled out the keys. "I can get in on my own. Just get us out of here," she said.

I ran around to the driver's side and jumped in. By the time I got the car started, Christine was in and had the door shut. I heard Kyle scream my name through the hotel door just before I punched the gas and tore out of the hotel parking lot. I needed to get out before he saw what kind of car we were in. I glanced back before I pulled out onto the Boulevard and didn't see him come out. He knew what Christine looked like, but didn't know her name or what she was driving. I didn't have a vehicle so it wouldn't be on the hotel registration card. We were safe for now.

CHAPTER SIXTEEN

When we were far enough away from the hotel, I took a few deep breaths to calm my shaking hands.

I looked over at Christine. She was wiping the left-over blood off her face and it was starting to swell. "Do you need to go to the hospital?" I asked.

She touched her face and winced. "No, nothing's broke. What the hell is going on, Julie? Is he a cop?"

"No. And calling them won't help. It'll just help him find me sooner."

Her eyes went wide. "Are you telling me that the cops are helping him?"

"Something like that, yeah."

She turned in her seat and looked at me hard. "I think you should stay with me."

I shook my head. "That's not a good idea. I can't chance him finding me at your place. You're safe for now and I want to keep it that way." The phone vibrated in my lap and I nearly hit the roof. "Shit!"

Chapter Sixteen

Her eye widened and she quickly turned to look out the back window. "What? Is he following us?"

"No, it's the phone."

"Don't answer it, Julie," she said. Her eyes pleading with me.

I pulled into a Seven Eleven parking lot and parked as far away from the store as I could get. The phone vibrated over and over. He wouldn't stop until I answered it. I wanted to throw it out the window and be rid of him, but I couldn't. I wouldn't be able to live with myself, if it was possible to help the two women I saw and I did nothing.

I turned the car off and looked over at Christine. "Believe me, I don't want to. I have to help if I can, and this is the only way."

Christine sighed heavily and nodded her head.

"First things first though," I said as I got out of the car.

"What're you doing?"

"I'll be right back," I told her and left before she could say anything more.

I went into the store, bought a cup full of ice and grabbed a handful of napkins. The phone had stopped vibrating by the time I got back into the car. He could wait till hell froze over as far as I was concerned.

I handed her the cup and napkins. "Here, use this for your face. It may be a little while before you get home and you really need to put something on it."

She dumped some ice into a couple of napkins, folded them up, and pressed it gingerly to her cheek.

The phone vibrated and I jumped again. "Damn it!" I said as I pulled it out, flipped it open and pressed talk.

"You realize this changes things," he said. His voice was somehow strained.

I wondered if he was still holding himself. I hoped that the "family jewels" were as swollen as Christine's face. Picturing it brought a smile of satisfaction to my lips.

"At least we agree on something, detective." My voice was as cold as ice. As if it could freeze the heart by the mere sound of it.

Silence. His breathing was quick and heavy, almost drowning out the faint clicking sound. I think I may have hit another nerve. Poor baby.

"I assure you our next meeting won't be as favorable for you," he said finally.

"Listen, I only answered to give you some information. Your idle threats aren't going to help."

"Damn it, Julie!" he yelled. He called me Julie. Not good. I really wished I could see his face.

I figured I'd better get the ball rolling or this conversation would never end. "It wasn't the same woman this time."

Silence. At this rate, I would have to call him back a few more times to tell him everything.

"What did she look like?" His voice sounded calm. He sure does change moods quickly. And they say women have mood swings.

"Dark-brown hair, my height, light-brown eyes, tanned skin, about a hundred and five pounds. I'm not very good at judging weight, so take it for what it's worth."

"It seems as though your friend may be right on this one."

The mere mention of Christine brought back the memory of what he did to her and it sent my blood boiling. "You mean the friend you nearly killed tonight?"

"If I wanted to kill her, she wouldn't be sitting next to you right now."

Chapter Sixteen

He said it so casually, almost as if the subject bored him. My stomach tightened. He was more dangerous than I imagined. I was in big trouble and now I had involved Christine.

Christine touched my arm. "What is it?"

I shook my head and went back to the phone conversation. I took a deep breath and ignored what he had said. "I saw more this time than the last time. I suggest you turn it off or this conversation is going to end right now." That irritating silence. This was not making me happy. "Okay. Fine." I took the phone from my ear.

"No." His deep voice came bellowing out through the ear piece. "Wait."

I brought the phone back to my ear. I knew he'd see it my way. I guess I had some kind of power over him. Small though it may be. The clicking stopped.

"What did you see?" he asked.

"I saw the back of a person in a black hooded robe with the same symbol on the robe as on the woman's forehead. I also saw lit candles around the room."

"Candles? What colors?" Christine interrupted.

I looked at her. "There were black and yellow ones scattered around the room. There was also a five-foot candelabra near the head of the altar that held four candles. Yellow, white, red and purple. That's about all I got to see before I brought myself out."

"How were they positioned in the holder?" she asked.

"Well," I said as I bit at my bottom lip, "from left to right, the yellow, white, red, then the purple one."

"Sunday, Monday, Tuesday and Wednesday," she said more to herself than to me. "But I don't understand why there are four."

"What?"

"Did you see if they were lit?"

I had no idea where this was leading, but it seemed important to Christine. "I think just the white one was lit, but I can't be too sure. I didn't really pay much attention to it."

She took the phone from my hand. "Those candles cold possibly symbolize the days of the week. Sunday, Monday, Tuesday and Wednesday. From what Julie has told me, this particular homage might be paid on Monday. It's quite possible that Julie's first vision was of the first to be paid. Which could take place on Sunday. The last on Tuesday. The only thing I'm not clear on, is the fourth candle. There are only suppose to be three." Silence. "No, I'm afraid I don't know that. Unless I have the ritual sitting in front of me, I can't tell you more than that." She shook her head. "No, I told you before I don't have the book. It's rare. That's all I can tell you right now." She handed me the phone. I guess she didn't want to talk to him any longer than she had to. Could you blame her?

"Yeah," I said as I tried to wrap the towel tighter around my wrist. The pain shot up my arm, hitting nerves I didn't know I had. "Shi-it!"

"Are you all right?" he asked from the other end of the phone. Was that concern I heard?

"That's none of your business."

"Your life is very much my business. I will not hesitate to get to you anyway I can and by any means possible." His voice was soft; somehow threatening. I knew what he meant.

I snapped. I was tired, hurt and frustrated. He would kill Christine if she got in the way again. She was the only one I had left whom I could trust and talk to. "If I ever see you again, detective, I will kill you," I said through clenched teeth and hung up.

And I meant what I said. With all my heart I did.

CHAPTER SEVENTEEN

I found another motel off Bonney Road, a short distance from the McDonalds at the corner of Independence Boulevard. It took a lot of persuasion to get Christine to leave. She gave me her home phone number and I had to promise not to call Kyle again unless she was with me. I couldn't really blame her. My visions come and go as they please and if it happened again while I was talking to Kyle, I would be in it deep.

The room I walked into was almost an exact duplicate as the last one. This one done in blue. Light-blue walls, dark-blue rug and bedspread with blue and pink flowers on it. It wasn't much of an improvement, but I could live with blue.

I undressed, put on an over-sized T-shirt and tossed my bag on the dresser. I went to bed, and for a second night, I slept without any incidents. It was the first time in a long time I actually felt rested.

I woke a little later than I wanted to. But I wasn't in a hurry to get anywhere so I took a long, hot shower, letting the water beat against my tight muscles. I wrapped my hair up in a towel and got dressed in a red sweater, jeans, and sneakers. My stomach was knotting up painfully. I couldn't remember when I ate last so I figured I'd better get something into my stomach. I grabbed my black jacket and left with my hair wet because it took too long to dry.

I walked out into the brisk October air and its cool breeze penetrated my wet hair sending a vibrating chill through my body. I shivered and hugged myself to bring the warmth back. I looked up at the clouds of dark blue and gray hanging motionless in the sky. I smiled thinking that for once the weather man was right. It did look like rain.

I walked down the street to the McDonalds. I ordered pancakes, a hot cup of coffee, and sat at the back by a window to eat. I looked out the glass window at the road watching cars fly by. I watched people I didn't know and wondered where they were going. To work? To an appointment? Maybe an interview for a first job or to the gym to work out. People who had the choice to go where they were going. It's funny how you don't think about things like that, unless you're in a position where your choices are limited.

I took my time getting back to my motel room. It was beginning to feel like a prison and wasn't that what I was trying to run from? I thought about whether this was better than the alternative as I shoved the key into the door.

As soon as the door was open, I was shoved roughly forward and landed face-first on the edge of the bed. I turned around when I hit, thinking Kyle had found me, but I found myself staring up into the stormy-gray eyes of the man I saw at the bus stop the other day. He kind of reminded me of the Mr. Clean guy.

Chapter Seventeen

He wore a black, leather jacket over a blue, cotton shirt. His muscular legs bulged out of tight jeans that looked like he poured himself into them. His long, blonde hair was tied neatly back in a pony tail. I stared into his eyes and used the bed to slowly get up. If I was going to die, it wasn't going to be in this position.

"Nice of you to return," he said. His voice smooth and rich. He closed the door and his lips curled up under a neatly trimmed mustache. Something moved behind his eyes as he reached behind his back. I heard a soft click. Not good. My heart skipped a beat and I could feel the cold rush of fear flowing through my veins.

I swallowed hard. "Who are you?" Why not ask? I thought it'd be nice to know who's going to rape and kill me. I could always come back and haunt him.

He took a step towards me. "You need to come with me."

My pulse came up into my throat and my stomach knotted. Well, at least I wasn't going to be raped and murdered. Right here anyway. "I'm afraid you'll have to take a number and I'll see if I can pencil you in."

He half laughed at that. "You really do need to come with me."

I kept my eyes on him as I stepped back. I hit the bed with the back of my legs and put my hands in back of me, feeling for the edge. I followed the edge around until I came to the end of the bed and stepped away from it. Getting through Shawn and Kyle was easy. They didn't see it coming. I didn't know what I could do against a two-hundred pound wall of muscle, but I wasn't about to go down without at least trying. I think some self-defense classes will be in order, if I make it through this one. . .or a gun.

I swallowed hard. Be brave. "Do I have a choice?" My voice sounded calm. That'a girl.

"No, you don't," he said and smiled widely showing even white teeth. He looked like someone right off the cover of Playgirl.

I shook my head slowly. "I don't think so."

"I was hoping you'd say that," he said half grinning. His brow coming up. He reached into the inside of his jacket and the leather creaked in protest from his movements. I think the jacket was about two sizes too small, unless he was trying to make a fashion statement. He pulled out a bottle of liquid and a red rag followed. I didn't have to be a rocket scientist to figure it out. Once again, I've seen a lot of movies.

He stared at me with those dark-gray eyes. There was a hunger in them that promised to give me things I wasn't willing to take. He opened the bottle, tilted it against the rag to wet it and took another long step towards me. I didn't think that was fair. I had to take two steps back to keep the same distance and I was running out of room. All that was left was the wall and I didn't want to be against it. I looked at him and glanced over at the bed. I didn't want to be there either.

I stood there frozen. . .waiting. Waiting for him to get close enough. I had only one chance and when I thought he was close enough, I did the same thing I had with Kyle. I swung my leg up and hit him as hard as I could between the legs. He went down like a tree in the forest, dropping the open bottle and rag on the floor. What'a ya know. That's twice now.

He lay on his side with his knees up and his hands between his legs. His breathing was loud and ragged. "You — bitch!" He growled through clenched teeth. His face was bright-red and large, blue veins popped out of his thick neck.

I stood there for just a heartbeat, then I jumped around him to get away. I felt him grab my ankle and I used my hands to soften the blow as I went face-first to the floor.

I turned sideways and kicked at him, trying to get my ankle free from his grasp. His hand was like a vise as he squeezed my ankle harder to stop me from kicking. I screamed and kicked his shoulder with my other foot. He let go with a grunt.

He looked at me and I kicked him square in the face. I heard the sound of bones breaking as his hands shot to his face to cover his now bleeding nose. I scrambled to my feet and grabbed my bag off the top of the dresser. I ran over, snatched the cell phone and ripped the cord out of the wall.

"Get back here you bitch!" he yelled as he held one hand on his nose and used the other to fumble his way to his feet.

I glanced back at him, ran out the door and slammed it behind me. I knew I would be okay once I was outside. I stood outside the door and decided to make a run for it down the road towards Independence.

When I was a safe distance from the hotel, I stopped to catch my breath and turned to see if he was following me. He stood near the edge of the parking lot with his hand over his nose. I felt my lips curve up and I did the first thing that came to mind. . .I flipped him off. I saw him stiffen and I waved a shaky hand at him before I ran towards the McDonalds.

I was satisfied. I knew I had the strength to take care of myself and to take care of Kyle. I liked it. I liked it a lot. The only thing that worried me was keeping Christine safe.

I used the pay phone at McDonalds to call Christine at home. I knew she wouldn't be at the store today because of her condition. It would've been nice if I could have given her some of my healing abilities. After I summed it up as much as I could about what happened, she agreed to meet me at the store. I walked up Independence and took the first bus that came by.

CHAPTER EIGHTEEN

Christine unlocked the door when she saw me walking up. She must've been waiting by the door since she got there. The left side of her face and lip were swollen, but it didn't look as bad as it did last night. The purple and blue bruise that covered her entire left side could still be seen under the heavy make-up she wore. She was wearing jeans and a red, pull-over, cotton shirt. She looked too thin in the jeans, which is probably why she wore loose skirts most of the time.

She locked the door behind me. "Goddess, Julie, is there no end to this shit?"

The picture of Mr. Clean holding his nose flashed through my thoughts and I smiled. I couldn't help it. "I do seem to be pretty popular lately."

She frowned at me. "And you're happy about it?"

I shrugged. "I can't change what's happened."

"He didn't hurt you did he?"

I choked back a laugh. "No, he didn't hurt me." I put my hand out to her face and stopped short of touching it. "The question is, how are you doing? You're the one who's hurt."

"I've actually had worse than this."

My eyes widened at that. "You're kidding right?"

She smiled, but it didn't quite look right with her swollen lip. "No, I played softball for three years in high school."

"Well, I guess that explains it."

Her smiled faded. "What are you going to do now?"

"I'm going to have to find another motel. At this rate, I'm going to run out of places to go."

"I wish you would consider staying with me."

"He's found me twice now, Christine. Do you think he wouldn't find me at your place?" I walked over to the glass counter and laid my bag on top. "This man is not fooling around."

"You never really told me who he is or why he's after you."

I looked into her deep, sapphire eyes and knew she was right. I involved her the minute I came in here and asked for her help. We were partners of a sort and partners shouldn't hold things back from one another. A clairvoyant and a witch. Quite the pair eh?

"You're right." I said finally. "You deserve to know what I know anyway, but let me make a call first, then we'll talk"

She nodded, went over to the register and jumped onto the stool. She knew by now that my phone calls to Kyle were less than desirable. Better to be out of shouting distance.

I flipped it open and dialed the number.

Chapter Eighteen

"To what do I owe the pleasure? Have you had another vision?" He asked. His voice was laced with sarcasm.

"No, not yet."

"That's good because I planned on being there for the next one."

"Well, if that henchman you sent over earlier today is the best you've got, you might want to re-think that. The only thing you've accomplished is to make me have to find another place to stay. It's no more irritating than having to hear your voice."

Silence. I could hear his breathing becoming heavy and quick.

"I would not send someone to do the very thing that I would enjoy doing the most."

That one sentence told me everything. He didn't send Mr. Clean. I swallowed my heart back into my throat. "Fuck," I whispered.

"What's wrong?" Christine asked from my side.

I just about jumped out of my skin. I took a breath and put my hand over the mouth piece of the phone. "I'll tell you later," I whispered. She frowned at me and I stared hard at her. "Later," I said.

She didn't go back to the counter. Instead, she backed up a couple of steps to let me finish the call.

"Someone tried to harm you today?" It wasn't a question. His voice was deep and savage as if it could cause immense pain in just one breath.

It sent my pulse into my throat and I had to catch my breath. "I didn't say that. Did I say that?"

"Julie, please. Tell me where you are."

"I can't do that."

"Someone is after you, Julie." That was twice he called me Julie. I was guessing his veins were straining in his neck by now. I didn't care.

"That's one more to the list." I tried to make it sound casual. I hoped it came out that way.

"This is no joke!" He yelled. His voice vibrated through the phone.

"I'm not joking, detective."

Silence. I was wishing I could at least hear some soothing elevator music.

"I can keep you safe." His voice was calmer. Not much mind you.

I choked back a laugh. "You? Keep me safe? As far as I'm concerned, you're no safer than the slime-ball that attacked me today. I'll take my chances on my own, thank you very much."

"What about those women? Are you just going to sit there and let them die?"

I shrugged, and realized he couldn't see me. "If need be, yes." I didn't really believe that.

"I don't believe that," he said. I must've been thinking too loudly.

"Believe what you want, detective. No matter what happens, I'm not giving myself up to you and your damn experiments."

Christine touched my shoulder, I glanced at her and she pointed to her watch. I hung up before he could say anything else and slipped it into my pocket.

"Thanks. I lost track of time."

"No problem. I knew it was important and I could see that you weren't paying attention."

"You might as well have a seat," I told her and motioned towards the counter.

Christine sat down and waited patiently while I figured out how I was going to tell her everything.

"I met Kyle on Monday, the first day I came in here. He claimed he was a detective for the police department here. He told me later that he's a part of some kind of organization. He didn't get into the specifics, but he pretty much can do what he thinks is necessary to get his job done."

"You're a part of that job aren't you?"

"Apparently a big part of it. He said that they look specifically for people like me and there aren't many around."

"He's not going to stop coming after you is he?"

"No, I'm afraid not. He also told me that Mr. Clean wasn't sent by him."

Her brows rose. "Mr. Clean?"

I smiled. "The man who attacked me in my room. Mr. Clean is my nickname for him. It's a joke is all."

"I'm glad you can joke about all of this. It only means that someone else is after you."

I shrugged. "What's one more? Maybe, if I keep it up, I'll have a whole list by Christmas."

She hopped off the stool, knelt down by my chair and stared hard at me. "This is serious, Julie."

"I know it is, but if I think about it too much, I'll go nuts."

She looked at me then her brows creased.

"What?" I asked.

"Would you like to try a little experiment?"

I raised my brow at that. "What kind of experiment?"

"No, its not what your thinking. I know you don't want to be drugged up. It's a natural way to tap into your visions. You can go there on your own and possibly see things the normal visions are holding you back from seeing."

"How are we going to do that?"

"Trust me. With the right herbs and incense, we just might be able to do it."

"Okay, lets try it."

Truth was I was willing to try anything. I wasn't sure if I could have two more deaths on my conscience. Giving myself up to Kyle was a definite last resort.

CHAPTER NINETEEN

I sat in the chair watching intensely as Christine scurried around the shop; grabbing this off a shelf, snatching that off a cabinet. She was making me dizzy. I only hoped she knew what she was doing. If this didn't work and I had another vision, I would have to resort to calling Kyle. Do you think there's a place around called "Options R Us?"

She spread a brown and white blanket on the floor in the middle of the store. It was the only place that there was any room. Her store was roomy, but well stocked. She put a brass incense holder in the center of the blanket and placed brown and white candles around the blanket along the edges. Her brows furrowed and she bit at her bottom lip as she surveyed the area.

She went to sit down, but got back up again. "Oh wait, one more thing. Julie, would you get the lights please?"

I nodded and went over to the door. I flipped the switch so that the only light to be seen were the faint rays of sun coming in through the small windows. Christine ran into the back room, coming out a minute later with a portable CD player and a disc.

She sat down, placed the player next to her and slid the disc inside. "I think that's all we need." She said and motioned to the spot opposite of where she was sitting. "Come over and sit down here."

I hesitated at first. I wasn't sure if I really wanted to do this. I didn't want to go back there. I was tired of seeing the panic in their eyes...the hopelessness...the fear.

"Julie?" she asked.

I walked over and sat down, crossing my legs Indian style. It was the only way to sit when you were on the floor with no back support. "Okay, what next?"

She must have seen the apprehension on my face. "There aren't any drugs, Julie. Trust me."

I sighed heavily. "Okay, let's do it."

Christine took some powder out of two different bags and let the powder fall into the incense holder. She lit the candles closest to her and handed me the candle lighter. I lit the candles nearest to me and handed it back. The candles glowed brightly in the soft darkness of the store. I watched as Christine lit the incense and turned the CD player on. A thin line of smoke came floating out of the holder. The smell of it drifted up and caught in the back of my throat. The tranquil music that came floating out of the player sent shivers down my spine and I felt my body relaxing without my willing it to.

"Now sit and relax. Breathe in deeply and let the music take you where it will. Don't be afraid of anything you hear or see."

I nodded.

Chapter Nineteen

She took a deep, cleansing breath and let it out through her mouth slowly. She closed her eyes and began to hum softy, the sound coming from deep within her chest. I sat and let the music and incense fill my senses and overtake my mind until my breathing became soft and even. Christine's soft voice penetrated my body and I found myself transfixed on her closed eyes.

Her soft humming stopped, but it didn't affect me as I sat staring blankly at her. I was looking at her, but somehow beyond her. The music drifted through my mind and my body felt detached from itself somehow.

She opened her eyes then and they were eyes the color of ebony. Those eyes looked into mine and penetrated my mind. . .my very soul. . .and I wasn't afraid.

"Send visions of truth. Visions of present time." Her voice was barely a whisper. *"Promitto visum of verum. Visum of tendo vicis."*

I fell into the blackness of her eyes and descended slowly to a place I knew I had been before.

"I'm here," I said.

I looked around the room. There was an oak door to my left that I hadn't remembered seeing before. It was closed and it gave one the feeling of finality. The black, velvet curtains hung from the walls and the altar was covered with the same material as the curtains. The black and yellow candles scattered about the room looked like they hadn't been used, as well as the candles in the candelabra. I looked at the floor around the altar and saw a nine-foot circle painted in black with another eight-foot in diameter painted inside the larger one. Between the two were different symbols and inside the smaller circle was an upside-down triangle. Everything was painted in black. The altar was in the center of it all and the room looked like nothing had happened in it. It was empty and for the first time. . .I didn't feel fear.

"What do you see?" Christine's voice came from somewhere outside my consciousness.

I looked around at each thing and described in detail what I saw. I started to walk towards the curtains, curious to see if they covered windows.

"Go to the door, Julie," she prompted.

I stopped and could feel a frown forming on my face. "I'm afraid."

"It's okay. I won't let anything hurt you."

And I believed her. I walked towards the door and the sound of my footsteps echoed off the walls. I reached out, turned the knob and walked through the heavy door.

I stood outside the room I was in and found that it was just a small building. The whole area was wooded and looked as though there was no one around for at least a half-mile or so. In front of me, about twenty yards away, was a small, two-story house. I couldn't tell whether it was beige or brown. The late hour and shelter the trees provided covered the house in blackness as if it were trying to hide some dark secret from the world.

"Tell me what you see, Julie," she urged.

I stood outside the door and described again what I saw. I was beginning to feel a tightness in my stomach. It was as if I knew there was something inside that house that could take the very breath from my body. Don't make me go in there.

"Walk towards the house, Julie."

"I don't want to."

"It's okay, you don't have to go in. Just walk towards it. To the front. A closer look at it is all I ask. I won't let anything hurt you. I promise."

I nodded. "Okay. Don't let anything hurt me."

"I won't," she said. Her voice was calming.

I started to walk towards the very thing I wanted to turn and run from.

A cool breeze ran across my body sending a chill across my skin. I shivered and hugged myself trying to get warm. Then I stopped. . .Someone was here.

"What's wrong, Julie?" she asked.

"Someone's here," I whispered.

"Who?"

A coldness only death could bring rushed through me and penetrated my flesh as a crack would spread along a pond of thin ice. And I knew she was gone. Thrown out as if sucked out by a vacuum.

"How nice of you to visit me." Came the soothing voice of a woman from somewhere nearby. Her voice embraced me and I felt like a newborn baby wrapped in its mother's arms for the first time. I felt safe and loved.

I said, "Yes, I came."

"You came on your own, little one?"

"Yes, on my own."

"How very special you truly are." Her soft voice caressed my skin as a soft wind on a warm starry night.

"Yes, special."

"You shouldn't have come here on your own, little one. It could have ruined everything."

I frowned. "I'm sorry."

"I will see you soon."

"Yes, soon."

"Hear the words I say, little one and I will see you very soon."

"I'm listening."

"Your mind to me. . ."

Her voice cut of abruptly as I was hit with a rush of darkness that surrounded me like a thick, warm blanket. I was pulled downwards as if invisible hands were grabbing my spirit and forcing it back into my lifeless body.

Christine's face although blurred, appeared in front of my eyes. Gotta love it. Her eyes were closed as if in sleep and as my focus came clear, she opened her eyes. She stared at me, took in a deep breath and let it out in a loud sigh.

I jumped up off the blanket and stepped quickly back, sending lit candles rolling about on the floor. "What the hell was that all about?" I yelled.

Christine got up and came over to me. "They pushed me out, Julie."

"They who?"

"The people that are doing this. They're not amateurs. I just barely brought you back." Her voice held an edge of panic. It wasn't reassuring.

"But you did. That's all that matters."

She grabbed my arms. "You don't understand. They were going to cast some kind of spell on you."

I shook away from her hands. "A spell? Come on Christine, do you actually expect me to believe that?"

"Think about it, Julie. You were there. Think about what was said to you." Her voice was calm as if she was trying to get through to a person getting ready to jump off a bridge.

I thought about that. "I don't remember what was said to me."

"You can't go back there on your own again. It's too dangerous. They know who you are and what you're capable of. They'll stop you and possibly even gain control of your mind."

"But those women will die. The only time I ever see anything of real importance is when it's actually happening."

"We'll figure something out, Julie. Going in on your own is not the answer right now."

I pulled from her grasp, walked away and turned back around. "So, that's it? I have to sit here and do nothing even with this "gift" I have?"

Chapter Nineteen

She just looked at me for a few breaths and then at the floor.

"Can't you do anything?" I asked.

"I don't have the ability against that kind of power. I just barely brought you back from their influences."

"Then what the hell good are you?" I yelled as I walked over to the cabinet and slammed my fists against the top of it. I was frustrated and scared now. What the hell good was I to anyone. I just couldn't sit back and wait.

I turned around to look at her and when I looked at the bruises Kyle had so easily put on her face, I immediately regretted what I had said.. "I'm sorry. I had no right to say that to you." I pulled the cell out of my pocket and flipped it open.

Her eyes went wide. "What the hell are you doing?"

"I'm going to tell Kyle where I am so he can come get me."

She grabbed the cell out of my hand and closed it. "That's not the answer. They're only going to use drugs to do the same thing that we've already tried here. The results won't be any different and they won't be able to keep those people from doing you harm. It won't accomplish anything but possibly get you killed right along with those women."

I thought about that and I didn't care. I felt lost. I had no money, no home, and now I would have at least three more deaths on my hands. "I'd rather die then have to live with the guilt." And it was the truth.

"It's just a wall we've run into. Walls can be brought down. We just need a little more time to figure it out."

I grabbed the cell back from her. "Time isn't a luxury in this case."

"Julie, no. Please don't give yourself up to that animal." She held my hand with the cell down from my face. "Just a little more time. Please?"

I looked at her pleading sapphire eyes and once again at the bruises on her swollen face. . .and realized she was right. Giving myself up to Kyle wasn't the answer. I slipped the cell back into my pocket.

"You're right, it's not the answer."

She sighed heavily. "We'll figure it out. I promise you that."

"You'd better be right about that. The only thing left for me to do at the moment is to find another place to stay." I held my hand up before she could say anything. "No, that's still out of the question. I actually do have some funds lying around. I just have been too afraid to try and tap into them. I have no idea how much he knows and what I have available to me."

"Would you like to at least try?"

"I'm pretty much open at this point."

I grabbed my bag and we headed for the lawyer's office.

CHAPTER TWENTY

We drove down Phoenix Drive, to the lawyer's office that had gotten in touch with me after my parents died. It was a four-story, glass building with windows that reflect the outside off of them. For privacy I guess. If you get close enough to the windows, you can see inside anyway. Kind of defeats the purpose unless you're on any floor other than the first one. I figure if you want privacy, put blinds up, but who am I to tell them how to do things.

Christine waited in the car for me because we were afraid the bruises on her face would bring too much attention. . .that is one thing we were trying to avoid. We didn't need anyone asking questions we couldn't answer.

I walked though a heavy revolving door. I always thought they were put in to make it easier. There was a hallway with see-through, glass walls showing the bank that took up the whole first floor. How convenient for me eh?

The office was on the fourth floor so I took the elevator. Figures, lawyers wanting the highest floor. Most think that highest floor is supposed to be the best. Like the penthouse. I just think it's irritating to have to wait in an elevator to get to my destination. The lower the floor, the better.

I walked through glass doors into the front office and that phrase "people in glass houses" kept coming to my mind. I stepped up to the desk where I was greeted by an older woman in her late sixties. She was frail looking and had mousy-brown hair with large streaks of gray flowing through it. It looked as though someone had taken a paint brush to it. I was thinking she was in bad need of a dye job. Maybe she was trying to start a new trend. Her face was heavily lined like she had spent too many hours in the sun. She had small pinched lips and dark-brown eyes that were sunk in her face making her look almost skeletal.

"Can I help you?" She asked. Her voice was quite pleasant. You wouldn't have expected it. I was never good at putting faces with voices anyway.

"Yes, I'd like to see Mr. Miller."

She opened a large green appointment book. "Do you have an appointment?"

Why did I know she was going to ask me that? "No, I don't. Is he busy? This is kind of important."

"Well Miss. . ." She looked at me and her brow rose.

"Julie Summers."

"Miss Summers. He's in with a client right now and I don't know how long he'll be. His appointments are pretty much back-to-back today."

"That's okay, I'll just sit here and wait, if you don't mind. Just in case he has a few minutes to spare." I wasn't going to wait any longer than I had to. You have to be pushy with lawyers sometimes. Especially their secretaries.

She frowned. It didn't help her face any. "He may be a while."

Chapter Twenty

I don't discourage easily. I smiled sweetly. "That's quite all right. I have all day," I said and walked into the reception area before she had a chance to say anything else.

It was a roomy area and had three, powder-blue, leather couches along the walls. Oak end tables were placed in between them with vases that held white carnations. There was an oak coffee table in the center of the room with a variety of magazines and a few of the area newspapers. The walls were covered with beige wallpaper that had tiny gold designs in it. The floor was dark hardwood and was polished to a glimmering shine. Whoever cleans the place must spend at least half a day on the floor alone. The over-all effect was elegant, at least to me it was. I sat down on one of the couches and the leather sank under my weight as it molded to my body. It was actually quite comfortable, which was good because I figured it was going to be a long wait. You know how lawyers are. They pretty much keep you waiting, even though it's your money they're going to be taking. Kind of like doctors eh?

Ten minutes later, he came out the door to his office with an older gentleman. He glanced my way and went back to talking to the other man. I stood up and waited politely for him to send his client on his way.

James Miller was a good looking man. . .for a lawyer. He was still quite young. He was six-feet tall with a medium build. His jet-black hair was cut just below the ears and was layered back to show his dark eyebrows that framed deep-blue eyes. He wore a blue sport jacket with a white, cotton shirt and blue dress pants. I didn't see a tie. It was nice to see a lawyer that wasn't afraid to be comfortable.

He came over to me with his hand held out. "Miss Summers, how nice to see you again. Nancy told me you were out here."

"How nice of her," I said and took his hand in mine for a quick hand shake. His hands were soft as baby's skin.

He motioned in the direction of his office. "I have some time before my next client arrives, won't you step into my office?"

"That'd be great," I said.

Although the room was small, it had the same hardwood floors and wallpaper. It was elegantly done with just enough furniture to make it comfortable. A large, oak desk cluttered with paperwork sat at the far wall. A soft, leather recliner chair was behind it. There were two bookshelves filled to the rim with every law book you could imagine. Two soft leather chairs sat on the outside of his desk. An oak end table, complete with vase and white carnations, separated them. Leather, oak and white carnations. At least the motif flowed throughout the place. The leather moaned under his weight as he sat down in the chair.

He leaned back and folded his hands in his lap. I guess that's a lawyer's, "look at me, I'm a professional," move. I resisted the urge to ask him if they taught him that in law school. . . just barely.

"I have to admit that I was surprised to see you here. If I recall right, our first and only conversation ended on a not-so-pleasant note," he said.

"That was a year ago, Mr. Miller and was soon after my parents died. I was not quite myself when you called."

He leaned forward on his chair. "Am I to assume you are here to sign the proper documents to receive what your parent's have left for you?"

"Yes, you can assume that."

"You do understand that this will take a day or two."

Chapter Twenty

"No," I said rather hastily. "Please. Is there anyway I could get it done today?"

"Today? Miss Summers, these things take time."

"It's been a year, Mr. Miller. Don't you think that's time enough?"

Maybe he saw the desperation in my eyes. "All right, give me a few hours. I'm sure I can get it done. Come back say around four?"

Four o'clock. The bank didn't close until five. Talk about cutting it close.

"Four will be fine, thank you."

He walked me out of his office, shook my hand and greeted a young woman who had been waiting for him.

I walked out of the building into a cold, bone chilling rain. I grabbed the collar of my coat and closed it up over my neck. Unfortunately, my hair was soaked by the time I got to the car.

"How'd it go?" Christine asked.

"He'll have it ready by four."

"Where to while we wait for Mr. Miller to do whatever it is he does."

Well, that was a good way to put it. I thought about that and the thought hit me. "I need to go get a replacement license."

"Huh?" Christine said.

"Kyle took my wallet Monday when he brought me to the hospital. I can't get to the money without it."

"Do you have anything that says who you are?"

I turned sideways in the seat. "I grabbed all my important papers when I went home that day. I think I have my birth certificate and maybe a copy of my social security card in my bag."

"That's all you need."

I smiled. Maybe, for once, something would go right.

I was hoping we'd make it back to Miller's before four. The lines at the DMV could be long at times. You know, the kind that you pack for the whole day. Kind of like an outing. Birth certificate, picnic basket, thermos and blanket. All set. Yep.

CHAPTER TWENTY-ONE

As with the lawyer's office, Christine waited in the car for me while I went into the DMV. It turned out that there weren't many people there. It was either the weather or the time. I didn't care which, I was just glad we didn't have to wait too long. I found that I had a couple of bills, my birth certificate and an old copy of my social security card in my bag.

The three things I had were enough to get a duplicate license. I told them my wallet was stolen, which wasn't far from the truth. I walked out of the DMV with another license and twenty minutes to spare. Just enough time to get back to Miller's and get the very thing that would give me back some feeling of independence.

As we made our way back to the lawyer's office, the sky had started to clear and the rain slowed down to an annoying drizzle. The kind where there is no setting on your wipers to handle it. It either doesn't clear it off often enough or the wipers screech across the windshield because there's not enough moisture on them. So, you either have to grit your teeth or keep turning your wipers on and off.

We made it to his office at five minutes to four. Talk about timing.

I walked up to the front desk where Nancy was staring at a note pad and pounding away at her keyboard. She seemed to be oblivious to anything around her except the work she was doing. It reminded me of Elaine. The computer hacker is what I called her. She could do a lot more on a computer than I could even dream about. I missed talking to her. She was the only friend I had up until a few days ago and had no idea what was happening. All she knew was that I was being tenderly cared for in the hospital where she left me two days ago. I figured I could chance calling her when I got settled, once again, in another motel room.

I cleared my throat to get Nancy's attention.

She glanced up, then back to her keyboard, then back up again. "Oh, I'm sorry. I didn't hear you come in," She said in that pleasant voice that didn't quite match her face.

"I'm. . ."

"Julie Summers. Yes, I know. Mr. Miller will be out shortly to see you. Please have a seat in the reception area," She said and smiled.

"Okay."

Once again, I sat down on the soft, leather couch. Except this time, I knew I wouldn't be waiting long.

He walked out of his office ten seconds before four o'clock. I had to hand it to him, he was punctual, if nothing else.

He walked over towards me with his hand out. "Miss Summers, you're right on time."

Chapter Twenty-one

After a brief handshake, we walked into his office again. I sat in the same seat as before and watched as he sat slowly down in his leather chair behind the desk. He reclined back and folded his hands across his stomach in one smooth movement. I was going to have to ask him where they teach stuff like that.

"I believe everything's in order," he said.

I must have looked confused because he leaned forward and slid the paperwork that sat on his desk closer to me so I could see it. I took the stack of papers and sat back in my chair, glanced at them, then back up at him.

"As you can see there, after a small fee, the figure is correct. All you need to do is sign on all the spaces marked with red check marks and you're done."

My fingers flipped through the papers one by one until I got to the last page, where a check had been paper clipped to it at the bottom. My jaw just about dropped to the floor. I sat speechless as I looked at a check worth a hundred and seventy-five thousand dollars. Yep. That's one hundred, seventy-five and three zeros. If I played my cards right, I could live quite a while off this.

"I assure you the amount is correct, unless you think it should be more, we can go through it together," he said.

My eyes widened as I looked up at him. "I'm suppose to get *this*?"

"Yes, you are. You never gave me the opportunity to tell you this when we talked over the phone that day. That is just from the policies."

My brows rose at that. "What do you mean just from the policies?"

"Your parents were very wise with their money through the years. You also have other funds available to you. There are other investments that are only available by withdrawals through the investment company. But I suggest, if you do feel the need to use them, that you withdraw on the interest. It should be quite sufficient."

"My parents never told me. About these investments I mean. I know they both worked hard all their lives, but I never figured they would be able to accumulate this much." Great, now I had investments I could live off of.

"I assure you, they did. With a little discipline, anyone can invest and be more the wiser for it when it comes time to retire."

"All I do is sign?"

"Yes, then you're free to go."

This was my chance to have some kind of freedom back. "All right. Where did you say I had to sign?"

"Sign in all the places that have red check marks. I might suggest you put this in an account as soon as possible. The check is drawn from the bank downstairs, if it is more convenient for you."

I nodded and started to sign on all the dotted lines I was suppose to. When I was finished, I handed the paperwork back to him. He went through them all one by one and when he was done, he handed me the check.

"Now, if you'll just wait here, I'll go have a copy made for you."

I smiled. "Okay."

He smiled and walked out of the room.

I hadn't a clue how much there was. He called me about three months after my parents died. It was too soon for me and I didn't want their money. So, I just forgot about it, until now. But I never realized it could be this much. I looked down at the check in my hands and frowned thinking that it didn't take the place of my parents. I would rather have them than all the money in the world.

Chapter Twenty-one

Miller came back into the room, stood by my chair and handed me a stack of papers as thick as the one's I had just signed. "There's also the paperwork containing the information on the investment companies for you to look over and do with as you will."

I got up from my seat and shook his hand. "Thanks for doing this for me so quickly."

"That's quite all right. It was nothing really."

With one less thing to worry about, I breathed a sigh of relief when I walked out of his office. Now I needed to get it in the bank in time to withdraw what I needed to get by on for the next week.

I took the stairs instead of waiting for the elevator. I can beat any elevator to a floor with my eyes closed no matter how far it is. They just don't make them so you get there faster. I think it's just for people who can't walk well or are just plain lazy. Most of the time it's the latter.

I went through the glass doors that led into the bank. Glass doors for a bank? Beats me. There were only two people waiting for tellers. I walked over to one of the service desks instead. I was opening a new account and didn't have to wait in line for a teller.

The woman at the desk saw me coming and smiled as I approached her. You know, that "let us have your money and we'll make more than what we'll give you for interest" smile. It's too bad we need banks.

She was a pretty woman. Long, dark-brown hair pulled back in a barrette so you could see her dark-brown eyes. She had very little make-up on. I didn't think she needed it anyway. Her features were quite lovely. She had a small, narrow nose, and full lips. Her medium toned skin was smooth and flawless. I needed to know her secret. She wore a beige sweater and a tiny gold chain hung around her neck that glittered when she moved the right way

"Can I help you?" she asked in a pleasant voice. I wonder if her and Nancy, the secretary, took the same class.

I smiled. "Yes, I would like to open an account with this and possibly draw from it today."

I held the check out for her to see then I sat down on the stiff seats they provide for their customers. They needed Miller's decorator.

She took the check. "I'm afraid that it takes several days for a check to clear before funds can be drawn from it."

I waited for her to really look at the check. Her eyes widened slightly, not much mind you, then she looked back up at me. Professionalism at its best.

"Well," I said and glanced at the nameplate on the desk, "Laura, if I can't open an account and take only what I need, I'll just go ahead and cash it then." I smiled sweetly at her. "Nothing larger than a hundred if you can."

Her brows rose ever so slightly and her mouth parted just a little. Don't you just love shocking people at banks? It works for me.

"No, you can open an account and withdraw from the funds today."

"That'll be fine then."

"Let me just get the necessary paperwork together and we'll take care of it for you."

"Yes, you do that." I said and watched as she rummaged through her desk and pulled out a rather lengthy form for me to fill out. And you wonder why I don't like bank accounts.

"Just fill this out, and with the proper ID, we can get you squared away as soon as possible."

The form didn't really take as long as I thought it would and by the time the bank was closing, I walked out with money of my own. I hadn't had any to call mine since Monday.

It was only five o'clock and already the sky was as dark as if it were nine. Courtesy of daylight saving's time. It made the days seem shorter, if you were a late sleeper. I didn't know if I liked the idea at this particular moment. It made it seem as though time was running in fast forward and time is something that I couldn't afford to waste. The wind sent a chill all the way to my bones. It may have stopped raining, but it didn't improve on the over-all conditions. It seemed to have made it a little worse.

"Everything go all right?" Christine asked.

"Better than all right."

"So, it's enough to help you out then?"

I smiled. "Yeah, it's enough."

"Okay, then. Where to now?"

"I'd like to go shopping for some clothes, but I guess I can't have everything so let's find another motel."

"Okay, but I need to stop at the store to check for messages first, then we can grab something to eat before we find you another place to stay."

"Sounds good."

With the lawyer out of the way and having something that says who I am, I felt a little better. I finally had some kind of control.

CHAPTER TWENTY-TWO

We got to the store in less than ten minutes. Not the greatest record considering Miller's office was pretty close to her store. When it rains in Virginia Beach, people pretty much panic. You would think they never got rain out here. Throw in some snow and there's all-out chaos. Defensive driving is the norm most of the time.

While Christine fumbled with her keys to unlock the door, I stood in the chill of the evening air. I was still pretty damp from the rain earlier and the cold went right to my bones because of my wet hair. Unfortunately her building didn't provide much cover from the elements. Christine walked in first and I was quick on her heels to get some place warm.

Christine flicked the lights on and headed for her message machine. I turned to close the door and just before I got it shut, it was flung open forcefully. The door hit me in the shoulder and threw me backwards. I fell to the floor, sliding to a halt against one of the bookshelves along the wall. The pain in my shoulder blades was sharp and immediate. For a few breaths I saw blotchy patches of white in front of my eyes. I blinked back the fuzziness and when I could see straight, I was looking up into the stormy-gray eyes of Mr. Clean himself.

He stood with his legs open and arms folded across his chest. He couldn't quite get his arms to close because of their size and it didn't quite look right. He had on his normal tight jeans that could pass as a second skin and a black shirt under his leather coat completed the outfit. His waist-length hair was in a braid that fell over his shoulder, although the over-all effect was ruined just a tad with that bandage on his nose. A slight purplish color formed under his eyes that looked like he hadn't slept in days.

"Not so cocky now are you?" he said. Although his voice had a slight nasal pitch to it, the dangerous edge didn't go unnoticed.

My pulse quickened and my stomach tightened. Oh, this is classic. I know the experiences over the past few days have given me new strength, but this was getting ridiculous. I've gone from a pin cushion to a punching bag. Not a very good trade-off. If this was another test, I wasn't going to get through this one. Whatever it was he wanted, he was probably going to get it.

The door clicked shut. Christine was over by the register. Not a good sign. I glanced around Mr. Clean and saw someone looming near the door. He was tall, although I couldn't tell at my present location how tall as everyone looks large when you're on the floor. His legs were big, but didn't bulge through his jeans. He had broad shoulders and his muscular arms stretched the seams of the cotton in the sweatshirt he wore. Do all muscle men buy shirts and coats two sizes too small? He had a thick mustache that covered his thin lips and his short brown hair was mass of damp curls. He looked like the Brawny guy straight off the paper towel package.

My heart felt like a large lump in my throat and I swallowed hard to put it back into my chest. I was afraid. Afraid not only for myself, but for Christine too. If it wasn't for me, she wouldn't be in this situation. The only thing I did know was that they weren't going to get what they wanted without a fight. I was beginning to think that being with Kyle would probably be better than going through this on a daily basis. Needles or boxing gloves. Some choice huh?

"Stay right there lady or I'll add to those bruises on that pretty face of yours," Brawny said.

Mr. Clean stared down at me and his lips curled up into a sneer. I peered around the other side of him and saw that Christine was scooting back away from the register. I was guessing she probably had a gun back there and was trying to get to it without notice. Her brows creased and her eyes went wide. She knew as well as I how grave the situation was. I knew they probably wanted me alive, but Christine was a whole different story. What would they do to her? I didn't think they would want to have to deal with taking her with them also. With that thought, I had a new sense of survival. Not for me, but for Christine. I wouldn't let her be harmed because of me. Not if I could help it anyway.

"Get up," Mr. Clean said. His tone left no room for argument.

I wasn't going to push the pencil just yet. I needed some kind of plan first. I got slowly up from the floor and when I was to my feet, I leaned against the bookcase I was so casually thrown into a few moments ago. Maybe I could do an encore of this morning's little rendezvous.

He must have seen the thoughts moving behind my eyes because he grabbed me by the hair and pulled me

Chapter Twenty-two

into him so my back was to his chest. I think I actually heard some of my hair separating from my scalp. He put his hand around my waist and pulled me roughly so my whole body was against his. I could feel the lumps of his braid pressing against my back.

"Don't even think about it," he said through clenched teeth.

He pulled my head back by my hair so my neck was bent back at a painful angle and I was staring into his eyes. I had to bend my neck back to look up to him anyway. I don't know why he thought I needed any help doing it.

Even with the bandaged nose, his eyes held a murderous glare to them. If I even twitched, he would snap my neck. I just stared into his eyes as my breathing became labored. It's hard to breathe normally with your neck bent back.

"Don't hurt her!" Christine yelled.

I heard her coming towards us. "Christine, no!" I screamed. My vocal cords strained against my neck.

Mr. Clean turned around sharply, flinging me around with him. I heard my neck crack with the force of it and cried out as the pain shot up through my head. The side of my face felt like tiny needles were jabbing at it. I saw Brawny out of the corner of my eyes as he ran towards Christine. He picked her up and threw her towards the side wall. She hit the floor first, saving her from the full impact when she slid into the wall. It looked like a repeat of what had happened to me just minutes ago.

I heard her hit with a loud thud and her breath came out in one large gasp.

"Leave her," Mr. Clean said to Brawny. He eased up on my hair so that I could bring my neck back up and tightened his grip on my waist. "Just get the gun she was headed for."

Mr. Clean and I shuffled our way towards the glass counter. You can't really walk in any dignified manner when you have someone pressed against the front of you. We stopped near the counter and watched while Brawny searched for the gun they thought Christine had. I glanced over at Christine, who was slowly and unsteadily getting to her feet. I breathed a silent sigh of relief and thanked God she used to play softball. She was going to be okay, for now.

I watched as Brawny searched the desk and noticed that there was a heavy pewter statue of a dragon on the counter. It's scales and wings were heavily detailed and had two large rubies for eyes. The dragon sat on a crystal ball with its talons wrapped around the sides as if it were some treasure it would pick it up and take back to its lair. I was close enough to grab it. I glanced over at Christine, then at the counter towards the statue. She nodded with her eyes. Good. She knew what I was thinking. And she says she can't read minds. It was our only hope. The only plan I could think of. Probably the only one we had.

I watched Brawny and when he bent down behind the counter, I inched my hand in the direction of the statue. I glanced back over at Christine. She had her eyes closed, her lips moving and faint murmurs were coming from her mouth. I had no clue what she was doing. If it would help, I was all for it.

"I found it," Brawny said and popped up with the gun in hand. Whata ya know. She did have one.

"Good," Mr. Clean said. His voice vibrated through his chest against my back. "Get the stuff outta my pocket so we can get outta here."

Brawny lifted his sweatshirt up and pulled the waist band of his jeans out showing the beginnings of what looked like a beer belly. He stuffed the gun in his pants, leaving the butt of it sticking out and pulled his shirt down over it. He started to come around the back of the counter and stopped to look over at Christine as her voice got louder.

Christine's eyes were still closed as she raised her head and hands skyward. "Nuit, Goddess of Air. Lend me your powers to fight the evil which presents itself."

Brawny's eyes widened. "What the fuck is she doing?" he said and looked over at Mr. Clean, then at me.

"Didn't you know? She's a witch you asshole," I said as I snatched the dragon statue off the counter and swung it straight up over my head. I knew I would hit something. Mr. Clean went down. . .for the second time today. He still had hold of my waist and took me with him as he fell backwards onto the floor. I landed on top of him and his body softened the blow. I took a breath, struggled out of his arm and rolled off of him. I stumbled to my feet and saw Brawny come rushing around the counter. His face was flushed and his mouth curled up in a sneer as he headed in my direction. He scowled as his hands stretched out in front of him to grab for me.

"*Planto aer lucus*!" Christine yelled in a hoarse voice.

Brawny's eyes widened as he ran into some invisible wall and was pushed back a step.

I looked over at Christine. She was walking slowly towards the counter with one of her hands held out in our direction.

"Get out, Julie," she hollered.

I glanced back at Brawny, my eyes went wide and my jaw dropped. I didn't really think anything would happen. There he stood, pushing against a barrier that rippled under is fingers like a calm lake when a leaf falls to its surface.

"Go," she urged.

I glanced at her, then down at Mr. Clean sprawled out on the floor. He had an imprint of the statue's base on his forehead. I looked back up at Brawny, turned and ran out of the store. Christine was a few heartbeats behind me.

We both jumped in the car at the same time. Christine threw the car in gear and peeled out of the parking lot; the smell of rubber burning stung my nose. When we were safely out of the parking lot, I turned and looked through the back window. Brawny came running out to the edge of the parking lot and stared at our taillights as we made our way down the road. I didn't flip him off. I didn't think it wise at this point. I had the feeling if Mr. Clean caught up with me again, it wouldn't be as pleasant.

When I knew we were completely safe, I let my body relax. The adrenaline slowly melted away and left me shaking. I closed my eyes and hugged myself to stop the shivering.

I took a deep, shaky breath. "That was some pretty heavy shit you laid out back there. I thought you said your abilities weren't that great."

She glanced at me before looking back at the road. "That was small stuff, Julie." Her voice came out a bit unsteady.

I raised an eyebrow at that.

"No, really, it was. It doesn't last very long either. My spells are small, but can be quite effective when need be. Believe me, if I could do more to help, I would."

"It may seem small to you, but it served the purpose at the time." I could feel a grin forming on my lips. I thought that alone I was doing pretty good. Between Christine and I, we could pretty much handle anything that came along. Optimism is my middle name.

Christine smiled back with a satisfied look on her face. "Let's get you a place to stay for the night."

Chapter Twenty-two

She was right when she said for the night. I didn't seem to be able to stay in one place for any longer than that.

CHAPTER TWENTY-THREE

I got a room at a motel near the beach this time. They weren't that expensive this time of year. Virginia Beach is a tourist city and during the late fall and winter seasons things pretty much come to a stand still for the beach area. I actually chose it because I wanted to be able to open my curtains and see the ocean. It was something that was untamed. Something wild and powerful. No one could alter or contain its fierceness no matter how hard they tried. I liked it. It gave me a sense of strength.

When we went into the room, I wanted to turn around and walk back out. Everything was done in burgundy and pink. It looked as though it had been coated with Pepto-Bismol. It's a good thing pink isn't my favorite color. It won't bother me not to buy anything in that color.

Chapter Twenty-three

The room was furnished like any other motel room. There was a bed, dresser, night stand, chair, and a TV. Do you think they all shop at the same place?

I threw my bag on the dresser. No sense in unpacking huh? I flopped down on the edge of the bed and looked up at Christine. "You can't go back to the store for a while. At least until we know who those men are and what they want."

She shrugged. "It's okay. I work too much anyway. Just get a good night's sleep and I'll see you tomorrow morning."

"I'll try. At least I haven't had any other visions since..." I stopped myself when I realized it. I usually had several in a row before it actually happens. I didn't have one today.

Christine was at the door with her hand on the knob. "What?"

"When these visions start, they usually come on a daily basis until the actual event occurs."

She came over and sat next to me. "How many do you usually have?"

I thought about that. "The last two times it happened, they came in three's. Two visions before and the last is when it's actually happening. The only one I've had today is the one we induced. Does that count?"

She shook her head. "No. We took you to present time. That was not like your normal visions. I think I should stay with you tonight."

"No, I've already almost gotten you killed once yesterday and once today. I think you've met your quota for the week. I don't want you getting hurt again." She opened her mouth to say something. I put my hand up to stop her. "If it happens again, I'll be all right. If I need help, I'll call you. The last time wasn't so bad. I stopped it and my wrist healed pretty quick."

"You are a very stubborn individual."

I smiled. "So I've been told."

I pulled an envelope out of my back pocket and handed it to her.

"What do you want me to do with this?" she asked.

"Hold onto it. I lost everything I had once already. It's not going to happen again."

She looked inside. It held the papers from my house and the lawyers, my license and money. I figured it would be safe with her until all of this was over. If I should get caught again, I wasn't going to let them take what I fought so hard to get back.

She put the envelope into her coat pocket and I gave her a quick hug before she got up.

She went to the door and turned around. "I'll see you tomorrow." She locked the door from the inside and left.

I plugged the cell in and took a long, hot shower. I wiped the steam away from the mirror to see myself better. I looked awful. My skin was paler than usual and I had the beginnings of dark circles under my emerald-green eyes. With all the commotion at the store, we never stopped to get anything to eat. I was going to starve to death, if someone didn't kill me first.

There was a greenish bruise on my shoulder where the door slammed into me today. I wondered if it was already healing or just starting to come out. Tomorrow would tell me the answer to that question. My hair had been wet most of the day so I used the blow dryer, supplied by the hotel, to dry my hair. Do you think they charge extra for such a luxury?

An hour and a half later, I was in my over-sized T-shirt, a pair of white socks and ready for bed. Maybe a hair cut would be in order. I was just about tired of having to

Chapter Twenty-three   135

spend so much time on it lately. If I cut it short, it sure wouldn't give Mr. Clean much to grab hold of.

The bed was hard and when I hopped onto it I just stayed where I landed. See, no springs here. I can't sleep on a soft mattress anyway. I stared at the motel phone on the night stand, sighed and picked it up. I needed to talk to Elaine.

"Hello," Elaine said through the phone.

It was so good to hear her voice. It was, in a way, a symbol of my life or what it once was. "Hi, Elaine."

"Julie! How are you feeling?"

"I'm okay, I guess. I just needed to hear your voice."

"I would have come to see you sooner, but they said I couldn't come until tomorrow."

"I'm not at the hospital anymore."

"Huh?"

"It's a long story, but I haven't been there since Monday evening."

"I don't understand. Why didn't you call me? Or come over? Have you been back to work?" she asked. Her voice was getting louder. I could tell she was getting upset.

"Elaine, please. It's just too complicated to explain. I wanted to call you before you went to the hospital and found I wasn't there."

"You have to tell me something. You just can't call me like this and leave it at that."

In that way we were alike. I never liked being left in the dark and it frustrated me. You have to feel sorry for the poor fool who doesn't explain something to me when I want an answer. Where would I start? It would take all night if I started from the beginning and I didn't know what parts to leave out. Leaving certain things out would just lead to more questions. She wouldn't stand for bits and pieces. I didn't want to involve her. I should never have called, but if I didn't, what would they have told her? It was just too scary to think about. It felt like I was in some kind of James Bond movie. That's classified information ma'am. Ri-ight.

"Julie? You still there?" she asked.

"Yeah, I'm here. I was just trying to figure out how to tell you is all."

She sighed heavily into the phone. "It can't be that bad. Can it?"

"Worse."

"Well, I'm not going anywhere."

That was her subtle hint that she wanted to hear it all. Great. I had to figure out how to summarize it and still tell her everything. "You know that detective? Kyle Sanders?"

"Yeah, he came over here Tuesday."

That figured. I knew he would try her. After all, she was my only contact he knew of. "What did he say to you?"

"That you were being taken care of. He thanked me for helping him with you."

Of course he would thank her. She had no idea she was helping an asshole lock me up and take my freedom away from me. What a slime bucket.

"He's not who he says he is, Elaine. He works for some organization and they want to use me and my abilities in any way they see fit."

"You're kidding, right?"

"I wish I was. I've been hiding from him since I escaped the hospital."

"This isn't making any sense."

I could tell this wasn't going to be easy unless I started from the very beginning. From the day they took me to the hospital. I looked at the clock on the TV. 8:45PM. I was glad I took the time to get ready for bed before calling her. So, I took a deep breath and started from the very beginning.

She let out a deep breath. "God, Julie. You should've called me. I could've helped you in some way."

"I didn't think involving you was a good idea, but I had no idea what they were going to tell you tomorrow when you found me gone. And I wanted to talk to you first."

"I'm glad you did, hun. But I'm still not happy that you didn't trust me enough to call me sooner."

"This guy is dangerous, Elaine. I didn't want to put you in any danger is all."

"You have to let me help you."

I knew that was coming. "Listen, I've already almost got Christine killed. Remember I have more than just Kyle after me now. I don't want to add you to my list of people to worry about."

"So, what am I suppose to do? Sit here and twiddle my thumbs while I wonder if you're dead or alive?"

"I don't even know what I'm going to do yet. Listen, just sit tight until I come up with something. If there's anything you can do to help, I'll call you."

"I don't know what to make of all this."

"I don't either and I'm the one in the middle of it all."

"Just be careful."

"Always," I said and hung up. I was glad I called and was upset that I didn't do it sooner.

I walked over to the window and drew the blinds. The ocean's muffled rumbling was like music to my ears. I closed my eyes, let it sink into my mind and calm my body. I opened my eyes and a smile formed on my lips. Things were going to work out no matter what. I now had two resources. Sure Kyle knew about Elaine, but there are ways around that. If she was careful, the three of us could get together and do what needed to be done.

The wind blew outside the window, howling like some lost lover morning for the fisherman who never returned. I looked out at the waves as they crashed against the wooden pier sending spray into the air. The spray and foam seemed to take on a bluish-white hue as if it actually glowed in the dark. It was beautiful. I think maybe that's why I never moved back home after my split with Scott. The ocean calmed the mind and soothed the soul. It's exactly what I needed right now.

I pulled the covers back from the bed when the motel phone rang. I just about knocked the lamp over on the night stand when I turned towards the sound. I stared at it for a few breaths. Christine was the only one that knew where I was. If it wasn't her, I was going to end up leaving the motel in my T-shirt.

My hand shook as I reached down, grabbed it and slowly brought it to my ear. "Hello?" My voice was just barely a whisper.

"Julie, turn your TV on!" Christine yelled. She sounded out of breath and alarmed. As if the button was pushed and we only had ten minutes to live.

"Huh?"

"Just do it. Put it on channel four."

There wasn't a remote so I had to put the receiver on the table by the phone. I walked over to the TV to turn it on. It was already on channel four when the screen came to life. My eyes widened and mouth fell open. My stomach felt like it was tied in a knot and the cold chill of fear rushed through my body. It was her. The first woman I saw on the altar with the soft, velvet cover.

Her dark-auburn hair was pulled back away from her face and fell in loose curls over her shoulders. It was her eyes I looked at. It was what I remembered the most.

Chapter Twenty-three

The one's that were wide with fear and the knowledge of an assured death in my vision. These pale-green eyes were so full of life. These eyes held the happiness of what she thought would be her future.

I reached over and turned the volume up. ". . .who has been missing since Sunday evening was found in the North Landing River late this evening. Investigators say. . ." I turned it off. I heard everything I wanted to hear. I over-heard Kyle that night in the hospital say she had been missing the night before. That would have been Sunday and I hadn't had any other visions about her since Monday. It was like Christine had said. They knew about me and were keeping me out somehow and if I went back on my own, they would control my mind. I believed her now. I was helpless to do anything for these women. I told Kyle everything I saw and knew. They would have to solve it on their own.

"Julie?" I heard Christine call through the phone.

I went over and picked it up. "Yeah, I'm still here."

"Is it the same woman you saw? She fits the description you gave me."

"Yes, it's her." It sounded so final. "She's dead."

Silence. I was guessing she was feeling the same way I was. I know she said that it would probably be impossible to help them, but I knew. I knew she felt the anger and frustration just as I was.

"I'm sorry, Julie," she said finally.

"Didn't you say it wouldn't take place until Sunday?" My voice sounded harsh.

"I said it was possible. It wasn't a fact. The fourth candle is what throws it off. There are only suppose to be three sacrifices not four. They obviously don't represent the days of the week. It was the only explanation I had at the time."

"So, now we have to sit here and watch as they announce one woman at a time on the news?" My voice was flat; lifeless. I was emotionally drained. "Tomorrow there will be another and Friday, another."

"We still have some time. Maybe we can figure something out before it's too late."

Figure what out? We could only go on what I knew and that seemed to be squat as far as these people were concerned.

"Maybe we should try to induce another vision," I said.

"It won't work, you know that."

I felt the stirrings of anger growing in my stomach. "Why the hell not? I was there once. Couldn't I be there again without being noticed?"

"Now that they know? No. It would just give them power over you. They wouldn't want you interfering anymore. If they can murder these women without conscience, do you think they wouldn't do the same to you?"

She was right. I wasn't any good to anyone dead. "You're right, but that doesn't mean I have to like it."

"I don't like it anymore than you do. The only thing that would help us is the Book of Olakla. Unless we can find it or a copy of it, we're pretty much screwed."

I thought about that. One book standing between us and those people. A book that was practically non-existent. Then, an idea hit me. "Do you think it's possible, through the computer, to locate a copy of it?"

"I've already tried that. I didn't find anything."

Ahh, but she wasn't Elaine. "I know someone who probably can."

"Who?"

"My friend Elaine. I called her this evening. I know I was taking chances doing it, but I really needed to talk to her. She's a beta tester, but she can do a whole lot more than that."

"She's a hacker then."

"I didn't want to put it that way, but yeah. I'll call her tomorrow morning."

"We actually have a plan in the making here." Christine said. Her voice sounding hopeful. "Get some rest and I'll see you in the morning."

"Okay," I said and hung up. I breathed a huge sigh of relief. There was actually some hope. A thread of it mind you, but it works for me.

I slid into bed and settled in to go to sleep. I reached out, turned the light off and for the first time since Monday, I wanted to dream.

CHAPTER TWENTY-FOUR

There was a movement in the room. Not much, but just enough to shift the air across the skin of my arms. Just enough to alert my senses that something was wrong. There it was again. It moved across the side of the bed I was on. This time it sent a chill through my body causing the hair on my neck and arms to stand up. I opened my eyes slowly to see if there was anyone there. It was dark after all and if there was someone there, they might not see my eyes open.

I lay looking at the legs of someone standing by the bed. I followed the legs up and although it was dark, I could tell it was Shawn. My pulse went into my throat and I felt a tightening in my stomach. Kyle was here. I was in bed and it was too dark to see where he might be. I was defenseless.

Shawn moved towards the bed and my instincts took over. I took a deep breath, threw the covers off and jumped to the other side of the bed towards the door.

Chapter Twenty-four

Before I realized it and could stop myself, I ran into something large and solid. My breath came out in a loud gasp. Two large hands grabbed me, picked me up like I was just a doll and tossed me backwards onto the bed. Right back where I started from and exactly where I didn't want to be. My adrenaline was starting to kick into high-gear as fear over-took my body.

I sure as hell wasn't going to sit here so they could pounce on me. I got up on my hands and knees and crawled across the bed to the edge. The light flicked on and I was momentarily blinded from the sudden invasion of its brightness. I sat back on my legs and squeezed my eyes shut until the darkness from behind my lids faded to match the light inside the room.

"I told you I wasn't going to play your games for very long," he said. There was a tightness to his voice.

His deep voice sent a shiver up my spine and I fought the urge to shake it off. There was only one voice that could do that to me. I didn't have to see him to know it was Kyle. This was turning out to be one hell of a week.

I opened my eyes, blinked the fuzz away and found myself staring into dark, steel-blue eyes. Eyes that stared back at me as if with one look, could pull the very heart from my chest. My heart leapt into my throat and I felt every muscle in my body tense. I was that wild animal trapped in a corner. Willing to fight for freedom. . .or die trying.

He stood there. In all his glory. He wore black jeans, a dark-blue, button-up shirt tucked into his jeans and a black jacket. He looked exquisite. It was too bad we hadn't met under different circumstances.

"I only wish I could have found you sooner. The woman is dead — and it's the same as if you did it yourself, Julie." He added. His voice was low and dangerous.

How dare he blame me for any of this. That arrogant son-of-a-bitch. I felt the anger building like a dormant volcano awakening after a thousand years. This was not my fault and he would not make me feel guilty about this. I snatched the anger that was building and held onto it. I could do anger.

My eyes narrowed as I pushed a tangled mass of hair from my face and took a deep breath through my nose. "Fuck you," I said through clenched teeth.

He stared at me hard and his brows furrowed down. The muscles in his jaw were working feverishly. He glanced over at Shawn and I fell for it. I looked that way just for a heartbeat and I was down on the bed with Kyle on top of me. His whole body covered the length of mine. I didn't think someone his size could move that quickly. I screamed as I struggled under him and pushed at his chest with my hands. My legs were pinned under his and I couldn't move them. He grabbed my wrists one at a time, held them up above my head and transferred them both into one hand.

"Get—off—me!" I yelled as I tried twisting my body under his to get some kind of advantage. He squeezed my wrists tightly in his hand. I tried to scream again and it was cut off when the air was pushed out of my lungs from the increasing pressure of his body against mine. My breathing came in short pants and it blew at the hair that lay in my face. We lay there, faces barely an inch from each other.

His steel-blue eyes stared down into mine. Something moved behind them and his lips curled up. With his free hand, he gently pushed my hair out of my face. I didn't even flinch. Good for me.

He lowered his face to my ear. "You are not getting away a second time. You belong to me, my little Jewel," he said. His voice was a deep, soft whisper.

Chapter Twenty-four

I felt a sharp sting in my arm. He kept his face near my ear and held me tighter when my body tensed as I felt the liquid being pumped into my vein. As the feeling of peacefulness flowed through my mind and my body slowly relaxed, he whispered in my ear again. "You are mine."

He brought his face back to mine. So close I could feel his soft breath against my skin. I looked into those beautiful steel-blue eyes and they made me feel safe. I sighed contentedly and smiled. He leaned in, touched his lips to mine, and kissed me so softly; so tenderly. It sent a wave of desire down my spine, reaching deep into the areas of my body that hadn't been touched in a very long time. I opened myself to him and kissed him back. I didn't want the feeling to end. Then the blackness engulfed my mind and took me away from the one that made me feel protected.

The darkened tunnel swallowed me up as if I was sinking into a black pit of quick sand. I knew it would take me to a place sleep could never promise. I could feel myself being set down gently and my feet touched a coldness only stone could bring. I knew where I was before I saw it. The darkness faded and I opened my eyes.

The room was empty again. I knew why I was here. I looked around and saw that the black and yellow candles had been used as well as the yellow one on the candelabra. The altar with its ebony cloth covering it was still there. It held no signs of anyone ever being laid upon it to give their lives unwillingly for another's purpose. The circles and symbols painted in black were still there as well as the curtains. This room would be here until it had served its purpose.

My T-shirt brushed the velvet cloth that hung over the altar as I walked along side of it. I stopped near the head of it where the woman's hands would be. My fingers traced a line along the blood stains that dried on the edge. Terrified pale-green eyes flashed before my eyes and I pulled my hand away. "This is her blood," I whispered.

It was not a vision of what was to come. I was in present time. Just as before. My stomach tightened when I remembered what Christine had told me about coming back. I didn't want to be here, but I couldn't go back. Something was keeping me here and I couldn't remember what it was.

"Where are you, Julie?" Shawn's voice asked from somewhere above me.

I looked up at the ceiling. "In the room."

"Does it look the same?"

"No, there's blood on the altar now." I looked down at the blood and felt a frown form on my face. I wished I could have helped her. "It's her blood."

I walked over to the candelabra and brought my finger up to touch the wick of the used yellow candle. I yanked my hand away as the image of the first woman's eyes came before me. Her pale-green eyes holding the truth of what had passed. I frowned wishing I could see through her eyes what she had seen. And in a heartbeat of time a dagger flashed before my eyes. It was silver and engraved with the same symbol as was put on the woman's forehead. A large ruby was set into the top of the hilt. My skin crawled with dread. This was the last thing she saw. Dear God.

"Anything else, Julie?"

"The candles." My voice was barely a whisper

"What's wrong with the candles?"

"They show me."

"What do they show you?"

"Eyes. The dead woman's eyes."

My trembling fingers touched the wick of the white candle that waited to be lit during the sacrifice of

Chapter Twenty-four

another innocent life. The image of the second woman's golden-brown brown eyes came forth to my sight. Her visions of doom lay bare for all to see. I didn't jerk my hand back this time. Instead, I brought it back slowly as the realization hit me. I was seeing what was and is to come with each thing I placed my touch upon. This had never happened to me before. The visions were usually just random and of whatever they wanted me to see. I realized that I could now see these things with just a thought and the touch of my hand.

If only the dagger I saw were here. It was possible I could see who held it. . .or maybe just the person's eyes. I wasn't sure. I needed to touch the red candle to find out if it would show me.

"Is there a way out of the room?"

"Yes, the door I went through before."

"The door you went through before?"

"Yes."

"Go through the door, Julie." Shawn urged.

"Wait. I need to touch the candle first. I need to see."

"No, Julie. The door."

I hesitated. I didn't want to go through that door again. "I don't want to. I'm afraid." I looked up towards the ceiling and pictured Christine's deep-sapphire eyes. "Christine? Where are you? Please, help me."

"Go through the door," Shawn repeated.

"Yes," I said. I couldn't stop myself as I walked slowly towards the large oak door. The door that would surely seal my fate if I walked through it. My hand hesitated over the knob as that rush of cold air blew at me and ran a chill through my whole body.

"Julie, my special gift," the woman said. Her voice covered me like the warmth of a hot summer day, making the chill melt away from my body. "You came to me again."

"Yes, again."

"I'm so glad you did, but you didn't come alone did you?"

"No, not alone."

"Where were you going, little one?"

I frowned. "Through the door. Please, don't make me go through the door."

"Don't worry. They are gone. You don't have go through."

I smiled. "Thank you."

"I would never let anything happen to you. You are very special to me."

I smiled. She was the one that would keep me safe. "I'm special to you."

"Yes, I will make you his special gift and you will no longer feel the pain of this life."

I believed her. "No more pain." She would be the one to make everything go away. She would bring me to a safe place where I would be happy and free for all time.

"That's right, little one."

"Can I come now?"

"No, sweetie. Not yet. When it's time I will call you and you can come."

"When it's time." I sighed. "But how will I know where to go?"

"Don't worry. I will know where you are. When I call you, someone will be there to show you the way."

"Okay."

"Now close your eyes and let me give you what you need to hear me."

I closed my eyes. "You will give me what I need. Yes."

Chapter Twenty-four

"Your mind to me I bind, not in part but in whole. From this moment and henceforth I take control," she said. Her voice caressed my skin and filled my mind with peace. *"Vestri mens ut mihi EGO redimio, non in secui, tamen in universus, ex is moment quod iam Capio imperium."*

Her words filled my mind and embraced my thoughts as if we were two becoming one. I felt protected and content.

"Now go child. Go back until I send for you."

"Until you send for me," I said. And a cool breeze blew at my face as the blackness flowed over me like a waterfall over a cliff. Then a pair of invisible hands pulled me from that dark void and lifted me up towards the faraway light.

CHAPTER TWENTY-FIVE

"What the fuck happened, Shawn? Why did we lose her like that?" Kyle's deep voice came from somewhere in the distance.

"I don't know. Nothing like this has ever happened before." Shawn's voice echoed back.

"Can't you keep her under longer than that?"

"No, not without increasing the dosage and we've already given her more than we should have."

"Don't start that shit. You know anything less wouldn't work on her."

The voices were getting clearer as the muck in my brain started to drain away. I tried to open my eyes and they fluttered shut. I was so tired. Why were these two yelling? Couldn't they see I was trying to sleep? Then, as the confusion of a drug induced sleep lifted. . .I remembered.

I opened my eyes again and blinked a couple of times to get them to focus.

Chapter Twenty-five

"Welcome back, little jewel. That was quite a trip you took," Kyle said. There was a hint of humor in his voice.

I found myself sitting in the chair by the window with my wrists handcuffed to the arms. Was there something funny about all of this? I sure didn't think so. The anger welled up in the pit of my stomach and I felt my heart start to beat faster. I had been hit by doors, my neck stretched to the point of breaking, shoved on beds and stuck with needles. I think that would try anyone's patience.

My eyes narrowed as I slowly looked up at him. I met those steel-blue eyes, and let my murderous thoughts of him show in mine. "Go—to—hell," I said through clenched teeth.

He laughed, rich and deep. Guess he thought that was funny too. He'll learn. Naaaw.

He smiled and sat on the edge of the bed. "Not until you tell me where you went."

I looked over at Shawn, who was standing near the door. He was just a few inches shorter than Kyle, but was thin with long legs and arms. His blonde hair was cut close to his head and looked as though he had been too busy to shave lately. His gray dress pants and blue shirt were wrinkled like he hadn't changed in days. He looked at me with tired, gray eyes. I guess when you're looking for someone who doesn't want to be found, you don't get much sleep. Kyle sure looked like a fresh daisy though.

"What the fuck did you do to me?" I spat at Shawn.

Shawn hesitated and shifted from one foot to the other. Did I make him nervous? Little ole *moi?*

Kyle leaned towards me, putting his arms on his thighs. "We used a little persuasion and brought you exactly where we wanted you to go. Except you took a little trip on your own after we got you in."

"I asked *him*," I said and motioned towards Shawn with my eyes, then looked back at Kyle, "Not you. Unless, of course, the question was a bit over his head." Sarcasm at its best. Point for me.

"He understood the question," Kyle said.

I raised my brow and gave him my "oh really? Is that so?" face.

"You deal only with me from now on. No one else. I'll answer your questions, if I feel the need to."

Oh, that hurt. Who the fuck did he think he was? Let's not go there just yet. I decided to let it slide. . .for now anyway. Let him think I was giving up. I gave him my best blank face. I didn't practice that one much, so I hoped it worked.

He sat back up and a smile formed on his lips. Yep, it worked.

"You avoided my question," he said.

My brows rose. "What question would that be?" Now I was trying for innocence. Ri-ight.

He smiled. "Where did you go while you were under?"

Okay, this wasn't going the way I wanted it to. I was angry and he was smiling. Not quite the effect I was looking for.

"I don't remember." It was the truth, I didn't remember. But I knew what probably happened. He didn't ask me *that* question, now did he?

"You're lying."

"It's quite possible she doesn't remember, Kyle. She never said anything while she was gone," Shawn said softly from near the door. Was he planning a quick get-a-way?

Chapter Twenty-five

Kyle got up and glared at him. "Shut up, Shawn. This is none of your business."

Oh goodie, anger. I feel better now.

He turned his attention back to me. Great.

"Where—were—you?" he asked. His voice going deeper with each word he spoke.

"I'll answer your questions, if I feel the need to."

His eyes faltered. A frown formed on his forehead and a flush began to crawl up his neck. "You do know, don't you?"

"No, actually I don't know. But if I did, I wouldn't tell you anyway."

He bent down and put his hands on the arms of the chair. His face just inches from mine. "I don't believe you."

My brow rose at that. "I don't give a shit."

"There *are* other ways to find out." His voice was dangerously low and it sent an icy feeling through my body.

I resisted the urge to shiver. That's it, be a brave soldier while you're handcuffed to a chair. I leaned forward so my face was barely touching his. "Fuck. . .you," I said calmly.

He put his face to my ear and I could feel his hot breath on my skin. I didn't move. I wasn't going to let his presence affect me and I wanted him to know that.

"It's not in my contract, but I'm sure I can work something out." He spoke softly and his voice sent a wave of fear down my spine. He pulled back enough for me to see his face. There was a darkness to his steel-blue eyes and his mouth curled up in a sneer.

I glared at him for a few heartbeats and I felt a smile forming on my lips. His eyes widened and at that moment I cleared my throat and spit right into his smug face. "Go to hell," I said.

He never took his eyes from mine as he stood up, reached into his pocket and took out a handkerchief. He wiped his face and stuffed it back into his pocket. "Shawn, take a walk," he said in a "calm before the storm" voice.

Shawn stood there and shifted on his feet. I was guessing Shawn didn't think it was a good idea.

"I said, take—a—walk," he said through clenched teeth. His voice a deep rumbling; somehow threatening. The muscles in the sides of his jaw were working frantically.

Shawn opened the door, stood there for a few breaths and left. The door clicked softly behind him. My pulse quickened as if that one sound had sealed my fate.

I kind of expected it, but didn't have time to prepare myself. He swung his hand and backhanded me across my left cheek. My head jerked to the side from the blow and my hair fell into my face. My cheek stung like a hot iron had been pressed against it. I could hear the sound of its impact echoing through my head. I held back the sting of tears that threatened to come. Don't let him see me cry. I was stronger than him and I would beat this. . .or die trying. I wasn't going to be the property of this man.

I turned my head deliberately back to look him in the eyes. "Is that the best you've got?" My voice was calm. Goodie.

His eyes narrowed and my head jerked to the side as the other cheek was soundly backhanded. Well. . .at least they would match.

I turned my face around again and glared at him. "I guess so."

He stood there for a few heartbeats. His hands balled into fists and his jaw worked over-time. I must have hit another nerve. He leaned down and put his hands back on the arms of the chair in one fluid movement.

Chapter Twenty-five

"I know you know where you were. You've been through that door before. Did this Christine person have anything to do with it?"

I felt my eyes widen before I caught myself.

"You called out to her. She helped you get through didn't she?"

I didn't say anything. Pretty amazing eh?

He leaned into my face. "Answer me!"

I felt my lips curl up. I couldn't help it.

He got up, walked towards the dresser and turned back around. "Damn you! That woman would be alive right now if you had told me!"

"No, it wouldn't have done any good."

"We'll see about that." He walked to the door and flung it open. "Shawn, get in here." He went around to the other side of the bed and threw his hand inside a black, leather bag.

Shawn came rushing through the door. "What's. . ." He stopped short when he saw me.

My face must've looked as bad as it felt.

"Holy shit, Kyle. You didn't have to. . ."

"Shut up," Kyle said and threw a small black case towards him. It hit Shawn's chest and he fumbled with it in his hands until he got a firm hold of it. "Do it again," Kyle demanded.

Shawn glanced down at the black case, to me, then to Kyle. "It's too soon after. You know that as well as I do."

"Do it or I will myself."

Either way, I didn't like the choice. Looked like I was going on another trip. The problem is whether I would make it through it. According to Dr. Shawn, it wasn't a smart move. He's got my vote.

Shawn opened the black case and laid it on top of the dresser. He pulled out a syringe and a small bottle with liquid in it. My pulse quickened as I watched him fill the syringe. I was helpless to stop it and chances were slim that I would make it through a second trip so soon on the drug Shawn was about to administer. Kyle knew this and he didn't care. My life wasn't worth as much as anyone else's . . .to him anyway.

When he finished filling the syringe, he placed the bottle carefully back into the black case and turned towards me.

I think we all heard it at the same time because we looked towards the door. Someone's muffled voice came from the other side of it.

The door swung open and Christine stood there. She wore a black negligée past her knees and a long sleeved robe that matched. The robe was untied and it whipped around her body as the wind blew at it. Her short hair was wind-tossed and her sapphire eyes were as dark as coal. My eyes widened and before anyone could do anything, she held her hand out to Shawn.

"Vis aer sicco!" she said and it was as if a gust of wind pushed against Shawn. He flew into the air, landed against the far wall and fell on the floor in a heap. Kyle started around the bed for her and she quickly put her hand in his direction. *"Planto aer lucus!"* she said and Kyle ran into that rippling, invisible wall Brawny had earlier.

Kyle's eyes widened and he kept trying to push against the barrier that kept him from getting to us. "What the hell is this?" he yelled.

We both ignored him as Christine came over to me. Her eyes widened. "Goddess! What did they do to you? Are you all right?"

"I've been better. Just get me the fuck out of here." My voice was rushed and shaky. "How did you know to come?"

"You called to me," she said.

Chapter Twenty-five

My brows rose at that. "Called to you?"

"Never mind that, let's just get you out of here."

I glanced over at Kyle and my eyes widened as I saw him reaching behind his back. "Christine!" I yelled.

She looked at him for a heartbeat and threw her hand up in his direction. *"Vis aer sicco!"* she said and Kyle was pushed upwards and hit the wall by the same force of air that hit Shawn. He landed with a thud onto the floor.

"I should've done that in the first place. We've got to get out of here quick," Christine said.

"The keys. I think Kyle has them."

She ran over to where Kyle lay slumped over and searched frantically for the keys.

"Be careful Christine," I said.

My heart was pounding against my chest so hard I thought it would break through my ribs. I was going to get out of here and in one piece.

She held the keys up for me to see. "Found um."

"The gun. Get the gun," I urged.

She reached behind his back and came out with a gun. I knew it. He was going to shoot Christine. I knew now he would do anything to get his job done. It was just as he told me that night on the phone.

Christine rushed back over to me. She laid the gun on the floor by the chair and with trembling fingers, unlocked the handcuffs.

She grabbed the gun and was going to toss the keys on the bed, but I held out my hand to stop her. "No, give them to me."

Her brows creased as she handed them to me. "What are you going to do?"

"Just grab my bag and lets get out of here."

She grabbed my bag and followed me out the door, slamming it behind her.

We ran down the walkway of the motel and around to the front where the cars were parked. I searched for the black Durango. It was parked in a far corner of the parking lot.

"What are you doing?" she asked.

I felt my lips curving up into a wicked smile. "I'm going to take his car, drop it off somewhere and keep his keys."

A smile formed on her lips. "I'll follow you."

"Okay, let's get out of here."

She nodded her head and ran for her car. I ran for Kyle's. My breathing came in short gasps as I fumbled with the key to unlock the door. I got the door open, hopped in and sped out of the parking lot onto Atlantic Avenue towards Shore Drive. Christine followed close behind.

CHAPTER TWENTY-SIX

Christine followed me as I drove a little pass the military base on Shore Drive and dropped Kyle's car off on the side of the road. The medium that separated the highway was large and thick with trees. I'm sure he'd find it eventually. He'd have to get another key for it though. I hopped into the passenger side of her car and a satisfied grin formed on my lips.

I turned in the seat so I could see her better. "Now explain how you knew to come."

She glanced at me, then back at the road. "I heard you call to me. You asked me to help you."

"You heard me?"

"Yes."

"You have that kind of power?"

She shook her head. "No, you do. You actually entered my thoughts."

"This is getting to be a bit much."

"I told you that your powers were just beginning."

"So, what took you so long?"

"I only heard you about twenty minutes before I came. I don't live very close to the motel." She looked at me hard for a few heartbeats, then back at the road. "Did he do that to you?"

"Yeah, he did. He'll pay for everything he's put us through."

"It looked as though they were getting ready to induce you."

"For a second time."

Her eyes widened. "A second time? You mean I was too late?"

"You probably saved my life. I might not have made it through a second time on the drug they were using. You weren't too late when you look at it that way."

"You don't understand, Julie. There is no good way to look at it. You've been there again. They have probably gained control over you already. If they have, the end result will be the same." She looked at me and a deep frown formed on her face. There was a sadness to her eyes.

"I don't plan on being alone long enough for that to happen," I said. She looked over at me and her brow rose. I smiled. "I think it's time I stayed at your house with you."

She smiled back at me but her eyes still held that sadness. I think she believed this would not end well. "That's good because if you didn't come, I would have dragged you anyway."

"Something different happened this time, Christine."

She looked at me. "Different? What?"

"Well. . ."

Chapter Twenty-six

A muffled sound came from the back seat. I let out a soft squeal, Christine jumped and we both looked at each other.

I turned slowly towards the back seat, grabbed my bag and unzipped it. The sound got louder. I reached in and pulled the cell phone out. I held it in my hand and just stared down at it. "It was on the night stand when I went to bed. Kyle must have just thrown it in here." I flipped it open.

"Julie, don't," Christine said.

My pulse quickened as I pressed talk and put the phone to my ear. "So much for a second time aye, detective?" I said. My voice was surprisingly calm.

Heavy breathing and silence. I didn't hear that exasperating clicking sound. Guess you *can* teach an old dog.

"I have underestimated your available. . .resources," he said finally. There was a tightness to his voice.

"That's an interesting way to put it, but accurate."

"It would seem that your friend Christine has some abilities of her own."

I knew where this was going. "She has a few tricks up her sleeve, detective." I glanced over at Christine. "She's a witch you idiot."

"A witch?" His voice held a surprised edge to it. I guess he ignored the "idiot" part.

"Yeah and the next time she sees you, she'll turn you into the vermin you were intended to be."

Christine gasped at that. "You know I can't do anything like that," she said.

"You should be so lucky, my little jewel," he said.

He heard Christine. It was worth a try anyway. I needed to get his mind off of Christine. I didn't want him getting any big ideas in that small pea-brain of his. "I think my luck has been pretty good so far, don't you?"

"Yes, it has. It would seem as though your psychic abilities have also strengthened along with your luck. How long have you been able to use thought transference?"

He doesn't miss a thing does he?

"I don't know what you mean."

"Don't fuck with me!" His voice was deep and there was a dangerous edge that could pierce the skin with just the sound.

My heart flew into my throat. If he ever found me again, I may not get off as easy as a slap in the face. I swallowed my heart back into my chest. "Oh, that's right. That's not in your contract, is it?" My voice was flat; unaffected Great.

Silence. I was betting by now his face was scarlet, veins and all. I couldn't hurt him physically, but I sure found other ways to do it. I felt my lips curve up.

"There are two other women that will die you know," he said finally. His voice was unusually calm. He changed moods faster than I could change my clothes. And I change pretty fast. I pity the woman who marries him.

"I know that. Has there been a third missing yet?"

"No, why do you ask?"

"If you didn't interrupt me and order me through that door, it was possible I could have found out who the third woman was."

"Julie?" Christine cut in. "What are you talking about?"

I put my hand over the phone. "I'll explain later okay?" I stared at her and my eyes widened.

"Okay, later." She went back to driving and listening.

"Would you care to elaborate on that?" he asked.

Chapter Twenty-six

"No, I don't think it's necessary to discuss that with you."

"It is *very* necessary, my little jewel." His voice was getting deeper. I struck another nerve. "If you don't tell me what I want to know now, I will have the pleasure of getting the answers later." His voice held a cruelty to it that promised me pain in ways I had never seen before.

I shook off the feeling of dread in the pit of my stomach. I needed to change the subject again. "If I had any information that could help these women, I would have told you. You know as much as I do right now. Using your drugs to induce my visions has done nothing but make it worse for me."

"You never told me you went through the door. You haven't been totally honest with me. How do I know that information wouldn't have helped?"

He had me there. Okay, so I'll tell him most of what I know. "There wasn't much to tell. The house was in a wooded area and it was too dark to see from where I was standing. I don't remember anything after that."

"Now you can tell me how you were going to be able to see the third woman."

Does he carry a notebook around with him or something? "No, I can't."

"Can't or won't."

"Okay, won't. What difference does it make? You're never going to find out, if I can help it. I'd rather die than have you touch me ever again."

"I will find out because I won't stop until you are found. You can't hide from me for long."

"You're either in love with yourself or a legend in your own mind, detective." I just couldn't help myself. I hung up before he could say anything else.

"Tell me about seeing this third woman," Christine asked.

She doesn't waste time does she? "When I was in the room, I walked over and started touching the wicks of the candles. When I touched the white one, a vision of the first woman came to my eyes. The yellow one brought a vision of the second woman. I wished in my mind I could see why she was so terrified and I saw a dagger flash before my eyes."

"A dagger?"

"Yes, it was silver with a ruby on top of the hilt and had the same symbol engraved in it."

"So, you were going to touch the other two candles when they ordered you to go through the door?"

"Yeah."

"All this Kyle person seems to do is screw things up."

"Would seem that way. He's more of an inconvenience than a help. I just don't understand how he found me."

"You didn't call him did you?"

"No, I only called. . . Shit!" I glanced over at Christine.

"Elaine," she said.

"Elaine. Damn. He has her phone wired. I've got to call her at work tomorrow."

"Who's to say he doesn't have that one wired either."

"True. I'll just have to be careful is all."

"Very careful," she said as she pulled onto Holland Road.

Christine lived on Warwick Drive, off of Holland Road. By the time we got to her house, it was nearly six o'clock in the morning. Her house was a white, one-story with red shutters and a lone pear tree that stood in the center of a neatly trimmed yard. She had two rose bushes

Chapter Twenty-six

on either side of the entrance to a white porch with pillars painted the same color as the shutters.

I walked through the door behind Christine and into the living room. A rush of warm air filled with incense blew at my face and I had to swallow the lump in my throat to keep from coughing. It smelled the same as her shop did.

She had a spacious, two-bedroom home. Her living room was all white walls with a dark, hardwood floor. A white couch and chair to match sat in the center of the living room. There were two glass end tables framed with brass edges on either side of the couch and a glass coffee table to match. Both end tables and the coffee table had a brass incense holder placed in the center. No wonder it smelled the way it did. It wasn't an unpleasant smell, just overwhelming at first. A book shelf stocked with books was centered between the two windows on the front wall. She had a TV in a glass cabinet on the inside wall facing the couch.

"Make yourself comfortable and I'll make us some tea. I need something to calm my nerves," Christine said.

I sat down in the chair in the living room. I sank to a comfortable level and let the softness of the chair form to my body. I watched Christine as she pulled some tea out of the cabinet over the sink.

Her kitchen was almost an exact copy of my own. It maybe had a foot more room. The walls were light-blue and the floor was white, ceramic tile. Her counter was blue to match the walls and the cabinets were white to match the tile. There were two barstools with blue fabric that covered the seats. At least it was color coordinated.

She came in with two cups of steaming tea. The aroma drifted throughout the living room and I suddenly felt homesick for my own house. I would never be able to go back there. It didn't seem real until now. I still had no idea where I was going to go after all this was over. Kyle wouldn't stop looking for me, which meant never being able to settle down in one place. I thought about leaving Virginia after all was said and done, but I would end up alone. I think that's exactly what Kyle would want.

Christine placed a cup on the end table nearest me. "Julie? What's wrong?"

"Nothing. Just thinking. I need to get a couple hours sleep before I call Elaine."

"I hope the couch will be all right. My spare room doesn't have a bed and it's full of my things."

"That'll be fine. As long as I'm not alone anymore, I don't care where I sleep."

She smiled. "I'll set my alarm and wake you up."

We finished our tea and Christine actually tucked me in on the couch. I had a fluffy pillow and a warm blanket. I was all set for a couple of hours sleep. Looked like that's all I was going to get for the day.

CHAPTER TWENTY-SEVEN

Christine woke me up exactly two hours later. It felt like I hadn't slept at all. Considering all the interruptions during the night, it was pretty accurate. I took a shower and dressed in black jeans, red sweater and my comfy sneakers. I noticed that the marks that Kyle left on my face were already gone. Gotta love it. I wrapped my hair in a braid to keep it off my face and I was ready to face a day that started long before anyone thought of stirring from their beds.

I walked into the living room to see Christine in the kitchen. She wore blue jeans and a blue, pull-over, sweat shirt. Any color blue she wore brought her eyes out more. I sat on one of the stools at the counter sipping a freshly brewed cup of coffee and watched as Christine made eggs and bacon for breakfast. My first home-cooked meal in days. The smell of bacon made my stomach tighten with hunger.

Christine set a plate in front of me and sat down with her own. "When are you calling Elaine?"

"I'm going to call after I finish eating."

"You have to be careful what you say to her over the phone, who knows if they've got her phone at the office rigged or not."

"That's why I'm going to call her husband's cell phone instead."

We sat in silence through our meal, which was good because I wanted to savor every bite of my breakfast.

I helped Christine clean up and with a fresh cup of coffee in front of me, I sat at the counter to dial Frank's cell phone.

"This is Frank, how can I help you?" he said.

"Hey, Frank. It's me, Julie."

"Julie, how are you?"

"I'm fine thanks. I know it's strange of me to call your cell to talk to Elaine, but could you please put her on for me?"

"Well, sure. Hold on a second."

"What's going on?" Christine asked.

"I'm on hold."

"Julie? Have you come up with something? Has something happened?" Elaine asked.. Her voice held an edge of concern.

"Elaine, listen to me for a second. Okay?"

"Okay, go ahead."

"I need you to meet me somewhere."

"Sure. What's happened?"

"Kyle has your home phone wired. He knows that I called."

She let out a gasp. "Shi-it. Why didn't you just call me at my work number?"

"I couldn't take the chance he had that wired too."

"This guy is relentless."

Chapter Twenty-seven

"You don't have to tell me that. Is there anyway you can meet me without being seen? I'm pretty sure Kyle knows the vehicles you and Frank drive by now."

"Hmm. I could take the company car that's left here in the garage for employee use."

"Great. Meet me at Mt. Trashmore, near the wooden play area on your lunch break and bring your laptop. I'll explain everything to you when you get there."

"Okay, I'll see you around eleven."

"Bye, Elaine. And be careful," I urged.

"I will," she said and hung up.

Looked like our little group was getting larger. A psychic, a witch, and a computer hacker. What more could one ask for?

CHAPTER TWENTY-EIGHT

Mt. Trashmore is a large park. It had a huge mountain of grass that lay in the middle of the park surrounded by all types of equipment for children to play on. A wooden play area that looked like a small fortress with picnic tables scattered about was on one side of the park and a lake complete with ducks on the other. A bike and jogging trail outlined the park for those that were into physical fitness.

We sat in the car near the wooden fortress with our windows rolled down. It was a pretty mild day for once this week and I was glad for that. The unusual cold weather had passed and we were back up to our normal warmth of sixty-five. The sky was clear with a light dusting of a few feathery clouds. There weren't many people at the park this time of the day. Kids were in school and most people were at work. Except for a few joggers and bicyclists, it was pretty quiet.

Chapter Twenty-eight

I saw Elaine pull into the entrance of the park. There was no mistaking the car. It was a red, Lincoln Town car with tinted windows. It had the AT emblem on the driver side door that stood for Anderson's Technology. It looked brand new. Does everyone except me have a new car?

I reached out the window and waved her over to where we were parked. She pulled along side Christine's car and rolled her window down. She was wearing a red jacket with a white, button-up shirt underneath. I was guessing she had a short skirt on. She looked good in them due to the amount of leg she had.

"Hey stranger," she said and smiled.

I smiled widely. "Hi, Elaine." It was so good to see her again. I missed our morning coffee and just all-around girl talk.

"You weren't followed were you?" I asked

"No, not a soul behind me most of the way."

"Elaine, this is Christine," I said as I sat back for her to see. "Christine, this is Elaine."

"Hi, Elaine. Nice to meet you finally," Christine said.

"Same here." Elaine said back through her window. "Are we going to talk here?"

"No, follow us to Christine's house. I hope you don't have anything important to do at work because we may need you a while," I said.

"Nope, nothing that I can't put off till tomorrow."

"Okay, let's go," I said to Christine.

It took us about twenty minutes to get back to Christine's. Noon traffic, red lights and making sure Elaine was close enough behind took a little more time than it normally would have.

I heard Elaine suck in her breath and swallow hard as she walked in the door. I had to choke back a laugh.

Walking into a room heavily scented with incense was pretty much the norm for me lately. She took her jacket off and placed it neatly over the edge of the couch. Christine and I followed suit.

"This is a nice place you have, Christine," she said.

"Thanks. Would anyone like anything to drink?"

"No thanks. I think we'd better just get down to business," I told her.

Christine sat in the chair and I sat on the couch near Elaine as she readied her laptop.

"Do you have a phone line nearby?" she asked.

"Near the bookcase," Christine said as she grabbed the line from Elaine and plugged it into the wall.

Elaine powered the laptop up and connected to her online service. "Okay, explain what it is I'm supposed to do.

"We need to be able to find a copy of the book of Olakla," Christine said as she leaned forward to see better.

"Julie mentioned something about that to me last night. Do you need the book itself?"

"I really only need one particular ritual out of it. But to find it, I'd have to go through the book."

"Okay, let me see what I can do."

Christine and I watched as Elaine pounded away on her keyboard, cursing and restarting her search a few times as she accessed places that Christine had never been able to get to before.

Christine's eyes widened. "How did you get in there?"

Elaine smiled wickedly at us. "Trade secrets, my friend. Trade secrets."

I couldn't help but smile. Elaine was just about the smartest person I knew. It kind of made me proud. I was lucky to know her at this particular juncture in my life.

Chapter Twenty-eight

Elaine punched in some kind of code and up popped three copies of the book. Only one had a name by it.

"Oh my Goddess. You found them," Christine said.

Elaine's brow rose as she stared over at Christine.

I nudged Elaine's elbow. "She's a witch." As if that was supposed to explain everything.

"Okay," she said. Both brows rose this time. "If you say so." She went back to her computer and clicked on the only one with a name next to it.

"But there is no address or phone number," Christine said.

"I know. Just give me a second," Elaine said and clicked a few more icons then punched in another code. Up popped the address and phone number of the person who held one of the books we were so desperately looking for.

My brows rose. "England?"

"Don't worry, I'll get the information you need. I have to go back to the office to do it though. I'll make the call from there and get a copy of the ritual you need. If this person has the book, then he will know what I'm talking about." She looked at Christine. "Christine, write down all the particulars and I mean every detail so we get the right information."

"You got it." She got up and went into the kitchen. I heard her rummage through a drawer and she came back with a pen and pad of paper. She sat down and began writing everything in detail that this ritual entailed. As much as she knew anyway. She included all the information I had given her from my visions of the room.

I sat and watched as Elaine packed up her laptop and got up.

I grabbed Elaine's arm. "Elaine?"

"What, hun?"

"If you can get the address of this man like you did, could it be possible to get the information of the two others that have the book?"

Christine stopped writing, looked up at me and her eyes widened. She understood.

"I can't do it from my laptop, but it's possible. Why do. . ." She stopped herself. She jumped up and grabbed her laptop off the table. "I'm all over it." She snatched the paper from Christine and went to the door. "I'll get a hold of this guy first, just in case I don't come up with anything. Either way, I'll have something for you." Her lips curled up into a half smile and she was gone.

"Goddess, Julie. Why didn't we think of this sooner?"

"Because we've been too busy dodging bullets, is why. We haven't had two seconds to breathe, let alone think."

She nodded. "You're right about that."

"Time is running out here. I only hope she comes up with something before it's too late. We don't even know what time the next ritual will take place. For all we know we're already too late."

"Please, don't talk like that. We'll do it." She looked at me hard. She was confident. I only wished I could be so sure.

CHAPTER TWENTY-NINE

"Will you please sit down?" Christine asked.

I stopped on my way back from the TV. I pretty much wore a six foot area between the chair and the TV on her hardwood floor from pacing back and forth. "It's five o'clock. Why hasn't she called yet?"

"She'll call when she has the information we need."

I looked up at the clock on the wall. 5:01PM. I started my path once more from the TV to the chair. "We're running out of time here you know."

The phone rang and we both jerked in the direction of the sound. We froze for a few breaths then Christine rushed to the kitchen to answer it.

"Hello?" she asked. "Hey, Elaine. What's going on?" Silence. "I see. How long do you think then?" Now she sounded distressed. She looked over at me and I could see the anguish in her eyes. It wasn't reassuring to me.

"That long?" Silence. "Okay, call when you have it. Good luck on the rest of the search." She hung up.

She turned to me heaving a big sigh. "The reason she didn't call until now is because it took her this long to get a hold of the guy."

My eyes widened. "You mean she just found him?"

"Yeah, she couldn't reach him at the number she had and it took her this long to track him down. He is, at this moment, translating the ritual into English for us."

I must have looked confused.

"It's in Latin."

I sighed heavily. "Figures. So, how long did she say it would take?"

"It's going to be at least another hour or two by the time he's finished and its faxed to her office."

"You can't translate it?"

"I'm afraid I don't know enough to translate such a complicated piece. There can't be any room for error."

I closed my eyes and took a deep, cleansing breath. "We're not going to be able to save that woman. Even if we knew the time, we still don't know where they are."

"Elaine is still working on that part. She said things like that take time."

"Time? Everything takes time and it's time we don't have," I said. I stared at her and my brow rose. "Unless. . ."

She looked at me, "Unless what? Julie, what are you thinking?"

"Take me back again."

She shook her head vigorously. "No, it's too dangerous. You know what they'll do."

I rushed over to her, covering the distance between us in just a few heartbeats. "It's possible the damage is already done. What more could happen?"

Chapter Twenty-nine

She shook her head slowly. "I won't do it."

I could feel a flush creeping up my neck. "Do it or I'll get someone who'll be more than willing to." My voice sounded threatening. I pulled the cell out of my back pocket and flipped it open.

Her eyes widened. "Julie, please."

"Do it."

I started to push the talk button and she pulled my hand away from the phone. "Okay, I'll do it. But I'm going to make sure we have some kind of advantage first."

My brows rose at that as I slipped the phone back into my pocket. "Like what?"

She took me by the hand and pulled me towards the spare room.

I walked into the room and almost turned to leave. It wasn't like anything I've ever seen before. The whole room was done in a dark beige color. There was no light, yet it seemed to glow of its own accord. An altar with three shelves sat along the far wall and an antique table cloth of rust, gold and red covered its surface. Candles of every color, shape and size filled every inch of it. Along each side of the altar where two, small, cast-iron tables that also held a variety of candles. A black chest sat against the wall to the left. White candles covered every inch of its surface and a wooden bench sat in front of it. There were two, cast-iron candelabras on either side of the door. Each one was a foot taller than me and held five white candles.

Christine walked into the center of the room and motioned for me to follow. I looked down at the floor as it illuminated under her feet and I froze. My eyes widened and my pulse raced. I wasn't going near that thing. It was the same type of symbol that was in the room of my visions. One circle about nine feet in diameter with another inside it about a foot smaller. The only thing inside the circles was a star of some sort in the center with its points reaching out past the outer circle. It was made up of small blue, burnt orange and green stones that seemed to be embedded into the floor in a chain-like pattern. The stones seemed iridescent and took on a strange blue hue when movement was detected inside the circle's perimeter.

"Come, Julie. Nothing will hurt you here. Trust me." Christine said in a soothing voice. She held her hands out for me to come to her.

My breathing came fast as I walked slowly towards it. I hesitated at its edge, looked down into its soft glowing warmth and stepped in. I felt an immediate rush of electricity through my body and tiny pinpricks nipped at my skin. Christine grabbed my hands and held them as my body tensed. We stood there with our eyes locked together. She didn't let go until the feeling subsided and my body relaxed.

"Sit," she said and turned towards the large altar.

I sat. I didn't ask why. I knew she wouldn't do anything that would bring me harm.

She picked up a long, wooden match and lit it. When she touched it to one of the candles, every candle in the room came ablaze like she had lit them one at a time. I gasped as I looked around the room.

She came and sat down facing me. "I only hope you know what you're doing. I may not be able to bring you back this time. Are you sure you want to do this?"

"Yes, I'm sure."

She held her hands out to me. "Okay, take my hands. It's going to be the same way it was before. Only this time we are in my circle of power. I hope this is enough to keep them from influencing you. And just remember, you don't have to do anything you're not comfortable with."

Chapter Twenty-nine

I smiled. "I know. Just let me do what I need to do and don't worry, it'll be all right." Did I really believe that? No. But I needed to do this.

She nodded and smiled back, but it never reached her eyes. "Breathe in deeply, look into my eyes and concentrate."

I took in a deep, cleansing breath and let it slowly out my mouth as I stared into her sapphire eyes.

She closed her eyes and began to hum as she had done in the store and even though her eyes were closed, I could still see their dark sapphire depths in my mind's eye.

I let her voice fill my mind as I did the music in the store. Her soft humming penetrated my body and I felt my breathing come slow and even. The music of her voice somehow hypnotized me and when her eyes opened, I was staring into the depths of eyes the color of midnight. Eyes I knew would take me through the darkness nightmares could never touch. . .and I wasn't afraid.

"Send visions of truth, visions of present time." Her voice was barely a whisper. *"Promitto visum of verum, visun of tendo vicis."*

The blackness of her eyes engulfed me and I fell slowly to a place I knew I shouldn't return to.

"I'm here," I said.

The room was empty again. I looked over at the white candle and a soft sigh of relief escaped my lips when I saw it hadn't been lit yet. The silk cords on the altar were spread out so they could wrap themselves around its victim. There was also something on the altar that wasn't there before. Something wrapped in black cloth and tied with the same black and red cord. They were preparing for the next ritual. We were going to be too late. Dear God, we were going to be too late.

My heart sank into the pit of my stomach. The feeling of dread overwhelmed me as I touched the soft material of the cords that would be tied around the woman's ankles. A vision of someone's hand flashed before my eyes. I forced myself to stay fixed on it and let my eyes travel up the arm to the shoulders and then to the face. My eyes widened as his face flashed before me and disappeared.

I saw for an instant those stormy-gray eyes. The bandaged nose, a bruise on his forehead and his long, blonde hair tied neatly back in a pony tail. It was Mr. Clean.

"Julie, what's wrong? Are you all right?" Christine's soft voice came from somewhere outside the room. "I can feel your fear."

"We're going to be too late," I whispered.

"Are you sure? How can you tell?"

"I just know. I need to see, Christine."

"No, come back before they feel you," her soft voice urged.

"No!" I yelled. "I need to see first."

I knew where I was and who was with me. Kyle's drug induced visions were forced and I didn't have the control as I did now. I wasn't sure if I should tell Christine what I saw. I needed to see more first. . .needed to know what every nerve in my body was already telling me.

I walked slowly over to the cords by the head of the altar. The ones that would hold her hands back so her wrists could be bled for the purpose of appeasing some dark God. I let the vision come to me. . .the vision of hands. I followed those hands slowly up to the face and it didn't surprise me this time as his face quickly vanished before my eyes. There was no mistaking the deep-set, hazel eyes, thick mustache and short, brown hair of Brawny.

I swallowed my heart back into my chest. I needed to see everything. I needed to see who it was that would do this. I walked over to the object that was so carefully

Chapter Twenty-nine

wrapped in black velvet. I thought that maybe if I could see who it was, we could find them in time before the last sacrifice was given. I had to see before I touched the red candle. But what were a few faces in a city of so many? Would it be possible for them to be found in time? I could only hope.

"Julie, please talk to me." Christine pleaded from the other side of the wall.

"I'm okay. Just wait. I need to see everything."

The cord was loosely tied and I slipped it slowly out from under the velvet cloth. My hands shook uncontrollably as I opened each fold of the cloth to reveal the dagger with the ruby on its hilt. I brought my finger down to touch it ever so lightly. Her eyes appeared before me. The darkest brown eyes I had ever seen. So dark they were almost ebony in color. Then those dark-brown eyes seemed to be looking back at me, as if they knew I was here. I jerked my hand quickly away and my breath caught in my throat as I stifled a scream that threatened to escape my lips.

I looked over at the door and ran towards it. "I need to go through the door, Christine," I said.

"No!" she screamed.

I grabbed the knob and flung the door open. The house. I had to see the house. To see what it looked like. It was the only way.

The house stood in the gloom of the darkened sky. The surrounding trees cast black shadows over it as if it were something that could reach out and swallow you up. There was a flicker of light coming from one of the rear windows, as if someone walked through the room with a lit candle. Someone was there.

My pulse raced as I glanced around before I took off running towards the house. The thickness of the trees hid the house from view. It left no room for the moon's brightness to shine through and light a path for me to see. I ran blindly towards the small flicker of light in the window and my foot hit a large rock. I fell forward onto the ground and it knocked the breath from my chest. I lay there for a few heartbeats re-learning how to breathe.

"Where are you going, my precious gift?" the woman's voice asked from somewhere in the trees.

My breath caught in my throat and I jumped up to my knees. I felt like I was a child caught doing something bad. "To the house," I answered. I felt she deserved to know.

"Why are you walking towards the house?" Her voice was like a baby's breath blowing lightly on the skin.

I suddenly couldn't remember. "I think I was suppose to do something. I don't know."

"I did not call you, my child."

I frowned. "I'm sorry."

"It is not time yet. You need to go back until I call for you to come."

"Yes, I'll go back until you call."

"That's a good girl. I will call you soon, my special gift."

"Soon," I said and the gloom of the house faded as the darkness swept me up into that familiar tunnel and invisible hands pulled me up and out into the light.

CHAPTER THIRTY

The darkness faded and Christine's face appeared in front of my eyes. Her coal-darkened eyes stared blankly at me for a heartbeat and then her eyes slowly closed. She took a deep breath and when her eyes re-opened, they were the familiar sapphire color I recognized.

I saw recognition slowly enter her eyes and when she was back from the darkness a deep frown creased her brow. "Are you all right?" she asked.

I nodded. "Yeah, I guess so."

"Good," she said as she got up and stared down at me. "Cause I'm never going to do that again unless I know it's safe and you communicate with me at all times."

I got up and took her hands in mine. "It's okay, really. I needed to go through the door, Christine. It was the only way to find anything out." I pulled her in the direction of the door. "I need to get out of this room. It makes me nervous."

She let me pull her by the arm into the living room and we sat on the couch.

"Now tell me, did you see anything of importance?" she asked.

"I remember going through the door and running towards the light."

"Light?"

"Yeah, I remember a flickering light in the back window of the house. I ran towards it. I wanted to see the house, where it was and who was in it."

Her eyes widened. "Goddess, going up to it was enough, but in it?"

"It doesn't matter now. I fell and the next thing I knew, I was being pulled back out." I looked down at my hands so she couldn't see my eyes. "I don't know anything more than I did before," I lied.

"What about the candles? Did you see anything?"

I looked back up at her. "I didn't get that far." At least that wasn't a lie. I really didn't get that far.

Her eyes narrowed. "How could you not?"

I could feel a frown forming on my face. "I saw something on the altar that wasn't there before. That's why I knew we weren't going to be on time." I looked back up at Christine. "It was the dagger wrapped in black velvet and tied with the same black and red cord."

"Did you touch it?"

"Yes. I only saw eyes. A pair of the darkest, brown eyes I'd ever seen."

I didn't know whether I should tell her about Mr. Clean and Brawny. What were the chances of anyone finding them by tomorrow? I couldn't call the police because I would have to go down and give a description based on a vision. If Kyle was who he said he was, they would probably lock me up the minute they saw me anyway. I'd be put in a cell until my next jailer came to get me. It was quite clear that if I was caught again, I probably wouldn't be so lucky getting away. Would that be so bad considering what I thought was going to happen? Yes, it would.

The only way to stop this whole thing was to get the address of the other two people that had the book. Hopefully one of them turned out to be in Virginia Beach. We could give the information to Kyle and let him take it from there. I was not going to tell Elaine or Christine. They would be hell-bent on keeping me safe. That would get them either hurt or killed right along with me. I was either going to solve this thing or die trying. And there's no denying the latter.

Christine's brows creased. "Julie? What aren't you telling me?"

Maybe I was too quiet. Maybe my face was too readable. Oh well, I'd have to work on that. I took a deep breath. "I told you everything. Really." I tried for the "I'm innocent" look. Ri-ight.

She stared at me for a few heartbeats. "I guess I've got no choice but to believe you."

I silently let out the breath I was holding and glanced up at the clock. 6:30PM. I thought about the woman that would lose her life because I couldn't help her. I felt as though it was my fault. Kyle was probably right. It is as if I had done it with my own hands. My pulse quickened at the thought and a feeling of panic spread through my body.

It must have shown in my face because Christine's brows furrowed deeply into her forehead as she touched the side of my arm. "What is it?"

My eyes slowly widened as a vision of terrified golden-brown eyes flashed before me. My stomach tightened and I grabbed Christine's hand, squeezing so hard my own hand went numb. I felt her fear. . .her horror.

. .and I could hear her thoughts. "God, help me please!" she screamed in my head.

"Help me please!" I screamed and looked at Christine but only saw golden-brown eyes that were seeing the impending death that was forced upon her.

"Julie!" Christine's voice echoed from somewhere off in the distance.

I felt myself being hugged tightly and I held on for dear life as the golden-brown eyes faded from my view and I heard her last screams.

"Nooooo. God. Noooo!" I screamed into Christine's shoulder.

I cried as her eyes disappeared. Never to show happiness, sorrow or any other emotion in them ever again. She was dead. Her last feelings and thoughts etched in my mind and body for all time. I cried for her, for her family. . .and for myself.

The phone rang and we both pulled apart startled. Christine looked at me, wiped one side of my tear-stained face with her hand and went to answer the phone.

"Hello?" Silence. "We've had a little problem here, Elaine."

I sprung up from the couch and yanked the phone from Christine's hand. "Elaine?"

"Yeah, hun? What happened?"

"Never mind that," I said as I wiped furiously at my face with the back of my hand. "Did you find anything out?"

"This friggin ritual or whatever you call it reads like stereo instructions."

I sniffed. "What about the other two people who have the book?'

"Are you all right?"

"I'm fine. What about the other people?" It sounded a little rude even to me, but I needed to know.

Chapter Thirty

"I found one. Its locked up in the archives of a museum in Salem, Massachusetts."

Salem—witches—figures. "What about the other one?"

"That one has been eluding me. I'm still trying though."

"That's got to be the one these people have. We're coming over."

"What? We can't chance going over there," Christine said.

I took the phone away from my face. "I'm not sitting around here anymore and you need to figure out what that ritual is all about. According to Elaine, even in English it reads like another language. We don't have time to have Elaine come down here with it. She needs to stay there and finish this research. Although, I don't think the ritual matters anymore. It won't give us what we want at this point in time, unless it proves that there won't be four sacrifices." I put the phone back to my ear. "Did you hear that, Elaine?"

"Yes. You're taking a chance, but I think you're right. I'll unlock the garage elevator and see you in a bit."

"Okay." I hung up without saying good-bye. I looked at Christine. "Let's go."

"All right, but let me grab a few things first."

"I'll meet you outside." I snatched my coat off the couch, walked out and got in the passenger seat of Christine's Jetta.

A few moments later, Christine hopped in and threw some books in the back seat. She turned towards me holding up what looked like a necklace.

"What's that?"

She held it out to me. "I'd like you to wear this. It'll provide some protection against some of their influence over you."

I took it and brought the little sack that dangled from the end to my nose. My nose wrinkled at the smell. "Geeze, what the hell is in here?"

"It's my own little private blend of herbs and powders for protection against evil influences."

I put it over my head and lifted my braid out from under it, then pulled the collar of my sweater out and let it drop down to my chest. "If you say so. After what I've seen, I don't doubt it'll work."

"Okay, let's get outta here," she said as she started the car and pulled out of the driveway.

I reached in my pocket, pulled the cell phone out and flipped it open.

"What are you doing?" she asked.

I held my hand up for her to wait as Kyle picked up on the other end.

"Hello, my little jewel." His deep voice vibrated through the phone.

I took in a deep breath and let it out slowly. "She's dead, Kyle." Did I just call him Kyle?

Silence.

I didn't look over at Christine. I wanted to get through this call without interruptions. Instead, I looked out the side window and watched the streetlights and oncoming traffic pass by in a blur while I waited for him to digest what I had just told him.

"How do you know?" he said finally.

"I just saw it happen. She died around six-thirty." My voice was flat. I was afraid to feel anything at this point.

"We'll keep an eye out along the river where the first body was found. They might try to dispose of it there as they did the last one." His voice sounded strained. He was angry now.

"Could I ask you something?"

"Yes, I'll answer if. . ."

"Yeah, I know. If you feel the need to. If you had a picture of a person, could you find that person in just a day in a city as large as this one?"

Silence. He must be pondering if the need was there to answer it or not.

"It's possible. It depends on whether or not. . ."

"Thanks for being honest with me. That's all I needed to know. So, it's possible, not a definite thing?" It wasn't a question.

"Is there something else you want to tell me, Julie?" He called me Julie and his voice was taking on a dangerous edge to it. Not good for the home team.

"We're working on finding the owner of one of the books of Olakla. The first of three, isn't even in the country. The second is locked up somewhere in an archive of a museum in Salem, Massachusetts. I have a feeling the owner of that last book is here. When I have the information, you'll be the first to know. Hopefully we'll know before it's too late."

"That's quite a bit of information. You certainly have an extensive list of resources available to you. I thank you for at least including me in on what you have, but that's not quite what I meant when I asked you if you had anything else to tell me."

I felt an edge of panic come over me. This polite manner was something new to me. Somehow, I sensed this was probably worse than any of his other moods I've experienced. I didn't like it. Not one bit.

"No, I don't have anything else for you yet. I'm sorry I couldn't help more." I hung up without letting him respond and slipped the phone back into my pocket.

"That was just about the calmest conversation I've heard you two have yet."

I kept my eyes on the flashing streetlights, the passing cars and the sidewalk. "Yeah, it was."

"Why did you ask him about being able to find someone?"

I could feel her staring in my direction. I didn't want to look in her eyes because I was afraid she'd see the truth. "Nothing. It was just a fleeting thought I had is all."

"I'm sorry about what you saw earlier."

I sighed heavily. "Yeah, so am I."

"Talk to me please."

"No more questions." I looked over at her. It was safe now. "Okay?"

She sighed and turned her attention back to the road. There wasn't much time left and I didn't want to spend it arguing with anyone. We drove the rest of the way in silence. I was happy with that.

CHAPTER THIRTY-ONE

Elaine's was a large corner office on the top floor of a four-story, glass building. Although she had those tinted, "you can't see in" windows, she still had blinds put up. I guess she thought the same way I did about the privacy factor. I'm sure if she had met Frank earlier, the building would be all brick.

Her office was all white, right down to the white, tile floor. The temperature in her room never got above sixty-five because of the wall-to-wall desks with computers on them. She usually had one chair and just rolled from one to the next when she needed to. There were two extras in the room tonight. There was one book case along the back wall where her main desk was. Manuals of all sorts on computers filled all but one shelf which had pictures of her and her husband on it. She told me once that she hoped to add pictures of children to it one day.

She sat behind her main desk staring intently at the computer screen and pounding away at the keyboard when we walked in. She had been at that computer since she left Christine's at one o'clock, that was over six hours ago. It was amazing she didn't have migraines from staring at the screen for so long.

"Where can I sit with these?" Christine asked.

She looked up and pointed to one of the desks. "There will be fine." She held out a handful of papers. "Here it is. Good luck deciphering it."

Christine took the stack of papers. She left her coat on and made herself comfortable at the desk Elaine pointed to. She flipped through all the pages, glancing at each one, then opened one of her books and began scribbling notes on the sides of the top page of the stack of papers.

Elaine went back to her computer and I was left standing there. I took my coat off, placed it over the empty chair and sat along side Elaine. I was interested to see what she was trying to do. So, I sat there for the next three hours watching her click from one thing to the next, curse under her breath, then start all over.

"This has definitely been my best challenge yet," Elaine said as she clicked on an icon and began to type some code into a square box.

"Do you think it's possible?"

"Oh, I'll get it, if I have to spend all night here."

"What did you tell Frank?"

"That I had important research to do for a very important person." She smiled over at me and then back to the computer screen.

"This is some pretty serious shit here," Christine said as she flipped through the pages of another book.

I looked over at her. "I don't want to know the details. I've seen plenty already. I don't know why you're bothering with it. It can't tell us where they are."

She turned in the chair to look at me. "No, it can't, but it can tell us the exact time of the ritual and give us an estimate on how much time we have before the sacrifice is made."

"No offense to you, Christine," Elaine said without looking up, "but this is just too sick for words."

"None taken and I agree with you. This type of magic doesn't follow the same rules as I do."

"One of these days, I'm going to have to get you to explain this all to me." Elaine said. "Shit, I just hit another wall." She clicked on another icon to start over somewhere else.

"I'd be more than happy to when this is all behind us," Christine said as she went back to her paperwork.

I felt like a third wheel. Out of place and useless.

"Okay, I think I've made a bit of sense out of this. I hate to bring this up, Julie. It was around six-thirty wasn't it?"

"Yeah, it was."

"We don't know what time the first woman died, but the second was at exactly the right time."

I got up and went over to stand behind her. "What do you mean?"

The first was supposed to be exactly at the time Venus sets on the first day the moon shows signs of its waxing, crescent stage. That would have made it," she said as she flipped through a few pages in one of her books, "seven twenty-three last night."

"They didn't announce it on the news that they found her until around ten-thirty or so," I said.

"Right. So we can't be too sure about that. The second one, on the other hand, would be exactly at the time the sun sets on the second day. That would have made it six twenty-five this evening."

I remembered the vision and was connected with the woman just before she died. I felt her emotions and heard her screams. I knew it happened when I saw it. "So, when is the third to happen?"

"The third exactly at the time Saturn rises on the third day, which is ten twenty-four tomorrow night."

"Is there a fourth?"

"No, there are only three as I suspected. The candles don't represent the days of the week or the number of sacrifices to be paid. Each one actually has meaning during the sacrificial homage and is lit just before. . .never mind that. The yellow is to attract the God Olakla to the ritual through the sacrifice of the first. The white is to show their sincerity and loyalty to the God with the sacrifice of the second."

I felt my pulse quicken and my stomach tighten. "And the third?"

"The last sacrifice is the most important as it will give the God physical presence so that he will share his great powers with his followers. In other words, the red is for strength and the purple is for power. The last sacrifice will give the God the power to reveal himself to them."

"You managed to get all that already?" Elaine asked.

"Yes, once I have the ritual in front of me, it's not that difficult. Although this book does not use the planets as I do. It would have made better sense to me ahead of time if it did."

"I'll just agree with you on that one," Elaine said and went back to pounding the keyboard. "Damn!"

"Another wall?" I asked.

"Yeah, don't worry, I'm not going to stop until I have it."

Chapter Thirty-one

"I know." I looked at the clock. 11:00PM. I needed to get out for some air. I tapped Christine on the shoulder. "You want to go get some coffee?"

"Sure," she said.

I looked over at Elaine. "How about you, Elaine?"

"Coffee would be great right about now. Thanks."

"There's a Seven Eleven right down the street," I said as I grabbed my coat off the chair, pulled Christine away from the desk, and to the elevator.

"Are you in some kind of hurry?" Christine asked.

"All that talk of human sacrifice was getting to me."

"I'm sorry. I should have realized."

"No, it's okay. I did ask the questions," I said as the elevator chimed and we were on our way to some fresh coffee and some much needed fresh air.

CHAPTER THIRTY-TWO

We walked out of the elevator side-by-side and as I went through the door, I was grabbed by my arm and yanked face-first into someone's hard chest. My scream was cut off as strong arms pressed against my chest forcing the air out of my lungs. I immediately recognized the scent he wore and after a heartbeat of shock, I started to struggle.

"Don't fight me or your friend Christine will pay for your actions." Kyle's deep voice vibrated against my face.

My pulse went to my throat and panic tied my stomach into a tight knot. I couldn't let Christine be harmed because of me. There were already two girls dead and I blamed myself for not being able to save them. I stopped struggling and stood still in his arms. In one fluid movement he jerked me roughly around so I was facing forward. He had one hand tightly around my chest and arms with the other pressed firmly against my mouth.

Chapter Thirty-two

My eyes widened as I stared into Christine's terrified ones. Shawn had one arm wrapped around her as he held a rag over her nose and mouth with his other hand.

I took a breath to scream, but it was cut off when Kyle squeezed his arm tighter against my chest. The only thing that escaped my lips was a whimper through a forced rush of air.

"Don't," he said. His voice held no room for argument.

I let my body relax enough so he would release the pressure on my chest. My breathing came labored against his hand. My brows came down in a deep frown as I was made to watch Shawn force Christine into unconsciousness. I wanted to run to help her. . .to tear Shawn's eyes from their sockets, but instead, I was made to watch in horror as Christine struggled against him. Her eyes fought to stay open and they somehow told me she wished she could do something. Her grunts and groans became softer as she quickly lost the battle, her eyes fluttered shut and her body went limp.

"Put her in her car," Kyle said to Shawn.

Shawn bent down, picked up the keys she dropped and lifted Christine's limp body into his arms like she were just a child. "Which one is it?"

Kyle jerked my body against his. "Which one?" His voice held threats of worse things if I didn't answer.

He took his hand slowly from my mouth. I wanted to scream for help, to cry out to anyone that would be near. . .but I was afraid. Afraid my cries would bring harm to Christine.

"The blue Jetta," I said. My voice was laced with contempt.

Without another word, Shawn carried Christine over to her car.

"Now that your witch friend is out of the way," Kyle said and twisted me back around to face him. "We can get back to some unfinished business." He held the sides of my arms and dug his fingers painfully into my coat and sweater.

My heart went into my throat and my breathing came fast as I thought about the "business" Kyle was speaking of. I stared at his chest for a few breaths. I couldn't let him see the fear in my eyes. I wanted him to see my true thoughts of him. Thoughts of murder and a slow, painful death. . .his death. I swallowed hard, took a deep breath and when I met his eyes, I let those thoughts show on my face.

His eyes faltered for a heartbeat, then his brows furrowed in his forehead and his face twisted into a deep scowl. He turned and forced my body up against the brick wall near the elevator. He held me up against it at eye level by my arms, so our faces were barely an inch apart.

"Kyle?" Shawn asked from behind.

"Meet me there," he said through clenched teeth.

Shawn came closer, stepping to the side so he could see my face. "I don't think that's a good idea."

"You don't get paid to think, Shawn. Go!" His face was flushed and blue veins began to show on the sides of his neck.

Shawn looked at me for a space of heartbeats. His eyes somehow telling me he was sorry.

"Now!" Kyle yelled through his teeth. I couldn't help but blink from the force of his voice. That one word held all the promises of what was to come when Shawn left.

Shawn turned to go and my pulse quickened as I screamed in my head for him to stay. He stopped, turned his head to glance back at me and his brows creased his forehead. "Please stay," I said to him in my mind. His

Chapter Thirty-two

brows rose-then lowered as he looked at the ground and left.

"He will not help you," Kyle said.

I looked back into those steel-blue eyes. They were eyes that promised everything I have always dreaded. I didn't dare say anything. It was as if my silence was the only thing keeping him from doing what his mind screamed out for him to do.

"We found her body tonight." His voice was shaky as if he was holding some dark thing back from coming out and unleashing its fury.

I stared at him for a few breaths, looked down at the ground, then at his shiny black shoes. At anything but his eyes. I knew they would find her. I was the one who watched as the life slowly withered from her eyes.

"Did you hear me?" he yelled.

I kept my eyes fixed on his shoes.

"She's dead, Julie." I felt his breath blowing at the hair on my head.

Dead. Even with all the things I could do, she was still dead. I thought of what I saw. . .what I felt. . .what I heard. Her horrified golden-brown eyes, her panic and fear — her screams for help. I felt the hot sting of tears in my eyes and let them flow freely down my face. I deserved to die right along with them.

He jerked me against the wall. "Are you listening? I said, she's dead!"

"I know that!" I yelled as I brought my eyes up to meet his. "Don't you think I know that?" I felt a frown forming on my face as I stared into his eyes, but somehow not at them. . .to somewhere other than here. "I was there." My voice cracked with emotion. "It was as though I was one with her when she died. I saw her eyes. Eyes so panic-stricken and terrified. They saw the very thing that would take her life." My voice started to rise as the panic over-took my mind and body. "And her fear — God — the tremendous fear of never living those dreams she had as a child when she was growing up." My breathing came fast as my pulse quickened with thoughts of pain and death. My eyes went wide and I cried out, "I heard her thoughts. She screamed and begged for someone to help her!"

Then I felt something from somewhere other than where I was. I was being wrapped in strong arms. Arms that held me tight as if they could take away the pain of a recent nightmare.

"She begged God to please help her!" I screamed into his chest. "She died and I couldn't help her, Kyle," I cried, then I broke down and let my emotions flow freely.

He didn't say a word. He held me in his arms and loosened the braid from my hair so he could run his hand from my head down the length of it. He held me and let me cry. . .and I felt safe.

When he thought my tears were spent and I was calm enough, he pulled me from him so he could see me. He looked at me hard. The rage and deep scowl replaced with something I didn't recognize. I closed my eyes as he brought his hand up to my face and delicately wiped away the left-over tears with his thumb.

I opened my eyes as I felt him put his hands on the sides of my face. He slowly lowered his lips to mine and when I didn't pull back, he leaned in and kissed me. It was a soft, tender gesture and made places low in my body tighten. When he pulled back, I saw raw desire in those steel-blue eyes. . .and I wanted him — just as he wanted me.

He brought his thumb over to trace the outline of my lips, the gesture reminded me of something that I couldn't quite put my finger on. "Your lips curve up so sensually that I have wanted to kiss you since the first time

I laid eyes them." His deep voice was low and it sent a shiver of something other than fear through my body. He leaned in and stopped just before his lips touched mine. "I will keep you safe, my little jewel," he whispered.

I closed my eyes and felt his lips touch mine and it sent a chill of pleasure down my body. I felt his hunger grow and I met that hunger with my own as I opened myself to him fully. He put his arms around my waist and pulled me into him. I wrapped my hands around his neck and held him tightly to me. Not wanting him to let go. He was the one who would keep me safe. He would keep me. . . .then I remembered.

The thoughts came in a span of a few heartbeats. The hospital where he ordered Shawn to drug me regardless. He did the same thing in the motel. And Christine. He had hurt her badly. He was not the one to keep me safe. He didn't care about me, the only thing he cared about was what I could do for him.

I jerked back from his grip and swung my arm to slap him. He caught my hand in his and in one movement, my wrist was handcuffed. The other end of the cuffs were gripped tightly in his hand.

"I hate you," I said through gritted teeth.

Something moved behind his eyes, then they grew dark and his brows creased deeply in his forehead. "No more games." He turned towards the direction of his car, yanking my arm painfully in his direction.

"Let me go!" I screamed as I used both hands to pull free of his grip. He stopped and jerked me forward so I ended up in his arms again. Not any better.

He brushed my hair from my face, looked down into my eyes and his lips curled up. "If you continue to fight me, I will do this *my* way. I assure you, you'll be more. . .agreeable to my demands."

My pulse quickened at the thought of what his words were intended to mean. He had a way of saying things without really saying them. I had no choice. I would not be drugged up so I wouldn't know what was happening.

He must have sensed the defeat I felt because he let me go abruptly. I fell back a step, only to have him yank me forward as he walked the rest of the way to his car. He pushed me up against the side of it, unlocked the passenger side door and shoved me in the seat. I just barely caught my breath when I found myself handcuffed to a long chain that was screwed into the floorboard near the seat. I was betting that it wasn't something that came with the extras. I didn't remember it being here before. He slammed the door in my face and went around the front of the car.

I pulled on the chain and it didn't budge. I had to try.

He jumped in the car, put it in gear and we screeched out of the garage. The smell of rubber stung my nose and caught in the back of my throat. Seemed as though everyone was in a hurry lately.

I stared out the window because I didn't want to look at him. I felt betrayed. He tried to make me feel safe with him, but it was just all an act. His main concern was getting his job done no matter what the consequence.

I watched as we turned left onto Holland Road. I needed to keep track of where I was. Just in case.

"Where are we going?" I asked. Couldn't hurt, could it?

"That's none of your concern."

I felt the stirring of anger in my stomach. "I see you found your car."

"Yes." His voice sounded a little strained.

Chapter Thirty-two

I rattled the chain I was handcuffed to. "I don't remember seeing this in here."

"A little something I added...just for you."

I already knew that one. "Did you have any trouble getting another key for it?" I just had to.

"No."

Gosh we're talkative. "That's too bad."

I heard him take in a breath. Good. I accomplished what I wanted to. He was going to find out real soon how miserable his life would be, as long as I was with him.

I turned to look at him. "How did you find me?" Hopefully that was a question he felt I deserved an answer to.

"You knew quite a bit about the locations of two of those books and there was only one person you knew that could get access to that kind of information. I put two and two together."

Me and my big mouth. I turned my head to look out the side window. "If I had known you could add, I would've kept my mouth shut."

The feel of his gaze on the back of my head was overwhelming. I ignored it and sat in silence. When I didn't feel his presence against my skin, I pulled the little sack of herbs that hung on a thin piece of twine out from under my sweater. I hoped that Christine was all right. Then I realized I could talk to her in another way. I did it with her before and I was pretty sure that Shawn heard me too. I closed my eyes, took in a deep breath and pictured her deep-sapphire eyes. "Christine?" I said in my mind. "I'm okay, I hope you can hear me. I'll let you know where I am as soon as I get there." I felt funny talking to myself. I would just be grateful if she was awake and it worked. I stared back out the window, content with the fact that I would just go along and wait for the right opportunity to present itself.

We made a left on Dam Neck Road. I had no idea what could be down here.

"You're going to help us find them," he said finally.

Seems as though the only time he ever says anything on his own, is when it's in the form of an order.

I kept my eyes fixed on the blackness of the trees that flashed by the window. "That's what I've been trying to do."

"Which hasn't gotten us anywhere, except add another woman to the list."

Did he have to say that? "Is there another one missing yet?" I already knew the answer to that one, but I wanted to be sure.

"No, not yet. That's why you're going under again tonight."

I took a deep breath through my nose and let out a long sigh, leaving a circle of my breath on the window. "That's not going to be necessary," I whispered.

I felt his stare again. I knew that would get his attention.

"What did you say?"

"You heard me."

"And why won't it be?"

At least I got his interest peaked. I looked over at him finally. It was time to tell him everything I knew. Why not? It couldn't be too much more time before Elaine found out who they were and they would be caught. "I went in on my own today and saw at least two of the people that are involved. They were male."

Kyle's face frowned and it quickly turned into a deep scowl. He snapped the wheel of the car to the right and I had to hold onto the door as we flew off the road

Chapter Thirty-two

onto a large dirt shoulder. He slammed on the brakes and we came to a sliding halt. My hand on the dashboard was the only thing keeping me from kissing it. The sounds of tires crackling on rocky dirt pierced the heavy silence of the night air.

He slammed the car into park and turned to look at me. "Was that something that just slipped your mind? Why didn't you tell me?" His voice was deadly as he spoke each word through gritted teeth.

My stomach tightened with the beginnings of panic. I could feel the hair on my neck standing at attention. "You couldn't find them in time even if I told you. She still would have died."

He hit the seat with his fist. "That's not the point!"

I jumped. I couldn't help it. "It's exactly the point."

He came towards me and I backed up against the door; trying to melt into it somehow.

He grabbed my arms and shook me. "There's still another woman out there somewhere that will die."

I just stared at him. I was helpless to do anything and felt I deserved what he did to me.

He pulled me towards him so that our faces were just a breath apart. His steel-blue eyes were as dark as a summer storm waiting to unleash its fury on anything that lay in its path. "If this woman dies, I will kill you." His voice was a deep murderous whisper.

I choked back a laugh. I couldn't help it. It was kind of funny when I thought about it. "Take a number, detective, because the list seems to be growing. I just may need an appointment book soon."

His brow rose at that and he let my arms go. He was taken back by my reaction and what I said. He looked at me as if I was crazy. Maybe I was because of all of this and I was going to end up locked away as I feared when this whole thing started. I turned back to look out the side window. I didn't care. Dead or locked up — my life was over no matter how I looked at it.

"What do you mean take a number?" he said. His voice was a soft whisper. I guess he replaced his forty-watt light bulb recently. It didn't take him long.

"It doesn't matter now, detective. Elaine will find out who owns that third book and they'll be caught."

He grabbed me and turned me to face him. "Tell me!"

I felt a frown forming on my face and a flush creep up my neck. "Those same two men have attacked me twice this week. You claim you can add. You figure it out, detective!"

His eyes narrowed, then widened. "How long have you known about this?" he said through gritted teeth.

"Not until I went in again today. What does it matter now?"

He shook me again. "You could very well have gotten caught, that's what matters!"

I choked back another laugh. "Dead or with you, there's no difference as far as I'm concerned." And I meant it. It didn't matter to me.

The redness in his face turned a deeper shade and I thought for just a second he would put me out of my misery.

"Are—you—crazy?" he shook me as he said each word.

I looked at him and opened my mouth to say something when I saw a dark shadow outside his window. My eyes widened and I saw the realization in his eyes that he knew something was wrong.

"Kyle!" I screamed.

Chapter Thirty-two

He started to turn as his door swung open. He was pulled out of the car and onto the ground.

CHAPTER THIRTY-THREE

I yanked furiously at the chain trying to get free while I watched the two men roll around on the ground in the night shadows.

"Kyle!" I screamed again.

A second man came from nowhere, grabbed Kyle and pulled him to his feet. I crouched down to see through the door better. A knot formed in the pit of my stomach and my heart went to my throat. Even though they wore all black and it was dark, I knew who they were. Mr. Clean and Brawny.

I pulled harder at the chain, cursing under my breath as the cuffs bit into the flesh of my wrist. I crouched down again to see what was happening. My breathing came fast as the edge of fear crept up my body.

Mr. Clean held Kyle under his arms as Brawny punched him repeatedly in the stomach. Kyle grunted and his body doubled over with each blow. Then Brawny swung back and laid his fist into Kyle's left cheek. The

Chapter Thirty-three

sound of his fist hitting flesh made my stomach turn. Kyle went limp in Mr. Cleans arms and he let Kyle drop face-first to the ground.

"Nooooo!" I screamed.

Mr. Clean started around the back of the car towards my door. "Grab his gun and throw me his keys," he told Brawny.

I pulled frantically at the chain as I watched him coming closer to my door. Brawny threw the keys over the hood of the car and I knew I wasn't going to get out of this one.

Mr. Clean unlocked the door, opened it wide and smiled down at me. "What do we have here?"

"Fuck you!" I spat at him.

"Still the bitch even when chained to a car hey?"

I could feel the panic welling up inside me as I looked over at Kyle. He was getting unsteadily back to his feet. Brawny stood near him with his legs spread apart and a gun pointed at Kyle's head. I was guessing it was Kyle's gun.

"He isn't going to help you," Mr. Clean said then reached in to grab the chain.

I slid sideways on the seat as far as the chain would let me and kicked out at him with my feet. My foot connected with his shoulder and sent him back a couple of steps. I was hoping for the face, but at this point any part of the body would do.

"You little. . .," he yelled.

I got back up and tried desperately to catch the door to shut it. My fingers stretched out to the handle, but the chain stopped me an inch from touching it.

Mr. Clean took hold of my wrist. "You're going to pay for that," he said as he twisted my wrist back at a painful angle.

I screamed and grabbed at his hand to pry it loose.

He slapped me across the head with his other hand. "Shut up."

I dug my nails into his hand. "You bastard!"

He reached in with his free hand, wrapped it tightly around my neck and pushed my head against the back of the seat. "Stay still or I'll put you out to do it!" he said through gritted teeth.

I thought about smashing my hand right into his bandaged nose, but I didn't want to be unconscious. I let my hands fall to my sides as he unlocked the handcuffs. He yanked me out of the car and threw me face-first to the ground. I used my hands to soften the fall and the rocks in the dirt dug painfully into my palms.

He took a fistful of my hair and lifted me to my feet. I had to grit my teeth to hold back the scream that threatened to escape my lips. I stumbled on my feet as he jerked me around to the other side of the car. He stopped a few feet from where Kyle was kneeling and pulled me back by the hair so I stood against his body.

He tossed the cuffs to Brawny. "Use these on him."

Brawny tossed the gun to Mr. Clean. I was hoping maybe I'd get a chance to catch it myself.

Mr. Clean pointed the gun at Kyle's chest. "Don't try anything, pal."

Brawny pulled Kyle's arms behind him and I saw Kyle's eyes squint as Brawny closed them around his wrists. The gun was tossed back to Brawny who pressed its barrel against Kyle's shoulder and forced him to his knees.

My pulse went to my throat as I looked over at Kyle. His hair had come free to fall in loose waves around his shoulders and in his face. Through the darkness, I could see the blood at the corner of his mouth.

"Now it's time for you. Once more scream and I'll do your boyfriend right here."

Chapter Thirty-three

That was a tempting offer, but I would rather do him myself. . .my way. It's no fun unless I'm the one inflicting the pain, now is it?

He threw me head-on into the side of the car. I used my hands to brace myself when I hit its hard surface and the force of the impact pushed a grunt of air through my lips. I felt the first rush of anger building as my body trembled from the abuse. I turned around, leaned up against the car and pushed my hair out of my face.

"I don't think the old lady is gonna like this Chester," Brawny said.

Chester? Did his parents want him to make it through school in one piece?

I choked back a laugh. I couldn't stop myself. I knew it was going to get me into trouble. But if I was going to go down, I was going down the way I wanted to. I refused to die tied to an altar.

"Shut up, Randy," Chester said. He turned around to face me again. Wonderful. His brows furrowed down into a deep frown. "And what's so damn funny?"

"Julie, no!" Kyle yelled and I heard him grunt as he was shoved back to his knees. Could he possibly be reading my mind?

I glanced over at Kyle who gave me a "please don't do it" look, than back at Chester. "Frankly, *Chester*." I emphasized his name for effect. "I was just wondering how you ever made it through school with a name like that." I smiled sweetly at him. Begging him to do what I wanted him to.

Chester growled through gritted teeth and his open hand connected with my left cheek. The impact sent me to the ground where I landed on my hands and knees. The sting of the blow vibrated though my face and echoed in my head. I had to take a few breaths to clear the fuzziness from my eyes. I lifted one of my hands to find that they had been cut up a little more by the rocks I landed on. I had a feeling my knees would be the same. I thought Kyle had given me everything he had. Now I know he held back quite a bit.

"Shouldn't that thing be working by now?" Randy asked.

Chester grabbed me by the arm and brought me to my feet. "I'm glad it's not. I'm having too much fun," he said. He held me by my arms in a vice-like grip. "You think you're tough eh, bitch?"

"Julie, please don't," Kyle pleaded. I guess he knew me pretty good.

"Shut the fuck up," Randy said and hit him in the shoulder with the butt of the gun, sending him down on his hands.

I glanced over at him. He looked up at me and although I couldn't see his eyes, I knew he was begging me not to do it.

"Fuck-you," I said in a calm voice. Brave ole me. I did have an ulterior motive. I was hoping Chester would accommodate me.

He pushed me back against the car and put his hand to my throat applying enough pressure to keep me from moving. "Now that sounds tempting," he said and brought his face to my ear. "You are a pretty little thing." His voice was a low whisper and it told me things I didn't want to know.

I could hear Kyle grunt loudly. He must've tried to get up again. I guess he didn't like the idea of anyone else touching *his* property.

Chester kissed my ear and continued a trail across my cheek towards my lips. I fought not to flinch and when he put his lips to mine, I grabbed hold of his bottom lip with my teeth and bit down hard enough to draw blood.

Chapter Thirty-three

The feel of his skin breaking between my teeth almost made me gag. I don't *ever* want to do that again.

He pulled away and his hand flew to his mouth as he yelled into it. One more wound to add to the many he already had. You would have thought he'd know better to do something like that. Doesn't he ever watch TV?

His blood left a bitter metallic taste in my mouth. I spat on the ground and wiped my lips with the back of my hand. "I guess you can add that to the other scars I've given you this week. I'm surprised they sent you a third time. Being bested by a female and all," I said and smiled.

I heard Kyle gasp at what I had just said. I was guessing that he now knew who these two men were and what they wanted.

He rushed over to me so quickly I almost didn't see it coming as he swung and backhanded my other cheek. I went sprawling backwards onto the ground. God, that fucking hurt! That ringing sound echoed in my head as the burning sensation spread through my face. I tasted the bitter-sweet flavor of blood and I winced as my tongue ran along the large cut inside my mouth.

He didn't give me time to recover as he bent down, pulled me up and flung me against the car. He grabbed me by the throat and wrapped his hand tightly around it. "You're-going-to-die," he said through clenched teeth. His eyes went wide. The whites of them stood out through the subdued light of the night sky and his neck strained from his rage. Took him long enough.

I stood there with my hands on his wrist, more for support than anything else. It was time. I knew Elaine could find out who they were, but I didn't want to rely on her doing it in time. I couldn't take that chance. I looked into his dark eyes as my body fought to breathe through the pressure around my neck. Then he looked down at my neck.

"What's this?" he asked as his grip loosened. He ripped it off my neck and looked at it while he held onto me like I was some picture he was holding up and needed an opinion whether or not it was straight. "I think this is some kind of voodoo thing." He looked down at me. "Is this why it's not working?"

I looked at him and my brows creased. I couldn't talk with his hand on my throat. He let go and I fell to my knees. When I took my first breath, my lungs burned from the lack of air. I held onto my throat and bent over as I went into a series of coughing fits.

Chester left me alone until I was able to breathe without coughing. Mighty considerate of him eh?

When I was done, he pulled me back to my feet. "Is this why it's not working?"

"Why what isn't working?" My voice came out a hoarse whisper as I held onto my throat. Then the realization of what he was talking about hit me. The mind control. My eyes widened and I rushed at him. "Give it back."

"I don't think so," he said and took hold of my arm. He pulled me into his body and held me at the waist with his arm. He threw the necklace so it landed in the grass that edged the dirt shoulder.

"No!" I screamed.

Chester wrapped both arms around my chest and held onto me tight enough to keep me from moving. "Now stay still and it'll all be over soon."

Then I felt it. The first rush of blackness. It was as if once the necklace was out of reach, it was rendered powerless. I felt the fear crawl through my body and I looked over at Kyle. I needed to tell him before it was too late. Please let this work. I closed my eyes and pictured Kyle's steel-blue ones and I sent my thoughts out to him. "Kyle, if you can hear me, tell Elaine and Christine I love them. I'm okay, really. I knew this was coming and I accept it. It's for the best. Please, Kyle. Tell them for me."

"Julie, nooo!" I heard Kyle's voice echoing from somewhere above. He heard me.

Then the dark tunnel that would take me to places I've been to other than in dreams, washed over me.

CHAPTER THIRTY-FOUR

My feet touched a damp thickness that only the feel of grass could bring. The darkness faded and I found myself standing in a freshly cut field of it. Out in the distance I could see a grove of trees, their mixture of dark, light and yellowish-green shades blending to look like someone had painted them in small dots of color. The smell of plant life filled my senses and I let it flow through me to lift my spirits. The pale-blue sky was filled with clouds in the shape of large bundles of cauliflower. They floated idly in the sky and looked as if they could feel as soft as a ball of cotton when touched. I closed my eyes and breathed deeply the scent of fresh, warm air. I never wanted to leave this place. I could stay here forever and bask in its quiet beauty.

"Hello, my sweet child," her voice whispered along the wind that blew at my face.

"Where am I?" I asked the wind.

"You are in a safe place."

Chapter Thirty-four

I nodded and smiled. "Safe. Yes, I feel safe."

"I picked this place just for you, my very special gift," her sweet voice told me from somewhere above.

I sighed wistfully. "It's perfect," I said to the sky and closed my eyes as the soft wind blew through my hair.

"It's time to start your journey towards freeing you from the heartaches of this world."

"It's time?"

"Yes, take the hand that will lead you to a place of rest until I come for you, my very special child," she said from somewhere beyond the trees.

I held out my hand and felt something soft and warm wrap around it. It pulled me gently forward. . .and I let it. I wanted to go. To be led to the one that would wrap me in warmth and keep me safe for all time.

I was led through the grass to a soft, quilted blanket that had been spread neatly over its thick surface.

"Now rest, little one. Rest and I will come to you again soon."

"Soon." I smiled and lowered myself to the blanket and closed my eyes.

I let the coming blackness fold around my body as my mind floated down to a deeper part of nothingness. As I felt my body sinking further into the pit of darkness, something outside its barriers called for me to come back. No. . .it screamed for me to come back. I reached out towards the sound and it snatched at my body, bringing me quickly up towards the dim light that was slowly closing to seal me off from breaking through.

"She is fighting it," a soft voice echoed from somewhere in the light.

"Yes, it would seem so. She is stronger than we realized," another voice echoed as I went into the light and the darkness disappeared behind me.

I slowly opened my eyes as the haziness seeped from my brain and found myself staring up into the dark-brown eyes from my vision. The eyes that belonged to the very person who held the dagger. A wave of panic flowed through my veins and my breath caught in my throat. I sat up and quickly crawled as far back as I could on the bed until my back hit the brass headboard.

My eyes flew around the room. It was a small room, about a ten-by-ten. The walls were white and it had a carpet the color of rust. A white night stand sat near the bed with an oil lamp centered on top. The only other furniture was a rocking chair in the corner by the door. It was so old that it probably rocked at least a hundred babies to sleep in their mother's arms. The only escape I could see was the door and a window on the wall opposite of me. The window had bars on the inside and was boarded up on the outside. The flame from the oil lamp and the candle the woman held were the only things that cast any light in the room.

I looked at those dark-brown eyes for a second time and was now able to see who they belonged to.

She was an older woman of about forty or so. Her dark eyes were framed by delicately arched brows, her nose long and straight. She had thin lips. Perhaps due to loss of pigmentation from age. Her long, jet-black hair had thin streaks of gray through it making her look older somehow. She wore a tightly fit, long black dress with sleeves that flowed out at the wrists. It was cut deep in the front, so her small breasts were barely covered. Long, tapered fingers with blood-red nail polish held the candle delicately in her hand. I looked back up into those eyes that held no remorse for the taking of innocent lives.

Her eyes narrowed. "You've seen me before?" It wasn't a question.

Chapter Thirty-four

I felt a frown forming on my face. "Only your eyes." My voice came out barely a whisper.

Her thin lips curved up. "That was enough for you, I think," she said. Her voice held a hint of humor. I didn't think anything was funny.

I looked back up into those dark eyes and said the first thing that came to mind. "Go to hell."

Her brow creased and her smile faltered. Good for me.

"She's going to be a handful, Maria," the other woman said as she stepped out from behind her.

My brows rose as I recognized her as one of the women I saw at Christine's store. She wore the exact dress Maria had on, except she looked better in it. Her long, ash-blonde hair stood out against the darkness of the dress like the sun in a black velvet sky. The dress accentuated the curves of her body and her small, firm breasts pressed against the material as if begging to be released. But it was her eyes I remembered more than anything else. Those pale-blue eyes. Eyes the color of a cloudless winter sky. And I remembered the ocean — the cliffs — the feeling of peace. My eyes widened as I realized she was the one who pulled me into them and took me to that place I thought was so safe. . .so real.

I felt the anger tighten my stomach. "Stay away from me," I said through clenched teeth and she stepped back.

"I'm afraid that won't be possible. You are going to be our special gift in just a short while and you have to be prepared to give yourself to him."

A short while? How long did I sleep for? My pulse raced as the adrenaline pulsed through my veins. My eyes narrowed as I stared her straight in the eyes. "I wouldn't count on it." My voice was deathly low so that I didn't even recognize it.

Her brow rose. "Do not test my limitations, child. I am not opposed to showing you how to behave correctly."

She wasn't opposed to showing me how to what? I stared into those dark eyes. My brow rose and my lips curled up. "Give it your best shot you sick-fucking-ticket."

I heard blondie gasp. This was going to be worth it.

Maria's brows creased deep into her face; the candle trembling in her hand. "Come, Beth," she said and started for the door. "We need to get ready. Send Chester in so he can prepare her." She followed Beth out the door and closed it softly behind her.

The silence after the click of the lock slamming home sounded so final. Maybe I would have a chance to try again. . .with Chester. I was *not* going to die in that room.

I jumped off the bed and ran for the door first. I yanked on the knob using my weight as I pulled back and forth. It didn't budge. I supposed it was tried twice before by two other women. The bars on the window didn't give either. I tried to open the window, but it was nailed shut. I was beginning to feel like that wild animal again. The one that just had the cage door slammed in its face and it knows it will never have the feeling of freedom again.

My breathing became labored as panic started to rush through my body. I went over to the night stand, ripped the drawer out of it and dropped it to the floor. . .it was empty. I stood in the middle of the room and ran my hands through my hair. God. There's got to be a way out of here.

I sat back on the bed. I put my elbows on my thighs and my face in my hands. Then I felt it. That small mass in my back pocket that I had grown use to. Kyle's cell! I screamed in my head. I threw my hand in my pocket and pulled it out. Would he have time? I still didn't know where I was so he would have to trace the call. Maria told me a short while. How the fuck long was a short while? I flipped it open, my hand trembled as I pressed the talk button and peered over at the window. There was no light shining through any of the cracks in the boards. Shit! How much time did it take?

"Answer, damn it!" I cursed softly as I listened now to the fourth ring on the other end.

"Julie!" Came that all too familiar deep voice.

I breathed a sigh of relief. "Oh, thank God," I whispered.

"Are you okay? Do you know where you are?" His voice held an edge of panic.

"I'm in the house, but I don't know where. I woke up here," I said quickly.

"Leave the phone on, if you can."

I glanced up at the door. "Okay, I'll try. How long will it take?"

"About a half-hour depending on where you are."

I heard footsteps coming to the door. "Oh, God, they're coming, Kyle. They're coming." I jerked my head up when I heard the sound of a key in the lock.

"Julie!" I heard him yell as I brought the phone slowly down to the floor. I kept my eye on the door and slid it under the bed.

I was hoping Kyle wouldn't talk anymore. If he did, they may hear it. A half-hour. Dear God, let them find me.

CHAPTER THIRTY-FIVE

Chester walked in with a large washtub in his hands and set it in the center of the room. He wore tight, black jeans, black, silk shirt tucked into his jeans and his blonde braid was tied off at the end with a black hair tie. Looked like it was going to be a "black tie" affair.

A woman I didn't recognize walked in behind him. Her hips swayed provocatively through the material of the same dress the other two wore. She was about four or five inches taller than I was without the three inch heels that made her legs look longer than they actually were. Her shoulder-length dark, strawberry-blonde hair framed a face with deep-green eyes under a mass of thick, dark lashes.

She placed a tray on the night stand and began unloading its contents. There were powders, oils, a long wooden match and a brass incense holder. A small glass bowl along with a glass stirring stick were the last two items to be placed on the night stand.

Chapter Thirty-five

When she was finished, she looked down at the drawer I had so carelessly dropped to the floor. She looked at me like I was a child who just threw a stone at the neighbor's window. She walked over to the door and looked at Chester. "I'll go get the water," she said and closed the door softly, locking it behind her. Guess they figured by now that Chester was no match for me.

"Okay, Sheila," he said.

Great. I was alone with Chester. He didn't look as good as he did when we were waiting for the bus that day. Now he had a Band-Aid under his bottom lip. Along with the bandaged nose and the dent in his forehead, it was almost comical.

"Looks like you woke up a little early eh?" He stood there, legs apart, arms crossed over his chest as far as he could get them. "See anything you like?" His lips curled up as he flicked his braid over his shoulder so it landed with a smack on his back.

I ignored that. I wanted to know first. "How long was I out?"

"Almost twenty-four hours straight and I had the pleasure of keeping an eye on you."

My eyes widened and my jaw dropped. "A whole day?"

"That was some pretty heavy shit the old lady laid on ya huh?"

I stared down at the floor and didn't say anything. A whole day? My God. How was that possible? That would make it around nine or so. Ten twenty-four. Christine said the third would be at ten twenty-four! I felt the stirrings of anger again and my heart beat faster as I let it take hold and flow out. I needed anger. It was an emotion I could deal with.

"Yeah, pretty heavy," I whispered as I brought my eyes up to look at him.

"It doesn't even look like I touched you last night."

My tongue immediately went to the spot where there should have been a deep cut. It was gone. I felt my lips curl up.

"What are you smiling at?"

He asked didn't he? "Well, I was just thinking that I wish I could say the same for you."

I braced myself as he scowled and started for me. Pretty short fuse.

The door opened and Sheila walked in. She had a tea kettle in one hand and some purple cloth draped around her other arm. Chester stopped dead in his tracks. Shit, I took too long.

She gave the kettle to Chester. Chester looked down at me and his eyes narrowed before he went over to pour what looked like hot water into the tub. With these people, who knew what it was.

"This is for you." She took the material, draped it over both her arms and held it out to me. That was odd, but then again, is there anything normal about any of this?

I got up, took it from her arms and held it up to see it better. It was velvet and actually lighter than it looked. Judging its size you would have thought I went to the store and bought it myself. It was perfect and it would probably feel like a delicate piece of heaven against my skin.

"What's this for?" I asked.

"It's for you to wear."

Was she serious? I stared into those pale-blue eyes and tossed it towards the end of the bed so it landed on the floor. "I'll pass, thanks. It's not really my color. Besides, I thought I was going to do this in the buff."

"No, you are the special one. It is for Olakla to unwrap his gift once you are sent to him."

Chapter Thirty-five

Unwrap me? Okay, calling them sick was an understatement. They were whacked-out, gone over the edge, lunatics!

She glanced over at Chester. Great. Chester walked over, picked it up, came around me and placed it on the bed where I was sitting. He started to go back towards the tub when he paused and looked as if he were trying to hear something. Then I heard it too. Shit. The phone!

He got down on his knees and reached under the bed. He brought the phone out, stood up and flicked his braid over his shoulder again.

My heart sank into the pit of my stomach as I watched him put it to his ear. "Battery died." He said as he looked at Beth.

Great, the friggin thing had to have a low battery warning.

"How long has she been awake?"

They talked as if I wasn't even in the room. Pretty insulting if you ask me.

"About twenty minutes or so."

Shit! I was hoping that was enough time.

She grabbed the tray and held it out to Chester. Chester took the battery out of the phone and placed both battery and phone on the tray.

Okay everyone. . .you've just entered *The Twilight Zone*. Ri-ight.

She held her free hand out to Chester. "Give me that drawer, Chester. We wouldn't want our special guest to hurt herself with it."

Chester snatched the drawer off the floor, looked at me with a cocky grin on his face and handed it to her. She walked out the door. A few heartbeats later, the door locked again.

Time for round two.

"So, *Ches-s-ster*," I said and sighed as I grabbed the dress, flung it back onto the floor and flopped myself on the edge of the bed, "how is it that you came to work for these creatures that are passing themselves off as human beings?"

"That's none of your business," he said as he sat carefully down on the rocker and folded his arms over his chest. It creaked and moaned under his weight. I was hoping it would break and he would fall on his ass.

"Do you think you should be sitting in that thing?"

"You're taking this rather well."

"Well, it's not everyday I get to spend time with someone the likes of you."

His brow rose as he put his hands on the arms of the chair. Good.

"I mean, come on, Chester. People have been drilling through ice in search of Neanderthals for years and here I sit actually talking to one." I smiled sweetly.

His hands gripped the arms of the chair so hard that his knuckles mottled. His face turned into a deep frown and a flush was spreading up his neck. Yep. Definitely a short fuse. Goodie.

One more try. "It would seem by the wounds I've given you, the women are the dominant species in the area that you come from. Which is funny because I always thought it was suppose to be the other way around." I raised my brows giving him the "tell me it isn't so" look.

His face turned red and that tell-tale scowl told me to brace myself. He flew off the chair and came after me with his hands stretched out in front of him. His hands hit my neck and wrapped themselves tightly around it as I went backwards onto the bed. He jumped on top of me and straddled my waist. His face reddened with full-blown rage as his hands made to crush my windpipe.

Chapter Thirty-five

Fear and panic overtook my senses and I brought my hands up to his, digging my nails into his skin and kicking my legs furiously. I fought to breathe and fought for my life even though what he was doing was what I wanted. I could feel the blood rushing to my face and my eyes began to bulge from their sockets as my lungs fought to receive the air they needed to survive.

"Get off of her!" Maria yelled. Her voice came out more a low growl as if she were a dangerous animal taking that first leap towards an unsuspecting prey.

Chester jumped off me in a mere breath. It was as if her voice alone could tear him to shreds if he didn't do as she said.

I turned on my side and felt the fire in my lungs when I started to breathe again. I put my hands to my throat and practically choked up a lung as I coughed into the blanket on the bed. No one said a word. It was as if everyone was waiting for me to finish. A standing ovation maybe?

When my coughing lessened enough for me to breathe at least ten times in between, I turned to look up at her.

"Get out, Chester." Her voice was calm. And I thought Kyle changed moods fast.

I looked up at him and he was staring down at me. His gray eyes were dark and menacing as if to say he wished he could have finished the job. I stared hard up into his eyes and sent my thoughts out to him, "I wish you could have finished it too."

His eyes faltered, then widened. He heard me.

"I said, get out." Her voice rose an octave.

He frowned down at me and left.

"Yolanda, send Randy in please."

I heard the door open and close. Now I was alone with Maria. It had possibilities.

"I know what you are trying to do."

My brow rose at that. "Do you now?" My voice was a tad raspy.

"Yes, and it isn't going to happen. Randy will come in to tend to you now. It would seem that you have rendered Chester useless in aiding in your preparation." She turned to look at the dress lying on the floor, then looked back at me. Her lips curved up.

Randy and another woman came through the door. Maria turned and walked out, locking the door behind her. Is there a reason no one trusts little ole *moi*?

I glanced up and saw the other woman from the store. She had shoulder-length brown hair and again was wearing the same dress. You might think that's all they had in their closets. I only wished I looked that good in black. But then again, I would never wear something that low-cut. She fit the dress the same way Sheila had. Her full breasts looking as if they would rip through the thin material. She was tall and slender and although she wore heels, she didn't need them to enhance her long legs. This must be the "Yolanda person" Maria spoke of. Well, at least I knew everyone's names now. Not that anyone introduced themselves or anything like that.

She looked down at me with her hazel eyes and memories of waterfalls and cliffs on some faraway island came to my mind. And I knew that she had done the same as Beth did. She took me to a place that I could have only dreamed of.

I glared into her eyes. "You can stay the fuck away from me too."

Her eyes widened before she caught herself. Great.

She turned her attention to the things on the night stand. She took the three bottles of oil and poured the same amount out of each into the glass bowl. She used the glass mixing stick to mix them together and after she was finished, she walked over to the tub and poured all but a small amount into it. She put the glass bowl back and put her fingers into the powders, placing a pinch of each into the brass incense holder.

I sat up on the edge of the bed, watching quietly. Randy stood by the tub with his legs spread and his hands behind his back, waiting like some silent mountain. I was wondering when this low-budget, horror movie would end.

Yolanda lit the incense, placed the cover on it and turned towards me. "You must undress now so we can anoint Olakla's special homage."

Anoint who's friggin what? I laughed. I had to. "I don't think so."

Randy walked slowly over to Yolanda's side. I'll give you three guesses to what she was going to say.

"If you don't yourself, Randy here can assist you."

Yep, just as I thought. "Let me get this straight. You want me to undress in front of *him*?" I said and used my head to motion in Randy's direction.

She smiled. "That's the general idea, yes."

Now I think she thought this was a joke. Okay, anger's a good thing.

My eyes narrowed as the anger rushed to the surface. "Not until he leaves."

"I'm sorry, but that's not possible. Make your choice now or Randy will make it for you."

Randy shifted his weight and smiled down at me, his top lip disappearing under his thick mustache.

I sighed heavily, turned my back to them and started undressing. I would rather do it myself then have some asshole slobbering all over me. I threw my clothes on the bed and was glad now for my waist-length hair. It hid the most intimate parts of the front of my body. And then I thought about it. I wouldn't give them the satisfaction of seeing me ashamed or embarrassed in front them. I let my anger ride my thoughts. I straightened myself and turned around; my eyes daring anyone to comment or look at me the wrong way.

Randy gasped and I glared up into his eyes, my eyes promising pain if he did anything else.

He blinked my stare away and looked down at the floor. Good boy. Now roll over for me.

Yolanda looked into my eyes; hers held a certain admiration. My pulse quickened. I didn't like the feeling it gave me and it infuriated me even more. I wasn't some side of beef to be checked out and graded.

"You are truly as beautiful as you are powerful. Such a rare gift for Olakla. He'll be very pleased."

Give-me-a break. "I have a name, it's Julie," I said through gritted teeth.

She ignored that. "Now step into the tub so we may prepare you to be anointed."

Take your clothes off. . .get in the tub. What was next? A bedtime story? I was so enraged that my nudity was just a fleeting thought.

I walked over to the tub; my hands balled into fists at my side, waiting to be used for some brutal purpose. The water was barely warm enough for coffee. It sent a shiver up my spine and through my body.

Randy came up behind me and I turned quickly around to face him, splashing some of the water out of the tub in the process. "What the hell do you think you're doing?"

"He's just going to put your hair up for you," Yolanda said.

I turned to look at her. "Does he have a tongue? I mean, he does have a grasp of the English language, doesn't he?"

"Yes, I do," he said.

Chapter Thirty-five

I turned back to glare into his eyes. "Good. I can put my own hair up thank you very much." I snatched the hair clip from his hand, twisted my hair up and clipped it.

She picked the incense holder up and brought it closer to me. "Now Randy will cleanse your body."

My teeth were clenched so tightly my jaw ached. "I'm not an invalid you know. I can do it myself."

"No, you cannot do this yourself. Please, time grows short."

Randy grabbed the sponge from the water. I turned back to him and glared up into his eyes. "If your hands touch my skin in any way, shape or form, I will brake the offending digit from your body."

He stared hard into my eyes, his hazel eyes silently acknowledging my request. Satisfied, I turned back around and fixed my eyes on the door. Yolanda held the brass incense holder by its chain and waved it around the tub. Her soft voice came out in low murmurs. It reminded me of Christine. I closed my eyes and let my thoughts wonder to Christine and Elaine. It made it easier to endure as Randy ran the wet sponge along my skin. I breathed in heavily, letting the scent that drifted up from the water and the incense fill my senses and relax my body.

"It's time to put your robe on," she said from in front of me.

I never heard her stop chanting or move for that matter. It was almost like I had been frozen in time and everyone else kept going.

I got out of the tub, put the robe on and zipped it up. It hung down to my ankles; its sleeves came down to flare out at my wrists. It clung to my wet skin, but still felt velvety soft against it. I stood and let Randy tie a purple and red silk cord around my waist.

She grabbed the glass bowl, the stirrer and came over to me. She dipped the stirrer in the left-over oil and brought it up to my face.

I held my hand up to stop her. "Whoa. What the hell are you doing now?"

"It's just oil, it won't hurt."

I rolled my eyes and sighed. "Fine, let's just get this over with."

She dipped it once more and brought it up to my face. *"Recipero is proprius donum,"* she said as she smeared the cold, thickness of the oil along my right cheek. *"Nostrum donum of vires quod vox,"* she said and smeared it along my left cheek.

When she went over to the night stand I brought my hand up to wipe the oil off my face.

Randy grabbed my arm. "Leave it."

I stared at him hard and lowered my hand.

Yolanda opened the incense holder, added some different powder to it and turned to me. "Now lie down and rest until we come for you. Randy will stay with you." Oh how thoughtful.

Randy nudged my back with his hands, urging me to do as she said. I turned and glared at him for a space of heartbeats. I sighed heavily and did as I was told. That's a good girl. Lie down until we come to kill you.

I closed my eyes and heard Randy sit in the battered, rocking chair as it moaned in protest under his weight.

The scents in the room and the slow creaking of the rocking chair lulled me into relaxation. They will come. I know they will. And that was my last thought as I felt my body become lighter than it should be. It felt as though I was floating up from the bottom of the deepest part of the ocean. Then that deep blackness I was familiar with folded around my body like rolling in a thick blanket.

Chapter Thirty-five

I went down into a deep tunnel of darkness that would take me to places sleep could never promise. I could feel myself being set down gently until my feet sunk into something warm and yielding. The darkness faded and I opened my eyes.

I walked barefoot along a beach with sand as white as the untouched snow. My feet sank in its warmth, sending shivers through my body. I closed my eyes and listened to the rumbling sounds of the ocean's waves slapping against the rocky shoreline. I let its echoing beat fill my thoughts as I swayed to its grand melody. I raised my face, opened my eyes to see the pale-blue sky and watched the thin feather — like clouds glide slowly across its blue depths. The sun sent waves of heat down on my face and I welcomed its warmth. A warm breeze pushed against my body, blowing at my face and hair, wrapping its softness around my body. Somewhere, in that wind, I heard a voice call to me.

"Come little one, time grows short." The woman's voice called to me. It was soft and soothing; almost intimate.

I walked down the beach towards the voice that held promises of things I've only dreamed of. "Where are we going?"

"You're going to a place where you will be set free. Free from your troubles and heartaches."

"Yes, free." I walked further and in the distance I could see a forest of trees outlining the edge of the beach. I walked towards it, knowing that I would find peace beyond that barrier of trees. All I cared about was being free and being with the person who would give it to me.

"That's it, little one. Don't be afraid. We will pay homage to him and you will be free." Her voice caressed my body and I wanted to be held in it forever.

"I'm not afraid."

"That's it, come to us. You are our special gift to him."

I smiled. "His special gift."

I closed my eyes and felt my body being lifted upwards like I were as light as a feather floating along the barest of breezes. The wind blew at my face and tickled my ears with my hair. Then I heard that familiar scream from somewhere above as the light behind my eyes began to fade to darkness. . .that same darkness I had seen so many times before. I fell down into the abyss of nothingness and the scream started to fade. I reached out to it and it took hold of me, whirling me upwards and out through the opening that led to reality.

CHAPTER THIRTY-SIX

There was soft chanting from a distance not far from where I was. The smell of incense was overpowering and it left a bad taste in my mouth. The fog and mist that laid heavy in my brain blew slowly outwards as if the breeze of reality waved at it with invisible hands. My eyes fluttered open and when the fuzziness cleared, I felt a wave of panic and fear drown my body and senses. As my eyes came into focus, I found myself staring up at the ceiling of the room I had been to so many times before. The room I didn't want to be in.

I kept my eyes focused on the ceiling. Not wanting to see. I could feel the hard surface of the altar underneath my body. Could feel my ankles tied in the silk of the cord. My hands were bent down at a painful angle to be pierced with something that would make my blood flow freely.

My heart flew up to my throat and I took in a deep breath. "Nooooo!" I screamed until my breath ran out. I struggled furiously against the cords and their tightness cut into my flesh.

Their chanting got louder and longer. I took another breath. "God, nooo!" I screamed until my breath caught in my throat. I knew the time was growing near. I could feel it as a wind that came from somewhere other than outside began to blow across my skin and sent the chill of death through my body.

"With power there is a price. It is this woman who will pay that price. Olakla, take this woman as our last precious gift to you," the four women said in unison.

I remembered what Yolanda had said to me. I was their gift to him. He would unwrap me when I was sent to him. Sent to him where? My eyes widened and panic filled my veins as its meaning became clear. It was my soul that would be sent to him. Sent to that nameless place other than hell to be tortured for all of eternity.

"No," I whispered. Then I screamed, "Please, don't!"

I felt a presence at my side and turned to look up into the dark-brown eyes of Maria. The wind in the room blew at the large cloak she wore over her dress. It played with the edges of the hood that flowed around her face. Symbols made of golden-yellow thread had been sewn into its velvet material. It was the same one I saw in my vision.

She smiled down at me and used her thumb to paint a symbol on my forehead with something cold and wet. I squeezed my eyes shut. I didn't want her touching me. . .didn't want her near me. Anger flowed through my body as the thoughts of her death filled my mind. I could kill her. I could kill her and not feel guilt.

When her touch left my skin, I opened my eyes and stared hard up into those dark pits of nothingness. The thoughts of hatred and of her death flowed out through mine and into hers.

Chapter Thirty-six

Her smile faltered and her brow rose as she kept her gaze on me and lifted something heavy from my stomach that I hadn't noticed was there. She brought it slowly into view. My eyes widened and my pulse raced as she placed the blade of the dagger flat against her other hand. It was as if she reveled in the thought of spilling my blood and seeing my fear.

The other women began to chant again. Their voices were just a hoarse whisper that began to get louder as they walked towards the altar to form a circle around it. My eyes grew wider as I looked frantically from one to the next. They were all dressed in the same dark cloak, their heads covered with large flowing hoods and their eyes closed.

I looked back up at Maria. "Please don't," I whispered. "I don't want to die like this."

She smiled down at me and walked away. Beth came closer and stood where Maria had been. Her eyes were closed and her mouth formed words that made no sense. I could feel Maria's presence near my head and felt the softness of her robe brush against my hands.

They opened their eyes, looked in the direction Maria was standing and said together, "May her blood flow free to fill the vessels that will wake your spirit. So that we may be given your great gift of power. The blood of the final sacrifice."

"May your powers flow through your blood to give him life," Maria said from somewhere behind me.

They said together, *"May vestri vox flow per vestri cruor ut tribuo him vita."*

"God, nooooo!" I screamed as the pain came sharp and immediate. My breathing came in short gasps as I fought the gray spots flowing in front of my eyes that threatened to overcome my mind. I felt the hot thickness of blood flow down my wrist.

"May your powers flow through your blood to give him life," Maria said again.

They all said, *"May vestri vox flow per vestri cruor ut tribuo him vita."*

I screamed again and the sound echoed off the walls as I felt the fresh flow of immense pain in my other wrist. My heart beat wildly against my chest and I squeezed my eyes shut to keep the feeling of dizziness from overwhelming me. I could feel my blood rush to the surface of the wound like it were water in a dam that had just been released. The sting of hot tears flowed freely from my closed eyes.

The wind that came from some invisible place inside the room began to get stronger. I opened my eyes and looked up at what looked like a circle of clouds forming above me. The women held their hands and heads skyward. And while I lay bleeding to death, they began to mumble words that could only be understood by the one they were meant for.

I looked up at the clouds that assembled over my body. A mixture of grays, dark-blue and black swirled around to form a deep, endless funnel. . .I knew that this would take my soul to the place where there was pain that could never be described. A pain that was promised for all time.

The wind grew stronger and blew the material of my robe wildly about as I felt the blood in my wrists flowing thick and fast. It was as if this entity knew it was almost time. Time for my blood to give it the power it needed to breathe life into its body.

The women brought their heads and their hands back down. Their voices grew softer until all that could be heard was the wind's low howl. I felt Maria's movements behind me and I knew it wasn't over. The thought of what was yet to come plagued the back of my mind.

Chapter Thirty-six

Maria walked up to Yolanda and handed her a silver chalice with a rim outlined in rubies the color of blood and that all-too familiar symbol engraved in its surface. "Drink my sister. As you drink, he drinks. Through you his thirst will be quenched," she said as Yolanda drank a sip of its contents.

"Stop it, you fucking lunatics!" I screamed and tried again to struggle free of the silk wrappings. I screamed again as the blowing wind in the room sent a burning pain through the cuts on my wrists.

They never looked my way. It was as if I wasn't even in the room. I watched through tear-blurred eyes while Maria walked around to each woman in turn, repeating the same words as they drank from the chalice. She made a full circle and came back to stand behind my head.

I felt her movements behind me and then she came to stand by my side again. She placed the dagger back on my stomach and held another chalice in her hands. Its rim outlined in amethyst stones that came to life in the flickering light of the candles.

She glanced at me then lifted it towards the ever darkening tunnel of clouds where evil things that no one dare put a name to hide. "As I drink, you drink. Through me your thirst will be quenched." She glanced down at me again, then said, *"Ut EGO imbibo, vos imbibo. Per mihi, vestri sitis ero quenched."*

She brought the chalice down to her lips and drank heavily from its contents. When she was finished, she brought the chalice slowly from her lips and stared down at me. My eyes widened when I saw a hint of something red in the corner of her mouth. She used her tongue to wipe the drop away and her lips curved up as she saw the realization in my eyes. It was blood. They were actually drinking my blood! They did this to the other two? No wonder their eyes held so much horror. And I was made to watch that woman die. Made to watch those golden-brown eyes. . .to feel her. . .to hear her screams. I watched as her eyes slowly faded to nothing like snuffing out the flame of a candle.

I took those thoughts and let the familiar feeling of anger came up from that deep hole fear had sent it to. It was an anger I have never felt before and I let it flow through my veins until it turned into a rage I had no name for. A rage that sent an iciness through me that even death couldn't compare to.

I looked up into those dark, empty eyes of hers and let the unknown thing inside me speak its words through my lips. "I'm going to kill you," I said. My voice strained through the tightness of my throat. And I knew that even through the howl of the wind above. . .she heard me.

Her smiled faded and her eyes narrowed as she grabbed the dagger. She held it up for me to see. I stared at it for a few heartbeats and my eyes never faltered as I looked back up at her. I wasn't afraid anymore. Her eyes darkened before she held the dagger up to the fierce whirling of the clouds. The winds blew harder around that tunnel of blackness and its size grew quickly as if in answer. It spread along the ceiling like some obscure disease through the body of an unsuspecting victim. Within seconds it had covered the whole ceiling and looked more ominous than any fury nature could bring upon the earth.

The other women held their heads and hands skyward, humming loudly over the moaning of the winds above. Maria held the dagger in both her hands, brought it slowly down to rest over my heart and then looked into my eyes. The smile on her lips was one of pure evil. One that could come back in your worst nightmare and crush your

Chapter Thirty-six

mind. She concentrated on the dagger as she raised it skyward and mumbled softly under her breath.

I stared up at the dagger's blade and let that nameless rage build inside the very core of my body. It rushed forward and turned into a fierceness that matched the very fury of the storm looming above me. The feeling over-took me and I felt as though I would explode from its very presence. Then that familiar chill ran through me once again making the blood in my veins grow cold. And I knew there was something inside me. . .waiting. Waiting for me to call it out.

"Olakla, take this woman as our last precious gift to you. May her flesh fill your hunger her power give you life, and her soul fulfill your needs," Maria called out to the thickness of clouds.

When she looked down at me, her dark-brown eyes were the color of charcoal. She smiled and it was then that I release it. I stared at that instrument of evil. The very thing that took innocent lives before they were ready. The tool that would pierce through my skin and stop my heart from beating. I looked up at it and released an unknown force that came from my very soul. I sent it out and willed it to burn the hands that held it.

I felt a force push through my skin as it cast itself out towards the very thing my eyes were fixed upon. And I watched as its blade glowed a deep orange and then to fiery red. Then I called it back and my breath caught in my throat as I fought to hold in the growing hunger of the thing that would be released with just a thought.

Maria's mouth opened and a hi-pitched screech filled the room and echoed off the walls as she dropped the dagger to the floor. The other three women rushed to her side and she screamed again and her eyes widened with disbelief as she stared down at me. She held her shaking hands out. Hands the color of pink and bright-scarlet.

The palms of her hands were raw with blood as if her skin had been melted away.

"Noooooo!" Maria screamed as she watched the deep tunnel of darkness and wind slowly flow into itself until it disappeared.

I looked into her eyes and watched as they widened with a horror I couldn't describe. What she saw in mine I didn't know, but I fed off her horror and called to the rage once more. I brought my eyes to the bottom of her cloak and before she could think, a burst of flames appeared and engulfed her like she were made of kindling. The three other women backed quickly away and stared wide-eyed as Maria's body burned before them. They rushed over to the black curtains, ripped them down, and ran to put the fire out that would surely take her life.

I called it back and took in another breath, willing it to wait. But it wouldn't wait for long. It wanted and needed more. . .and I wanted to feed it. I looked down at the three women who covered Maria's struggling form on the floor who were trying frantically to put out the flames.

Yolanda glanced up at me and the fear in her eyes grew deeper as I stared down at her. She got slowly to her feet and shook her head vigorously. I felt my lips curl up as I released it once more; the force of it taking my breath away. An ear-piercing scream filled the air as the hood of her cloak went ablaze. It caught her hair and spread quickly to her head. The other two stood up and watched in terror as she backed away with her hands flailing about until she fell to the floor. Her screams of death echoed in my ears. . .and I was satisfied.

Beth ran for the door and I brought my head up to look at her as she tried desperately to unlock it. I stared down at her cloak and once more the invisible force rushed out of me to consume its next victim. She fell to the floor and screamed wildly as she rolled around trying to put out a fire that wouldn't stop eating until the life it attached itself to was no more.

Sheila ran to the other side of the room, knocking candles over as she crouched low in a darkened corner. But I knew she couldn't hide. If I could see her, I could feed it. There was no hiding from the fury of what was inside my body. It cried out for more.

I looked over at her and could feel the rage that was being restrained inside the core of my body. It beckoned to me to be released. I brought my eyes to meet Sheila's. I wanted her to see before she died. I wanted the rage in my eyes to be the last thing she would see. . .and I called upon it once more.

"Julie!" Kyle's smothered shout came from the other side of the door.

The sound of Kyle's voice brought my attention to the door. My breath caught in my throat and I gasped as I fought to keep it in. It sat just below the surface balancing towards release and consuming my very soul. I squeezed my eyes shut and pushed it down.

"Julie," Kyle yelled again as he pounded on the door sending a thunderous sound through the now silent room.

I took in a deep breath. "Kyle!" I screamed.

"Julie, can you open the door?" he yelled.

I turned and looked desperately over at Sheila. It wanted her. I choked back a breath and a low moan escaped my lips as I sent it back below the surface. "Untie my hands and stay behind me!" I yelled at her.

She looked at the bodies of her friends that were still smoldering with the thing I willed upon them and shook her head vigorously.

"Do it or I-will-kill-you!" I yelled.

She got up, hesitated for a breath and ran behind me.

My eyes searched furiously for something to give to it. I brought my head up and fixed my eyes on one of the cords at my ankles. It caught fire instantly. I pulled my leg free before it could burn me and did the same with the other one. When my hands were set free, I sat up and let out a small whimper as it crawled to the point of release.

"Julie, open the door," Kyle hollered.

I turned to see where Sheila was. She whimpered, backed up against the wall and shook uncontrollably. "Stay there," I told her as I turned back around.

"Kyle, get away from the door. Now!" I screamed.

I stared hard at the door and hurled the energy outwards. The door seemed to radiate heat at first like a paved road on the hottest of summer days. It creaked and moaned, then a ball of fire caught in its center and burst into a raging inferno as it blew outward off its hinges.

It came upon me again, but I couldn't let it out yet. Not yet. "Noooo!" I screamed.

Kyle ran in and stopped just over the entrance to the door before he hit Beth's smoldering body. Christine and Elaine were on his heels and bumped into him as his large frame blocked their way. He looked at the other two bodies and quickly scanned the room to make sure it was safe to go in. It looked like a room of total carnage. A room of death with the smell of burning flesh that left a sick taste in the back of your throat. The energy seemed to only burn for a short while, but it was long enough. . .long enough for death.

Christine let out a loud gasp and her hand flew up to cover her mouth and nose.

"Dear God," Elaine whispered from behind Christine.

Kyle's eyes widened as he started in my direction. "Julie."

Chapter Thirty-six

"No, stay back!" I yelled as I flew off the side of the altar and backed up to the far wall. My blood soaked hands stuck to it as I pressed my body against it.

He starting for me again. "Julie, Please let me..."

"No!" I screamed. I frowned as I choked it back and a whimper escaped from my throat. "Don't come near me." My voice strained with the effort to talk and hold the force at bay. It was there, under the surface. I had to release it or have it consume me.

My eyes flew to Sheila and she cringed back, trying to become one with the bricks of the wall. It wanted her. In the worse way it did. "Get out!" I yelled at her and took two quick breaths.

Sheila ran for the door and they gave her room to get out. Christine pushed pass Kyle, looked down at Beth's body and stepped sideways around it. "Please, Julie. It's all right now. Let us help you."

"Stay back!" I yelled and stopped her in her tracks. I frowned. "Please, Christine," I whimpered. Tears began to flow down my face as my eyes pleaded with her to stay where she was. The energy came bursting to the surface and I knew if it didn't find release, it would kill me. I quickly searched around the room. "God, please make it stop," I cried.

"Julie, there's no one here that can hurt you anymore," Kyle said.

I looked at him. No, not yet. Not him. Not like this.

He looked into my eyes and backed up as his own eyes widened.

"What is it, Kyle?" Elaine asked. Her voice held an edge of panic.

"Just stay back," he said as he pulled Christine back and held his arms out so they couldn't get by.

I looked over at Christine and Elaine and when they looked into my eyes, the color drained from their faces. Their eyes showing the same horror I had seen in Maria's earlier. Then I felt it...It fed off of it...It wanted them.

"Nooooo!" I screamed as my eyes flew to the altar...the thing that held two women until their lives were taken away and sent to that dark place that isn't hell, but worse. I stared hard at it, brought the force up with all the anger and rage I felt for this symbol of death and forced it up and out of my body. The force of it was so great that it took the breath from my lungs. I moaned loudly and dropped to my knees as I kept my eyes fixed on the altar.

The altar started to creak and moan as it radiated tremendous heat from the inside. And I kept my gaze on it. I wanted the force that could kill with just a thought to be appeased.

I could see out of the corner of my eye that Kyle was headed in my direction again. I held my hand up to stop him. "Don't, not yet," I said through gritted teeth.

He stopped within eye shot, but I couldn't look his way. I didn't dare look his way. I blocked out everything around me out so all I saw was the object of death.

Then it came like the force of a fast moving storm. The altar burst into flames as if it were made of mere paper and someone took a match to it. But it wasn't done. I could feel it wasn't done so I kept my eyes fixed on it. I willed it to finish. Then the last of the energy flew out and hurled the altar into the wall where it shattered into a hundred burning pieces.

I waited for a few heartbeats. I had to be sure it was finished. When I didn't feel the energy of rage flowing through my body, I looked over at the three people that came to help me and was glad I didn't hurt them. I put my blood-stained hands over my face and cried long and hard.

Chapter Thirty-six

When my tears were spent, I looked over at them, let the feeling of lightness take over and collapsed to the floor. I heard them come to me and a pair of strong hands lifted me off the floor and held me tight against a warm body. I shivered uncontrollably and looked up into steel-blue eyes that looked tenderly down into mine. He brought his hand up to my face and used his thumb to wipe my tears away. When he was through, I turned my head to find Christine and Elaine standing behind me. Their faces were ashen, their eyes wide as they looked cautiously into mine.

I turned to look back up at Kyle and frowned. "I killed them, Kyle," I whispered.

"Yes," he said.

I put my face into his chest and cried some more. I cried for those women I couldn't save. I cried knowing where their souls could possibly be. . .and I cried for myself. I had taken life and felt no remorse.

He ran his hands down my hair. "It's okay," he said softly. "Everything will be okay." He lifted me up and cradled me in his arms like a child. I wrapped my arms around his neck, laid my head against his shoulder and let the tears flow freely down my face once more. He held me closer to his body and carried me out of the room.

CHAPTER THIRTY-SEVEN

There was an ambulance and two other cars parked outside along with Kyle's. I didn't see Christine's or Elaine's. I figured they parked somewhere where I couldn't see. The other cars weren't normal police cars. I assumed they were probably unmarked. I saw Chester and Randy in one and Sheila in the other. I could see more cars coming in the distance down the entrance road to the house as Kyle carried me towards the ambulance. There were no flashing lights or sirens. I was so mentally and physically exhausted that I didn't give it a second thought.

Elaine and Christine followed close behind. After seeing the horror in their faces, I was afraid to even look their way. It seemed as though they were afraid of me somehow. As if they thought I would harm them. I didn't like the thought of that and I hoped it wasn't the case.

As we approached the ambulance, I could see that Shawn was standing by the open doors. I should have known that where ever Kyle was, Shawn wasn't far behind.

Chapter Thirty-seven

His posture seemed to have relaxed a little as we got closer to him. It was as if he had been holding his breath the whole time we were in the room. Probably not far from the truth.

Kyle started to step up into the ambulance.

"No," I said as I pushed against his chest and wiggled my body so he would put me down. "I don't want to go in there."

Kyle stopped. That surprised the shit out of me. He stood there for a few breaths and lowered me gently to the ground.

My trembling had ceased enough that I could stand without falling down and I pushed myself away from him. "I'll just sit here," I said and sat on the edge of the opening.

He looked down at me and his brow rose. "I just thought you may need to lie down so Shawn can tend to your wounds."

"I may need to, but I'm not going to." I looked up at Shawn and held my wrists out for him to inspect. The wounds were already beginning to clot up and only a small spot of blood fell from them every now and then.

He stood there just staring down at me.

"Well?" I said. "You *are* the doctor. Start doing what doctors do."

I watched him as he climbed into the back of the ambulance to get the supplies he needed and found the ambulance personnel consisted of one person....Shawn as the driver and attending physician. Did I expect it to be any other way? No.

Kyle leaned up against the door of the ambulance, legs crossed at the ankles and arms folded across his chest. Elaine and Christine stood silently to the side as Shawn cleaned my wounds to prevent infection.

I looked at both of them. "How did you find me?"

I saw Christine glance at Kyle. I looked over at Kyle and watched as he nodded his head. My stomach tightened with the knowledge of what was taking place. I didn't think I had strength enough to fight the battle that would soon take place.

"It was actually a combination of Kyle and us," Christine said.

"So, the cell phone worked?" I asked.

"It died before I could pinpoint your exact location, but it gave me the general area within a five mile radius," Kyle said.

I looked over at Kyle. "Those aren't very good odds."

"Christine figured out why I kept running into walls during my search," Elaine said.

Christine smiled. "There was an evasion spell on any information regarding that particular book."

My brows rose at that. "You're kidding right?"

"No, when I figured it out, I cast a spell of my own," Christine replied.

"Yeah, you should've seen it, Julie. It went right into the system and as soon as it took affect, I found the information in less than twenty minutes," Elaine said.

"Which was not too long ago I take it," I said.

Christine came over and hugged me. "I'm sorry I didn't figure it out sooner."

Her hug reassured me that she wasn't afraid to be around me and I felt relieved.

I hugged her back one-handed as Shawn bandaged the other. "I'm just grateful for all the help you two have given me is all. Please, don't be sorry."

She pulled back from me and smiled.

Chapter Thirty-seven

I looked over at Elaine. "I don't want you to be either, Elaine."

I was rewarded with another hug. It felt good to know they weren't afraid of me.

They both stood aside as Shawn prepared to bandage my other wrist. They were quiet. A little bit too much for my taste. Why was no one talking about what happened in the room? And why hadn't anyone come over to get a statement from me yet? Usually that's the first thing they want if the victim is able to do it.

I looked around the yard as Shawn tended to me and noticed there weren't any regular police cars to be seen. There were three more that added to the two that were already there. One was a black van that was being loaded with three body bags. The three I released my rage onto. I saw a few men going in and out of the house and that was about it. Something wasn't right and I had a feeling I knew what it was. These men were not from the police department.

My pulse quickened as I glanced over at Kyle. He was still in the same position as he surveyed the area and watched the going's on around the house. I looked over at Christine and Elaine and saw the apprehension in their eyes.

I did the only thing I knew to do so Kyle wouldn't suspect anything. I concentrated on Christine's deep-sapphire eyes and threw my thoughts out to her. "Christine, Kyle is not going to let me go is he?" I said to her in my mind.

I watched her eyes widen ever so slightly then she shook her head twice so that it wasn't noticed. Shit.

"If you have to leave me here, don't go far. I *will* get away. Do you hear me? I will get away," I said again to her in my mind.

She nodded her head in affirmation.

"There, how does that feel?" Shawn asked after taping the last of the gauze down.

I lifted my wrists up and twisted them around for inspection. The creme he put on them had some kind of topical anesthetic in it and they didn't hurt anymore. "They don't hurt anymore," I said and smiled up at him. "Thanks."

He smiled back, a warm smile that lit up his eyes. "It was my pleasure." He started picking up the left-over supplies to put them back in the first-aid box. I think I was actually starting to like him. Not everyone is an asshole.

Kyle pushed himself away from the door of the ambulance. "I need to have a word with Julie alone, if you two ladies wouldn't mind?" He asked.

Christine gave me the "we have to leave" look and I nodded my head slightly.

They both looked at Kyle and left without a word.

"How do you feel?" he asked.

"I'm okay, I guess."

Shawn hopped into the back of the ambulance to put the box back and to do whatever doctors do in the back of ambulances.

Kyle sat down next to me and pulled my hair behind my ear. "You surprise me, the perseverance you have."

I fought the urge to pull away from him. "Thank you, I guess."

He smiled. "Tell me, your pyrokineses, did that just happen tonight?"

I thought I heard Shawn gasp from inside the ambulance. I guess I would have to.

"Whatever it is you call it, yes. It happened just tonight."

"Do you know what triggered it?"

Chapter Thirty-seven

I looked up at him and felt my brow rise. "Why do you want to know?"

"I'm just curious." His deep voice was soft and non-commanding.

I thought about whether I should tell him. He knew about it anyway, so why not. "The fear of my soul going to a dark place worse than hell. But mostly I think it was Maria, the head bitch. When she looked at me with those dead eyes. Eyes that held no remorse for taking innocent lives. They were the last thing the second woman saw before they took her life. I actually felt and heard what her last thoughts and words were before they killed her. When those thoughts came to my mind, I wanted Maria dead. I think that's what really triggered it."

"So, it was a series of events then?"

I looked around to see if there was any possible way out of here. "Yes, I guess you could put it that way."

"Did you do it on your own?"

I thought about that. "No, not really. It was a feeling that ran through me. It's kind of hard to explain. It was a kind of rage I have never had or felt before. I fed into it and brought it out. I guess if this didn't happen, I wouldn't have done it. I'm not sure. But then I couldn't get it under control. I had to keep giving it something to lash out on until it felt it was compensated for its use." I sighed heavily. "I don't ever want to do that again."

He looked down at me and stared into my eyes. "I heard your words in my head last night."

"I wasn't even sure if it would work, but I had to try so Christine and Elaine would know. I only did it that one other time with Christine," I lied about that last part. He didn't need to know about Shawn and Chester.

"You know how to control your thought transference then?"

He knew about that too. So, why not? It's not like he's going to be able to benefit from any of this. I wasn't planning to stick around long enough for that to happen. I figured I would just play along so he didn't suspect.

"Yes."

His brow rose at that. "Would you care to explain it to me?"

No, not really. "I guess so. It's another thing that's hard to explain. I concentrate on the person's name first, then their eyes. If they're not near for me to see and I know what they look like, I picture them in my minds eye. I concentrate on their eyes and send my thoughts out to them. I guess it's right for me because it has worked so far."

His smile was one of pure satisfaction. I guess he thought I hadn't figured it out yet. He was in for a big surprise.

He got up, walked a few feet away and turned back around to face me. "I think that is the most information you've ever given me."

I watched him and a slight tingling of panic tickled my nerves. Here we go. "Well, you've never been this polite about it before."

He stood with his legs spread and his arms crossed over his chest. Must be a guy thing.

"If I had known that's all it took, I would have done it sooner."

"I still wouldn't have gone with you to be some kind of test subject for you to play with. I'd rather die first."

His smile faded. "You nearly almost did tonight because of your stubbornness."

I looked up at him and gave him my best blank face. "If I had died tonight, it was still better than the alternative." That wasn't really the truth. I didn't have a problem with dying, but I did have a problem with where my soul was going. After killing three people tonight, it was still questionable.

"I'm sorry to hear you say that." His voice was taking on that all too familiar tone I was used to. He looked back towards the ambulance. "Did you get all that, Shawn?"

"Yeah got it all."

I got up and looked inside the ambulance. Shawn had a tape recorder in his hand and was putting it in a bag. My bag. I see they packed for me. How convenient.

Kyle's lips curled up. "That should do until we get her in and do some proper tests."

I looked casually around and didn't see any immediate way out. "I guess this means I'm not free to go huh?" I sounded calm. Goodie.

He stepped closer to me. "No."

I stepped back and my legs hit the back of the ambulance. Not good. "This case is over with now. Why can't you just leave me alone?"

"This little problem may be over, but you still belong to me."

Okay. That pissed me off. "I happen to be a human being, not a piece of property to be sold to the highest bidder."

"You can look at it anyway you like. It would seem your abilities increase by the day and that makes you too valuable to be allowed to live life as you wish."

My stomach tightened and the hair stood up on my neck. I had to do something fast. I glanced quickly behind me and saw Shawn coming towards me. I stepped sideways so I was away from the back of the ambulance and I could keep both of them in sight.

"After what I did in that room, I would think you'd be careful not to try my patience, detective," I said.

"I'm not worried as you can't control it yet. Once we get you housed in our facility, we have methods to keep it under control."

It was just as I suspected. Housed in some friggin facility like an animal. "Fuck you," I whispered.

I braced myself as he came toward me. I didn't plan to struggle because I knew it wouldn't get me anywhere. He grabbed me and turned me to face the ambulance. He had his arms wrapped around my arms and chest, which was fine with me, as long as my legs were free.

I watched as Shawn came down from the ambulance with a syringe in hand. Shawn closed the distance in two steps. When I knew he was close enough, I brought my legs up, used Kyle to brace me and kicked out as hard as I could. My feet slammed into Shawn's stomach that sent him, Kyle and myself falling backwards in opposite directions. I heard Shawn hit something hard and then nothing. Kyle landed on the ground with me on top of him. I glanced up quickly and saw Shawn lying motionless near the ambulance. One down. I tried to struggle from Kyle's grip and he rolled us around so I was underneath him.

He grabbed my arms, held them over my head and pressed them painfully against the ground. "Not this time," He said through labored breaths.

That's what he thought. I felt a smile forming on my lips and as his eyes narrowed, I cleared my throat and spat in his face for the second time since I've met him.

His eyes darkened and his face formed a vicious scowl as a flush crept up his neck. I think that's a good indication of rage. Good. He was either going to kill me or I was getting away. I would make sure there was no in-between. My brows rose and I gave him my "is that supposed to scare me?" look.

Chapter Thirty-seven

He got up and in one fluid movement, yanked me to my feet and pulled me roughly to his chest. He glared down into my eyes. "It's not going to work."

My brow rose as I stared hard into those stormy eyes of his. "You're not getting me into that ambulance alive, detective."

"We shall see." He pulled me by my arm and dragged me towards the syringe Shawn had dropped.

This was my one and only chance to get away. I waited until he grabbed the syringe off the ground. When he got up and turned to face me, I swung my foot up hard between his legs. I was sure I would never get another chance at that again after this.

He let go immediately and his hands flew to his groin as he fell to the ground on his knees. "Damn it!" he yelled. His voice was strained.

I didn't stick around this time. Instead, I took off around the ambulance and ran into the woods. I had bare feet and the only other protection I had was a thin robe. Great. I stepped on rocks, twigs and tree branches as I flew through the thick forest of trees. I bit my lip and held back the cries that threatened to escape. I didn't care because any injuries I got were small in comparison to what would surely happen if I were caught again.

I didn't look back as I pushed myself to go faster, my face, arms and legs getting cut and scratched by things I couldn't see. My breathing came labored and the only thing I could hear was the pounding of my heart in my ears.

There didn't seem to be an end to the thickness of the forest as I ran in the direction I thought the road would be in. Something thicker than a twig hit the side of my right cheek and I could feel the blood trickle down my face. I ran with my hands out in front of me hoping to stop anything else from flying in my direction.

I couldn't fight the instinct to look back. I needed to know what my senses were already telling me. I glanced back and saw a dark shadow moving through the trees. God, no. Don't let him catch me. I tried to push myself faster but my legs felt weaker and heavier by the minute. I looked back again and when I did, I ran into a low lying branch of a tree. It knocked the breath out of me and sent me backwards onto the ground. I lay there for a few heartbeats re-learning how to breathe as the pain in my chest and ribs throbbed with every beat of my heart.

Then I heard it. Twigs and leaves breaking and crumbling under heavy footsteps. He was close now. I had to get up. I turned around on my stomach and as I lifted myself up, I noticed a fallen tree limb on the ground about a foot from where I fell. I grabbed it and got unsteadily to my feet. I stood there, feet spread apart with the limb held out to my side as if I were a tennis player getting ready to swing at the ball.

He stopped a few feet short when he saw me. We stood frozen for what seemed an eternity; the only sounds were our heavy breathing and the things that lay hidden in a dark forest.

Every muscle in my body ached from running and the cuts from the things that had lashed out at me, stung in protest from the cool air that blew at them. I had to take shallow breaths because it hurt to breathe. The tree limb felt like lead in my hands, but I was desperate and wasn't going with him alive.

"You need to come with me, Julie," he said. His voice was deep and laced with threats of what was to come.

"Why don't we just skip that part, detective, and get down to business," I said. My voice was calm. Good for me. I held the limb up a little higher and let out a whimper as the pain shot through my chest. When this is

Chapter Thirty-seven

over I think I'll skip the self-defense classes and just get the gun.

He took a step towards me. "I'll carry you out of here, if I have to."

I held my ground. "The only thing you'll carry out of here is your sorry, beat-up ass."

He took another step forward. That's it, keep coming.

"You can't escape this time, Julie," he said.

That was the second time he called me by my name. Good. Angry people don't think before they react. I've already proven that fact more than once.

"I'm glad they left you alive, detective. I really did want to kill you myself." My voice sounded low and deadly.

I saw him stiffen. He reached into his pocket and took another step towards me. Just one or two more steps. I knew what he had in his hand. I saw Shawn do it that night in the hospital. I had to keep my calm because I needed to be able to think before I did anything rash.

"You're not even going to get close enough to use that," I said.

"I'm not letting you leave here." His voice was somehow strained. I was wishing it wasn't so dark.

"Then one of us is going to die," I said and meant it.

His breath caught in his throat before he could stop himself. He knew I meant it. Good.

"You don't mean that," he said. It's nice that he can lie to himself like that.

I needed to hurry this up. My arms were starting to tremble from the position they were in and I was feeling light-headed from breathing so shallow. I knew I wouldn't be able to hold it for much longer.

"Try me," I said in a "if you think your man enough" voice.

He stiffened again and I prepared myself for the onslaught as he rushed towards me. He was angry so I had the upper hand.

I waited a few breaths and swung with all the strength I had left. His eyes went wide and didn't get his arm up fast enough before I slammed it into his shoulder. The syringe he held went flying somewhere into the dark of the night as he fell to his back like dead weight to the ground. I grabbed my side and moaned loudly as a stinging pain shot up through it. I looked down at Kyle and knew I didn't have time to waste. I took in a small breath, walked cautiously up to him and nudged him with the limb. Not even a groan.

I dropped the limb and knelt down beside him. When I could hear his breathing, I fished around his waist, yanked his keys from his belt loop and his cuffs from their holder. His gun was next. I rolled him onto his stomach and heard him moan. Shi-i-it. I swallowed the panic back down my throat and fumbled with trembling fingers to get the cuffs open. He moaned again and I struggled furiously to get his hands inside them. When they clicked shut, I grabbed the gun and keys, got quickly to my feet and backed up to a safe distance.

He moaned and rolled slowly onto his back. "Fuck!" He yelled. "My shoulder's dislocated."

Considering what I've been through this week, a dislocated shoulder is a piece of cake.

"You should be lucky that I didn't smash your face in, detective."

"Take these," he stopped and groaned when he moved his arm, "things off me, Julie."

I fished around for the safety I knew was on the gun and clicked it off. "I'm thinking, no."

"Don't fuck with me." His voice was a deep growl.

Chapter Thirty-seven

He started to get up. I winced as I brought the gun up in both my hands and aimed it down at his chest. "Stay down, detective."

"You're not going to use that."

Sounded a lot like a dare. Not good for him I think. "I think we've been through this before too."

He stopped and looked up at me. I couldn't see his face, but I knew that his veins were probably beginning to show. He laid back down but never took his eyes off me. I felt my lips curving up. I need to buy some doggie treats.

"Julie," he said. His voice taking on that threatening tone. As if he was in any position to threaten anyone.

"I'm sorry, detective. I just don't have time for idle chit-chat." I put the safety back on the gun and tossed it with the keys as far as I could throw them. I didn't want the gun and didn't want to have to hold onto the keys.

He started to rise again so I took off into the woods in the same direction I was headed before.

"Julie!" I heard him yell. And I knew by his voice, that I had gotten the best of him again.

I smiled as I ran towards the freedom that lay just beyond the forest.

CHAPTER THIRTY-EIGHT

It took me another twenty minutes or so before I finally stumbled my way out to the road. My breathing was labored and my muscles shook uncontrollably from pushing myself so hard. I knew that I wasn't free yet. Not until I was safely away from this place and out of his reach. I pictured Christine's deep-sapphire eyes in my mind and threw my thoughts out to her. "Christine, I'm on the road. Please help me." I thought as I held onto my side and headed slowly down the road. I stayed as close to the woods as I could in case I needed to hide.

The road's cold surface felt good against the cuts I knew I had on my feet. The night's stillness was deathly quiet and the only thing I could hear was my heart pounding in my ears. Then I saw it. Lights from a car coming behind me. I felt a rush of panic overcome my senses as I turned to look. Please don't let it be him.

I turned to see headlights not too far in the distance and I waited. I needed to see what it was. My eyes

Chapter Thirty-eight

grew wider as its shape came into view. "No," I whimpered.

It was an ambulance. . .He was coming. I looked frantically up and down the street and when I didn't see anything else coming, I ran back into the woods. The only place there was to go. I fought back the tears that threatened to come as I stumbled on shaky legs through the thickness of the forest once more.

I heard the ambulance's tires skid to a stop on the soft shoulder along the side of the road. Tears of frustration and defeat fell down my face. I knew I wouldn't get away this time. They were too close and I didn't have the strength to go much further. My legs gave out from under me and I fell to the ground on my hands and knees. I hung my head down as I heard his footsteps come up behind me.

"I told you, you weren't going to escape this time," he said from above me. His deep voice was calm. He grabbed my arm, lifted me slowly to my feet and turned me to face him. My legs trembled just from the weight of my body and I fought to keep myself up.

He didn't have a sling on his left arm. "How's your arm?" I asked casually.

His eyes narrowed. "Not as bad as I thought."

He was actually taking everything I did quite well. Unless this was the calm before the storm.

My brow rose. "I'll have to try harder next time."

His brows furrowed deep in his forehead. "There won't be a next time."

I guess I hit another nerve. I'm batting a hundred where he's concerned.

"Don't bet your life on that one, detective."

He grabbed me by both my arms. "This is the end, Julie. Do-you-hear-me?" He shook me hard as he said the last through clenched teeth.

I cried out as the pain shot though my ribs and side with each jolt and the threat of blackness overwhelmed my mind. My legs buckled from underneath me as I fought the darkness that would leave me helpless. His grip tightened on my arms to keep me from falling to the ground and then he lifted me up into his arms.

I put my head against his shoulder and my breathing came in short, shallow gasps. I was too weak to struggle and I had no fight left in me. I squeezed my eyes shut to keep the darkness from invading my brain as he carried me back the way I came.

"I hate you," I whispered into his neck.

I felt him stiffen and take in a breath. Did I hurt his itty, bitty feelings?

"I know," he said as we came out from the cover of the trees.

A cold chill ran up my skin and I felt another wave of dizziness wash over me that made my head spin. I squeezed my eyes shut again and a low groan escaped my lips as we approached the back of the ambulance.

I heard a deep gasp come from someone close by.

"Holy shit, Kyle," Shawn said.

I opened my eyes again and through blurred vision, I saw Shawn standing just inside the ambulance.

"Help her, Shawn," Kyle said. His voice held an edge of panic. Guess he was afraid he was going to lose his asset.

Shawn moved back into the ambulance as Kyle climbed in and gently lowered me onto the gurney. My body shivered uncontrollably as I watched Kyle kneel down by my side. He moved my tangled hair away from my face and I jerked away from him. He looked down into my eyes and I saw something move behind them that I couldn't quite put my finger on.

Chapter Thirty-eight

"Move aside, Kyle so I can tend to her," Shawn urged.

Kyle backed up and sat on the bench opposite of where I lay. A worried frown creased his brow as he watched Shawn pull supplies out of a metal cabinet above my head.

Shawn sat by my side and brought out a small flash light to shine in my eyes as he held my lids open.

I looked up at him. "I'm s-sorry if I h-h-hurt you," I said. My voice shaking along with my body.

He smiled down at me. "Shhhh. Don't try to talk."

I felt a wave of dizziness and the sick taste in my mouth overwhelmed me. "Oh, God. I'm gonna be sick."

Shawn grabbed a metal bowl from the floor and brought it quickly to the side of the bed as I leaned over and went into spasms. I cried loudly during each one as it sent waves of pain through my ribs and chest.

"Christ, Shawn. Is she going to be all right?" I heard Kyle say.

"I don't know the answer to that yet," Shawn answered.

When I thought I was finished spilling an empty stomach into the bowl, I got back up and dropped my head onto the pillow. I closed my eyes and fought back the cloudiness that threatened to overwhelm me. "Please, just let me die," I whispered.

"Please, Julie, don't talk like that," Shawn said as he checked my heartbeat, took my pulse and blood pressure. "Kyle, grab a couple of blankets from up over your head quick. She's going into shock."

Kyle jumped up and did as Shawn said. He came over and covered me with the blankets. When he went to cover my feet, he let out a gasp and his eyes widened. "Geezus, Shawn. Her feet are tore up bad."

I looked over at him. His frown deepened when his eyes met mine.

"It's o-k-kay. It doesn't hurt m-m-much," I said and grit my teeth to fight back the violent shiver that overtook me.

Shawn took his hands and started to feel the back of my neck and worked his way to my arms. I screamed out in pain when he pressed his hands against my ribs.

"What is it?" Kyle yelled.

"She's got three broken ribs as far as I can tell."

Shawn pulled the covers down and pressed his fingers against my robe.

"F-fuck!" I yelled and pushed his hand away. "Stop doing that!"

He put the covers back over my trembling body. "We have to get you to a hospital."

"No. No h-hospital!" I yelled. I tried to get up and whimpered as the pain shot through my side and up my chest, causing me to fall back down. My breathing came in short gasps.

"Please, Julie, let me help you," he said. He stared down into my eyes and I saw the sincerity of his words. He wanted to help me and it wasn't because I was some kind of valuable piece of merchandise. He saw me as a person. I relaxed my body and nodded my head.

I lay there as Shawn cleaned the cuts on my face, arms, legs and feet. I kept my eyes on Kyle most of the time. I didn't want him near me. He just sat there in silence. His face still holding the same deep frown as he watched Shawn tend to my wounds.

By the time Shawn had finished cleaning and bandaging my cuts, my shivering calmed to a few twitches every now and again. I watched as he fished around in a box on the floor and I saw his hand come up holding another syringe.

I slid quickly away from him. "No! Stay away from me with that."

"It's only a pain killer. I have to bandage your ribs."

"No! No drugs."

He looked down at me and there was a sadness in his eyes. "I'm sorry, I have to do this."

"Please don't do this. Please?" I felt the tears of desperation stinging the backs of my eyes. I looked over at Kyle. "Please, Kyle. No drugs. I'll be good, I promise. Please?" I grit my teeth as another shiver ran though my body.

Kyle just looked at me as Shawn came towards me with the syringe.

I pulled back some more and stopped when my back hit the side of the ambulance. There was nowhere else to go.

"I'm going to need some help here," Shawn said.

Kyle reached out and grabbed Shawn's arm. Shawn looked over at him, Kyle shook his head and sat back on the bench. I looked into Kyle's eyes to see if this was some kind of trick.

He looked into mine and I could see the truth in them. "No drugs," he said.

I silently thanked him and settled back down.

Shawn put the syringe back into its case and closed it. "You'll have to take your robe down so I can wrap your ribs."

I looked from him to Kyle. Kyle's brow rose as if to tell me that I promised to behave.

I felt my face forming a frown. "Can you please look the other way?" I asked Kyle.

Kyle's eyes narrowed and then he turned his face towards the doors. I didn't care about Shawn seeing. He was a doctor after all and his main concern was helping me.

I sat up, unzipped my robe and let it fall to my waist. I concentrated on Kyle's back as Shawn rapped the bandage around my waist.

He pulled tightly on it and it sent a wave of pain through my body. "Shit! Can you take it a little easy?" I asked as I looked up at him.

There was a small movement of his lips as he looked down at me. "Sorry about that."

Did he think something was amusing? "You think this is funny do you?"

His eyes looked back down as he concentrated on what he was doing. "No, I was just thinking what a remarkable woman you are, Julie. And I'm not speaking of your abilities. I only wish I could have met you under different circumstances."

"Enough of the pleasantries, Shawn," Kyle said.

I looked over at Kyle's back. He sat upright and there was a certain stiffness to his posture. I frowned and looked back at Shawn. He refused to look me in the eyes as he finished and turned away from me to put the supplies back. I pulled my robe back on and zipped it up. Somehow the tension in the air grew thick enough to suffocate a person.

"All set," Shawn said.

Kyle turned back around and his eyes held something I didn't recognize.

Shawn came back over to me and pressed his hands against my ribs. "How does that feel?"

I turned at the waist and the pain seemed less than before. I smiled up at him. "It's much better. Thanks again."

He rewarded me with a brilliant smile back. "You're very welcome, again."

"Let's go," Kyle said. His voice was flat.

Chapter Thirty-eight

"Lie back down so I can strap you in," Shawn said. I felt my eyes go wide and he touched me gently on the shoulder. "It's just so you don't fall out during the trip."

I looked over at Kyle. His expression told me nothing. I sighed and did as Shawn said.

Shawn put the covers over me and I watched as he strapped my ankles, my waist and then put a strap over my chest and arms. He pulled the straps through the buckles and secured them tightly around my body. I glanced over at Kyle and saw his lips curl up. My stomach tightened and a wave of panic swept through my veins. Shi-i-it!

He looked down at me and stared at me hard. "Give it to her, Shawn."

My eyes narrowed as I felt the anger build. I knew it was too good to be true. And I let myself be talked into being strapped down like cattle for branding.

"But I thought. . .," Shawn said.

"I told you, I don't pay you to think."

My pulse began to race as I watched Shawn reach back down into his case to grab the syringe. I looked up at him and saw the grief in his eyes for having to do this to me after I had trusted him. He didn't want to do it anymore than I wanted him to. I glared over at Kyle and his lips curved up more.

"You son-of-a-bitch. I should have killed you in that room." My voice was low and deadly, as if my words could take life with just the sound.

His smile slipped. Point for me.

"Why didn't you?" he asked.

"Because I wanted to do it with my own hands."

He came over, knelt down beside me and pulled my hair out of my face. I turned my head away and heard a laugh escape from his lips. "A mistake I'm sure you will soon regret. Do it, Shawn."

I turned my head back to look as Shawn when I felt him pull the blanket away from my arm.

I looked up into his eyes. "Please, don't do this."

His face frowned softly. "Forgive me, Julie," he said and bent down to administer the drug that would render me useless. He stopped short of touching my arm when a soft click sounded from the direction of the open doors.

"I think that's about as far as you're going to go," Christine said. Her voice was low and threatening. She stood at the open doorway, legs spread apart and held a gun out two-handed.

I breathed a sigh of relief at the sight of her. "Christine! Thank God you're here."

Kyle made to move from my side, she looked into his eyes and brought the gun level with his chest. "I don't think so." That stopped him. "Sit down on the bench," she said and pointed the gun in that direction.

He got up slowly and sat down on the bench. Christine kept the gun aimed at his chest the whole time. Good doggie.

"He's got a gun, Christine," I told her.

"Take your gun out and slide it over here," she said. He went for the gun with his right hand. "Try the other hand," she ordered. He stopped short and I saw his face redden.

He reached in with his left hand, unsnapped the gun from the holster and slid it carefully towards Christine. She kept her eyes and gun on him as she reached down and grabbed it.

She looked over at Shawn, but kept the gun on Kyle. She knew who the monster was. "You've got exactly ten seconds to get her out of there."

Shawn didn't hesitate as he bent down and started to unbuckle the three straps that held me captive.

Chapter Thirty-eight

"Don't do it," Christine said. Her voice rising an octave.

I glanced around Shawn and saw Kyle had slid down closer to where Shawn was standing. His face was flushed, his brows were furrowed deep into his forehead and his jaw was working over-time. He was losing his asset once again and couldn't bare the thought of it. Poor baby.

Shawn moved aside once the straps were undone. I got up slowly so as not to upset the possibility of my escape. I slid sideways through the narrow walkway and kept my eyes on Kyle as I passed by him. My heart skipped a beat and my stomach tightened when my eyes met his dark, steel-blue ones. They held the promise of what would come when he caught up with me again.

I climbed out carefully as not to cause more injury to myself and once my feet were on solid ground, I let out the breath I'd been holding. "I'm so glad you came back."

She smiled but kept her eyes on the two men. "I waited just as you asked. I've been out here all along. I wanted you're injuries to be tended to before I did anything."

"I should've known," Kyle said through gritted teeth.

My eyes narrowed. "You can just shut the fuck up." I took Kyle's gun from Christine, clicked the safety off and aimed it at Kyle. "I've got him. Get the keys."

Christine moved her gun so it was aimed at Shawn. "Get out here. We'll go around to get them."

Shawn moved slowly as he climbed out of the ambulance and walked ahead of Christine to the driver's side.

"You are a very lucky individual, Julie," Kyle said.

"I don't think luck has anything to do with it. If I were you, I'd find another line of work. You don't seem to be cut out for this, detective," I said and smiled. "Now, if you don't mind, give me your cuffs and keys."

His veins started to strain against his neck and I knew that if I didn't get away tonight, he would probably kill me. Asset or not.

He reached around his back, pulled his keys and cuffs off his belt and slid them across the floor of the ambulance. I kept my eyes on him as I snatched them up just as Christine came back with Shawn.

"Where are the keys?" I asked.

"Out there somewhere," she said and nodded her head in the direction of the forest as she kept the barrel of her gun pointed at Shawn's chest.

I choked back a laugh. "Grab my bag, come out and close the doors, detective."

I thought I heard a growl come from his chest as he reached down for my bag. He walked slowly to the door, stepped down to the ground and closed the doors so hard that the ambulance shook.

"Toss my bag this way," I said. Kyle picked it up and tossed it by my feet. I picked it up and handed it to Christine.

"Shawn, stand over by that door," I said and pointed towards the door closest to the road. He walked over to it and turned so his back was leaning against it. Christine followed him with the gun to make sure he didn't try anything stupid.

Since I only had one pair of handcuffs, I tossed the cuffs to Kyle. "Cuff yourself to the door, detective." I knew who the monster was too.

"What about this one?" Christine asked.

"I'm not worried about Shawn," I said as I watched Kyle do as I asked. His face was a deep scowl and his breathing was becoming somewhat labored. Definitely rage. I was loving life.

Chapter Thirty-eight

When Kyle was done cuffing himself to the handle of the ambulance door, I cocked the gun and walked over to him. I looked up into his eyes and my lips curled up as I put the barrel under his chin. I kept my eyes on his as I reached over and tightened the cuffs on the door. My brow rose as I did the same to his wrist. I saw him flinch and it made me smile more.

The look in Kyle's eyes was one of pure evil as I backed up until I was standing beside Christine again.

"Where's your car?" I asked Christine. My eyes still fixed on Kyle's.

"It's on the other side, up the road a bit. I couldn't chance them hearing me pull up," she said.

"Go get it. I'll stay here until you come back."

"Are you sure?" she asked.

"Oh yeah, I'm sure."

"Okay, I'll be right back." She backed slowly away and left me alone with the monster.

I pointed the gun in Shawn's direction. "Shawn, come over here please."

His brows rose as he walked slowly over to stand about a foot from me. I stepped up to him, pressed the gun to his side and looked up into his eyes. "I want to thank you again for patching me up, doc." I said and smiled.

He smiled down at me and his eyes lit up. "You're welcome, Julie," he whispered.

I glanced over at Kyle and smiled before I stood on tip-toe and wrapped my arms around Shawn's neck to hug him. He didn't hesitate to bring his arms around my waist and hug me back.

I pulled back enough to look into his eyes again. "Remember what you said to me in there about meeting under different circumstances?"

His brow rose. "Yes, I do. I meant it."

"I know you did. I wish we could've also."

He smiled down at me again. I reached up around his neck, pulled his face down to mine and brushed my lips against his. His lips were as soft as silk and it sent a shiver across my skin. He pulled back and stared down into my eyes, the shock of my actions written on his face.

"What the fuck are you doing, Shawn," Kyle said. His voice was a low growl.

I kept my eyes on Shawn. "Shut up, detective. This is none of your business. I'm the one with the gun and Shawn will do as *I* wish."

I smiled up at him and pulled him closer to me. He brought his face back down to mine and when I didn't resist, he pressed his lips to mine and kissed me long and hard. His kiss sent another shiver though me and made things tighten low in my body. I opened myself to him as he pulled me closer so he could caress me tenderly with his hands. I could feel his need for me and I wrapped my arms around his neck to meet his need with a hunger of my own. I wanted to melt into him and savor this moment for all time.

When we finally pulled away, I was left breathless. I wanted him badly and wished things could be different, but I knew he had to stay here with Kyle.

"I'm sorry things can't be different," I said.

"So am I."

I turned at the sound of Christine's car pulling up beside us.

"Okay, Julie. Let's get outta here," she said through the window.

I looked over at her. "Hold on a second." I looked back up into Shawn's gray eyes and brought my hand up to caress the side of his face. "I'm sure I'll see you again."

Chapter Thirty-eight

Shawn glanced over at Kyle then back at me. "If I'm still breathing after this, yes, I'm sure you will."

I smiled and gave him one last, soft kiss before I ran over to the passenger side of Christine's car. I put the safety back on the gun and threw it into the woods on the opposite side of the road.

"Okay, I'm ready now," I said and got in.

"What was that all about?" she asked.

"Oh, it's nothing really," I said and smiled as we pulled away. I turned in my seat and watched as the ambulance faded from my view.

CHAPTER THIRTY-NINE

It turned out that the house was in a secluded area near Indian Creak Road, not too far from the North Carolina boarder, which is where Christine and I headed that night. There was no mention in the news or anywhere else for that matter of the goings on there. Imagine that. I don't know what became of Sheila, Chester, or Randy. The only one who could tell me is the one person I didn't care to see again let alone speak to, so I'll probably never know.

They blamed the two murders on an escaped mental patient. They gave him a name and a face. Although I think it was probably for the best, the one thing that haunts me is the fact that the families of those women will never know what really happened.

Christine and I called Elaine. We called her husband's cell phone after we got settled in a motel. We didn't talk for long or give any information on our whereabouts. We weren't taking any chances. When I unpacked my bag, I found the tape recorder Shawn had put inside. I took the tape out and destroyed it. I don't know what good it did because they didn't need a tape to remember what I had told them. I also found Shawn's cell. How convenient for Kyle huh? I didn't throw it away because it made me feel closer to Shawn. It rang that night and has every night since. I haven't answered it yet and don't know if I ever will.

We stayed in South Carolina for two weeks before we went back to Virginia. Christine insisted we were leaving too soon, but I needed and wanted to go back. I paid her Jetta off and we sold it to a used car lot. Kyle knew the car and I wasn't going to live off of public transportation for the rest of my life. I bought a used car and paid cash for it. Elaine registered it in her name so it couldn't be traced back to us.

Christine insisted on staying with me so she found someone to run her store and watch her house. I thought she was nuts, but it's her choice and I like the company. I paid off the rest of my lease on the house and just left everything I owned in it. I couldn't chance going back. I don't know how long I can live on a day-to-day basis, but I have the freedom to make my own choices and that's all that matters to me.

Three weeks after our return to Virginia Beach, I felt it was time to do what I had been wanting to do since the whole thing ended. Elaine brought Christine and I to the place where I could pay my respects to the two women who died by Maria's hands. If I didn't, I would never be able to put it behind me and go on. I went to visit Sandra Barrinton last, the woman who's golden-brown eyes I saw in my vision that night she died. I knelt by her grave and let the tears flow freely down my face as I remembered. Elaine and Christine stayed in the car to give me the time alone I needed. The time to cry for her soul that went to a place too horrible for words. I cried and wished I could have done something to stop it and hated myself for surviving.

When my tears were spent and I felt I could finally deal with it and go on, I got up and turned to leave. I stopped when I saw a man standing off not too far in the distance by a large, oak tree. I knew who it was before I lifted the black veil that hid my face to see him better. I stood there for what seemed an eternity, looking over at the very man I was trying to hide from. He never moved from his spot against the tree as I pulled the veil back down over my face. I turned slowly around and left. I don't know why he didn't stop me and hoped I would never meet up with him again to find out.

Shawn's cell rang that night. . .I didn't answer it.

THE AUTHOR

Teresa A. Leighton

Teresa A. Leighton was born in Worcester Massachusetts and grew up in the New England area. She is one of six children. She has been married for ten years, writes full time along with taking care of her two children and has lived in Virginia Beach, Virginia for ten years. She is currently working on her second **"Julie Summers"** novel.

Mirror To The Soul

It slipped through the portal that led to the dark place. The place that tortures souls for eternity. Now it would roam the place it inhabited, consuming the souls of its unsuspecting victims. It wouldn't stop until it found the one it hungered for. . .the soul that held the power that would give it form to cause total destruction.

Visions of black eyes and death came to haunt me once more. Now, for the second time, I face the fear of giving my soul to a place like hell. . .only worse.

Look for *Mirror To The Soul* coming in summer 2003

Dreaming Cross the Line...
The Final Sacrifice

Dreams are but a phase of sleep where images and thoughts pass through one's mind. But what happens when those images cross the thin line between fantasy and reality?

A little over a year ago, I had a dream. It came twice more after that and even though I tried to tell them it was some sort of omen, they told me it was just a dream and dreams aren't real. My parents died in that fatal accident. The very one in my dreams. I spent the next year building walls around the guilt I felt and talking myself into believing once again. . .that dreams aren't real.

That all changed the night I got up from the couch and walked to my bedroom. Even though I looked back at myself sleeping soundly in the very place I had left, I told myself it was just a dream. When I opened the door, I found myself in a bedroom I didn't recognize and saw a woman lying lifeless in bed. . .and the very man who had murdered her.

My life as I knew it ended that day when I woke with injuries similar to the woman I saw in my dream. The very woman the police found dead in her home. Visions of sacrificial murders to pay homage to a dark God followed that dream. A God who took souls back to a place worse than hell to be tortured for eternity. There were two women dead and it became a race against time.

I had to stay one step ahead of a man who worked for a secret government organization, that wanted to experiment and use my abilities for purposes I didn't care to know about. Most importantly, I had to find the people behind the murders before they could perform the final sacrifice.

Preview of Book 2 of the Vision Series:
Mirror To The Soul
From Teresa A. Leighton
Coming Summer 2003

We walked down a wide hallway that had three other doors similar to mine and I thought that Christine could be behind one of those cold, steel barriers. The elevator was to the left about half way down the hall with a door next to it that led to the stairway. The hall walls were brick and everything was painted white, except for the steel elevator and doors to the rooms. It was exactly as I thought a place like this should be. When you think of a facility used for test subjects, you always think white for some reason.

When we got to the elevator, Kyle pulled my arm so I stumbled to his side. I glanced over my shoulder to see Aaron standing behind us. He looked at me with dead eyes that told me nothing of where we were going.

As the elevator doors opened, I was swung by my arm face-first into the back wall of the elevator. I used my hands to brace myself and by this time I'd just about had enough. I felt the rising anger wash through me and my breathing came quick as the rush of adrenaline surged through my veins.

I heard the elevator door close as I pushed the damp hair out of my face and turned to look at Kyle. "Don't-ever-touch-me-again," I said through my teeth.

He grabbed me by the neck and in one smooth movement, I was shoved against the wall and held at arm's length by my throat. My hands flew up to the one applying steady pressure to my throat and I dug my nails in as hard as I possibly could.

His brows furrowed deep in his forehead and I saw his eyes squint ever so slightly from the gouges I knew my nails were leaving in his hand. "I will touch you anytime I please. Do you hear me?" His deep voice came out a low growl.

I glared up into his dark, steel- blue eyes that promised immense pain if I dare say otherwise. "I think not. Unless you don't value the use of your hands," I said. My voice sounded strained from the pressure of his hand around my throat.

His face turned to a deep scowl and as the elevator doors opened I was hurled forward into a small hallway. I couldn't get my balance fast enough to use both my hands and the side of my face slammed into the hard surface of the brick wall. I came away with the bitter taste of blood in my mouth. My tongue ran along the deep cut on the inside of my cheek and I winced from the burning pain that ran through my mouth. I wiped the blood from my chin with the back of my hand and I felt the first prickle of rage building inside my body.

I turned around slowly and pushed the hair out of my face. I brought my eyes up to stare into the ones that belonged to the man I wanted to take the very life from. "I wouldn't do that again, if I were you," I said. My voice was low and as deadly as a double edged blade.

I saw something move behind his steel-blue eyes before his brow rose. "You're in no position to give orders," he said then turned to Aaron. "Unlock the door."

There were two doors in the small hallway. One on each of the side walls. Aaron unlocked the one to the right and I was pushed roughly into the room and almost stumbled into a steel door. I was figuring that he wasn't taking my threats seriously. He will soon know the error of his way's eh? The real question was, will he learn from them? I'm thinking. . .no.

I found myself in a large white room. The steel door I almost hit belonged to a room that ran the length of the back wall. It had brick that ran about four feet up the walls, with thick, mirrored windows that covered the rest. The room I was standing in contained five items. Concrete blocks stacked six-foot high in the shape of a pyramid to my right. Near the right corner of the back wall was a steel door held up with metal braces. Near the left corner of the back wall stood a ten-by-ten wall of some sort that was set in a cement block to keep it upright. On the wall to my left a seven-foot block of ice sat in a shallow, steel tub. In the center of it all was what looked like a computer on wheels with a bunch of long wires draped over it.

"Whoever your decorator is, I'd ask for my money back," I said and turned around to walk back out the door.

Kyle grabbed me by the arm and pushed me towards the computer on wheels. "Wrong way," he said and pushed me again. "Shawn, get your ass out here!" he hollered.

His voice echoed back off the walls and I resisted the urge to press my hands to my ears as I was shoved and pulled until I was standing in front of the computer.

Kyle turned me around so my back was to it and I was facing the objects in the room. "Do as you're told or else."

That tingle of rage started to grow in the pit of my stomach and my heart started to beat faster in response to it. Rage was a very good thing at this point. I looked up into his eyes and swung before he knew it was coming. The force of it sent his head to the side and the room filled with the sound of it.

Kyle turned his face back to me, looked at something behind me and his lips curled up. "I don't think she'll need much persuasion on this one, Shawn."

I turned my head and saw Shawn standing behind me near the computer. He was wearing a long, white coat over a white T-shirt and jeans. Kyle walked by me and I watched as he unlocked the door to the extra room and disappeared behind the mirrored glass.

Shawn took my face in his hand and his eyes widened. "My God, Julie. What did he do to you?"

I looked up into his gray eyes and they held a look as though they wanted to take all my hurt away. I pushed his hand away and looked down at the floor. "Nothing. Let's just get this over with okay?"

Shawn grabbed little sticky discs that were connected to wires, placed them on my forehead, the back of my neck and my wrists. When he was done, he turned the computer on and it lit up like a Christmas tree.

"It's all set," he said to the mirrored glass windows. He put his hand under my chin and brought my face up so I would look at him. He brought his hand up to the injured side of my face and touched it gently. "I'll take care of this when we're through here."

I nodded and as he was about to leave I touched his arm to stop him. "Shawn?"

"Yes, Julie?"

"Is this going to hurt much?"

His face frowned softly. "A little, yes. I'm sorry, but please, keep the patches on. If you remove them, we'll only have to start over."

My stomach tightened and I let my hand drop from his arm. "Okay, I'll try not to touch them."

"Let's go, Shawn," Kyle's voice echoed in the room.

Preview: Mirror To The Soul

The mere sound of his voice brought the unfamiliar rage back to existence, sending the fear of pain to a place where it couldn't be found.

I heard Shawn gasp as the computer behind me started to come alive with chatter of its own as it reacted to my body's inner-most thoughts.

"Julie?"

My heart started beating faster as the rage I felt built deep in the core of my body. "Get out, Shawn," I said. My voice sounding low and deadly.

I heard his footsteps walk quickly away and the door to the mirrored glass room open and close. He was safe.

I felt something deep down inside me. It started softly and within seconds I felt a throbbing pain coming from within my body somehow. I balled my fists at my sides and gritted my teeth until my jaws hurt to keep from crying out. I took a quick breath and the pain caused a whimper to escape my lips.

My body responded to the pain and frustration of not being able to stop it and that unknown rage fed from it. It grew deep from inside my soul and when the next wave of pain came it rose quickly to the surface.

I took a quick breath and whimpered as it sat just below the point of release. It wanted to feed and if I didn't give it what it craved, it would kill me. I turned my head to look at the mirrored windows and wanted so badly to reach the man who would do this to me.

No. Not that. Shawn is there. Not Shawn. I took in a breath and frowned as it forced itself upwards. "Noooo!" I screamed. My eyes searched the room, fixed themselves on the concrete blocks and it came forward and out into the object it would feed upon.

The blocks did nothing at first and then they seemed to radiate heat from within. Within a few breaths they burst into flames as if they were made of mere wood. I called it back and took a deep breath to hold it in.

The pain had stopped after I had sent it out, but it wanted more. I didn't know how to stop it and it wouldn't until it was satisfied. It crawled to the surface just below my skin and I fixed my eyes on the steel door. I thought maybe if it couldn't consume it, it would go away. I released it out again and willed it to take the door. I stayed fixed on it, hoping the rage would be buried back down to the nameless place it came from.

The door started to heat up and I let a whimper escape my lips knowing it wouldn't stop after this. The door seemed to expand and moan until a ball of flame appeared in its center and then engulfed it completely.

My breath caught in my throat as the rage stayed just within release. "Please, stop!" I cried out as my eyes searched for its next source of consumption.

I looked over at the wall and sent it out from my body with a force that took my breath away. I kept my eyes on it and willed it to take it and be satisfied. The wall moaned and creaked and burst into flames within seconds. But I didn't stop looking at it. I willed it to take it completely and then the wall burst into hundreds of flying pieces.

I felt it build once more and I gasped from the force of it. I turned and looked at the mirrored glass.

"Please, help me," I whimpered and took in a quick breath to keep it at bay for another heartbeat.

The ice was the only thing left to send it out too. I looked quickly over at it, sent it out and the ice exploded, leaving pieces boiling on the cement floor. I kept my eyes in that direction and fixed them on the steel tub the ice had been on only seconds before. It radiated heat as a hot tar road would on a summer's day and a ball of flame burst in its center.

Preview: Mirror To The Soul

It still wanted more and there was nothing left to feed it, but to pull it into myself and have it consume me. I searched frantically around the room, my breath catching in my throat with the force of its greed to feed upon someone or something.

"God, noooo!" I screamed and saw the door that led out of the room. I fixed my eyes upon it and willed it to finish. I willed it to be complete as the door moaned and bent with the heat that consumed it. It burst into flames but I didn't look away, I forced what I hoped was the last of it out into the door. The last burst of energy knocked the breath from me and I fell to my knees as I still kept my eyes on it. The door ignited and a few breaths later exploded outward off its hinges.

I stared at the empty doorway for a couple of heartbeats to be sure it had been completely satisfied. When I didn't feel its power within me, I dropped to my hands and let the feeling of lightness wash over me. I let the tears flow freely as my body trembled from my ordeal.

A strong hand grabbed me by the arm and pulled me gently to my feet. My legs buckled underneath me as the blackness threatened to overwhelm my body. I was lifted up into a pair of strong arms.

I looked up through the darkened mist and saw steel-blue eyes. "I said, not to touch me," I whispered before I closed my eyes and was taken to a place that would relieve me of all my problems.

Printed in the United States
1015200001B/26